PAUL TEMPLE
AND THE
SPENCER AFFAIR

Francis Durbridge

WILLIAMS & WHITING

Titles by Francis Durbridge published by Williams & Whiting

Murder At The Weekend – the rediscovered newspaper serials and short stories

Also published by Williams & Whiting:
Francis Durbridge : The Complete Guide
By Melvyn Barnes

Titles by Francis Durbridge to be published by Williams & Whiting
A Case For Paul Temple
A Game of Murder

A Man Called Harry Brent
Bat Out of Hell
Breakaway – The Family Affair
Breakaway – The Local Affair
Melissa
Murder In The Media
My Friend Charles
Paul Temple and the Alex Affair
Paul Temple and the Canterbury Case (film script)
Paul Temple and the Conrad Case
Paul Temple and the Geneva Mystery
Paul Temple and the Gilbert Case
Paul Temple and the Gregory Affair
Paul Temple and the Jonathan Mystery
Paul Temple and the Lawrence Affair
Paul Temple and the Madison Mystery
Paul Temple and the Margo Mystery
Paul Temple and the Sullivan Mystery
Paul Temple and the Vandyke Affair
Paul Temple Intervenes
Step In The Dark
The Desperate People
The Doll
One Man To Another – a novel
The Teckman Biography
The World of Tim Frazer
Tim Frazer and the Salinger Affair
Tim Frazer and the Mellin Forrest Mystery
Two Paul Temple Plays for Television

INTRODUCTION

Francis Durbridge (1912-98) began his career in 1933 as a prolific writer of sketches, stories and plays for BBC radio, mostly light entertainments including libretti for musical comedies, but a talent for crime fiction became evident in his early radio plays *Murder in the Midlands* (1934) and *Murder in the Embassy* (1937). The *Radio Times* (11 February 1938) mentioned that Durbridge had by then written some one hundred radio pieces, and Charles Hatton commented in *Radio Pictorial* (28 October 1938) that "He is one of the very few people in this country who have succeeded in making a living by writing for the BBC."

So Durbridge continued to write plays and serials for BBC radio for many years, using his own name and occasionally the pseudonyms Frank Cromwell, Nicholas Vane and Lewis Middleton Harvey, while capitalising on a particular brainwave. In 1938 he had hit on the dream team of novelist/detective Paul Temple and his wife Steve, with the huge success of his serial *Send for Paul Temple* leading to Temple cases over several decades that built an impressive UK and European fanbase. Little wonder, then, that following *Send for Paul Temple* Durbridge responded later in 1938 with *Paul Temple and the Front Page Men* and began to gain confidence that Temple would prove to be an enduring radio favourite, with the result that from 1939 to 1968 there were another twenty-six Paul Temple radio productions of which seven were new productions of earlier cases.

Then in 1952, while continuing to write for radio, Durbridge embarked on a long sequence of BBC television serials that achieved enormous viewing figures until 1980. And additionally, from 1971 in the UK and even earlier in Germany, he became known for stage plays that have been produced by professional and amateur companies ever since.

Paul Temple and the Spencer Affair was broadcast on the BBC Light Programme in eight thirty-minute episodes from 13 November 1957 to 1 January 1958, and repeated from 11 July to 5 September 1958. As a special tribute it was broadcast yet again many years later, on BBC Radio Four from 29 October to 17 December 1992 to celebrate Durbridge's 80th birthday, and more recently it has been repeated several times on BBC Radio Four Extra.

This is one of the best and most enthralling Paul Temple radio serials, with plenty to tease the listener. Peter Coke (1913-2008) appeared as Temple for the fourth time, having taken over the role for *Paul Temple and the Gilbert Case* in 1954, and he remained for every other serial until the concluding *Paul Temple and the Alex Affair* in 1968. Indeed Coke and his co-star Marjorie Westbury (1905-89) are still regarded as the definitive pairing of Paul and Steve Temple – they appeared together in eleven of the serials, although Westbury excelled numerically as Steve with her twenty-three appearances overall. Before Coke, Marjorie Westbury had partnered Barry Morse in *Send for Paul Temple Again* (1945), Howard Marion-Crawford in *A Case for Paul Temple* (1946) and Kim Peacock on nine separate occasions. But special mention must also be made of the veteran radio actor Lester Mudditt, who appeared in *Paul Temple and the Spencer Affair* for the last time as Sir Graham Forbes of Scotland Yard, and who had occupied this role on eighteen previous occasions beginning with the original 1938 *Send for Paul Temple*.

A couple of random facts about the radio serial *Paul Temple and the Spencer Affair* might be of interest to Durbridge fans. Firstly, he originally intended to call this *Paul Temple and the Ambrose Affair* but was alerted by the BBC to the fact that Philip Levene's serial *Ambrose in London* was about to be broadcast. Secondly, 13 November 1957 was a particularly notable date for Durbridge because that evening saw the first instalment of two of his serials - *Paul Temple and the Spencer Affair* on the BBC Light Programme at 8.00, followed immediately by *A Time of Day* on BBC television at 8.30.

Unlike many of the Paul Temple radio serials, *Paul Temple and the Spencer Affair* has never been novelised. A recording of the original broadcast serial was, however, marketed on two audiocassettes (BBC Audio, 2000) and later on four CDs (BBC Audio, 2004). This was also included in the CD box set *Paul Temple: The Complete Radio Collection: The Fifties 1954-1959* (BBC, 2016).

On BBC radio during the mid-twentieth century, Durbridge vied in popularity with fellow thriller writers Edward J. Mason, Lester Powell, Ernest Dudley, Alan Stranks and Philip Levene, but always a new Paul Temple serial was eagerly anticipated. As well as their appeal at home the Temples acquired an enormous European following, with translated versions broadcast in the Netherlands from 1939, Germany from 1949, Italy from 1953 and Denmark from 1954. *Paul Temple and the Spencer Affair* was broadcast in the Netherlands as *Paul Vlaanderen en het Spencer mysterie* (19 January - 9 March 1958, eight episodes), translated by Johan Bennik (pseudonym of Jan van Ees) and produced by Kommer Kleijn, with Jan van Ees as Vlaanderen and Eva Janssen as Ina; in Germany as *Paul Temple und der Fall Spencer* (2 October – 20 November 1959, eight episodes), translated by Marianne de Barde and produced by Eduard Hermann, with René Deltgen as Temple and Annemarie Cordes as Steve; and in Italy as *Cabaret* (21 March – 1 April 1977, ten episodes), translated by Franca Cancogni and produced by Umberto Benedetto, with Luigi Vannucchi as Temple and Lia Zoppelli as Steve.

Although we have no novelisation to read, we can now enjoy Durbridge's original radio script. And maybe those of us of a certain age might be tempted to hum the familiar signature tune - *Coronation Scot* by Vivian Ellis – that was used to introduce *Paul Temple and the Sullivan Mystery* in 1947 and every Paul Temple radio serial thereafter.

Melvyn Barnes
Author of *Francis Durbridge: The Complete Guide* (Williams & Whiting, 2018)

This book reproduces Francis Durbridge's original script together with the list of characters and actors of the BBC programme on the dates mentioned, but the eventual broadcast might have edited Durbridge's script in respect of scenes, dialogue and character names.

PAUL TEMPLE AND THE SPENCER AFFAIR

A Serial Play for Radio in Eight Episodes

By **Francis Durbridge**

Paul Temple . . . . Peter Coke
Steve . . . . .Marjorie Westbury
Sir Graham Forbes . . . . Lester Mudditt
Det Insp Vosper . . . . . . Hugh Manning
Rupert Dreisler . . . . . .Brewster Mason
Charlie . . . . James Beattie
Peter Wallace . . . . . . .Frank Partington
Clutch Brompton . . . . Lockwood West
Adrian Frost . . . . .Simon Lack
Terry Gibson . . . . Isabel Dean
Judy Milton . . . . .June Tobin
Eric Lansdale . . . . .John Graham
Warren . . . . .James Thomason
Pete Roberts . . . . . . Thomas Heathcote
A Police Sergeant . . . . . Frank Windsor
Singer . . . . .Norman Tattersall
A Police Sergeant . . . . Haydn Jones
PC Johnson . . . . Frank Windsor
Ritchie . . . . .Hamilton Dyce
André Reynaud . . . . Denis Goacher
Other parts - Beryl Calder, Malcolm Hayes,
Will Leighton, Trevor Martin, Molly Rankin
and David Spenser

EPISODE ONE

"MY HEART AND HARRY"

OPENING MUSIC.
FADE DOWN MUSIC.

CROSS FADE to the sound of a Continental train:
CROSS FADE to interior with the background noises of a dining car.
OTTO, the dining car attendant greets PAUL TEMPLE and STEVE.

OTTO:	Good evening, sir – madam.
TEMPLE:	Good evening! Have you a table for two?
OTTO:	I'm sorry, sir – not at the moment.
STEVE:	(*Disappointed*) Oh dear!
OTTO:	There may be a table vacant a little later, sir – when we leave Innsbruck.
STEVE:	But we don't reach Innsbruck until nine o'clock!
OTTO:	(*With regret*) I know, madam …

CARL, a second dining car attendant arrives.

CARL:	Excuse me, Otto. A party has just left, there are vacant seats in the next car.
OTTO:	Oh good, thank you, Carl! (*To TEMPLE and STEVE*) This way, if you please.

TEMPLE and STEVE follow OTTO into the next dining car.

STEVE:	This is a piece of luck.
TEMPLE:	It certainly is! I didn't fancy walking all the way back to the carriage…
STEVE:	Not on an empty stomach!
TEMPLE:	(*Quietly; aside to STEVE*) Hello …
STEVE:	What's the matter?
TEMPLE:	I've seen that man before somewhere …
STEVE:	What man?
TEMPLE:	At the end table there.

OTTO reaches the table.

OTTO:	Here you are, sir.

TEMPLE:	Thank you. You go in first, Steve.
STEVE:	Thank you.

TEMPLE and STEVE take their places at the table.

DREISLER:	(*With an Austrian accent*) Good evening.
TEMPLE:	(*Puzzled*) Good evening.
DREISLER:	It is Paul Temple?
TEMPLE:	Yes?
DREISLER:	Dreisler. Rupert Dreisler.
TEMPLE:	(*Recognising him*) Why, yes, of course! (*Laughing*) I beg your pardon, I knew we'd met before somewhere. I was just trying to place you.
DREISLER:	Paris – Theatre Marignon, 1952.
TEMPLE:	That's right. You presented Hamlet – in modern dress.
DREISLER:	Unfortunately.
TEMPLE:	(*Suddenly*) Oh, Steve, I'm sorry! This is Mr Dreisler – my wife.
DREISLER:	I'm very pleased to meet you, Mrs Temple.
STEVE:	How do you do?
TEMPLE:	Mr Dreisler's an impresario. A very famous one. He's presented a great many plays on the Continent.
DREISLER:	(*Depressed*) Including Hamlet – in modern dress.

STEVE laughs.

DREISLER:	Are you on holiday, Mrs Temple?
STEVE:	Yes; we've been staying in Saltzburg for ten days. We're on our way home now.
DREISLER:	I see. (*A pause*) Well, what have you been doing, Mr Temple, since I saw you last? Have you written any plays lately?
TEMPLE:	No; I finished a book about a month ago. Since then, I've been taking it easy.

4

DREISLER:	Well, I trust you enjoyed your stay in Saltzburg?
STEVE:	Yes, we did. It's a lovely city.
DREISLER:	It's my – what do you say in English – home town?
STEVE:	Yes.
DREISLER:	(*After a pause*) Yes, you are right, Mrs Temple. Saltzburg is a lovely city. (*A note of regret in his voice*) It's a pity I don't spend more time there.
TEMPLE:	Where do you live – in Vienna?
DREISLER:	I have an office in Vienna – and one in Paris – and New York, but I seem to live in trains and aeroplanes most of the time.
TEMPLE:	Where are you off to now?
DREISLER:	I'm going to London for two or three days to see my daughter, then I'm flying to New York.
TEMPLE:	Does your daughter work in London?
DREISLER:	She's training to be an actress. She's at the British School of Dramatic Art.
STEVE:	Oh, they're doing a play on Saturday. I've just been reading about it in The Times.
DREISLER:	That's right. Mary, my daughter, is playing an important part so naturally Father has got to be there.
STEVE:	Naturally.
TEMPLE:	What play are they doing?
DREISLER:	(*Depressed*) Hamlet – in modern dress.

TEMPLE laughs.
Bring up the noise of the train.
FADE.

FADE UP of background noises and general babble of voices and atmosphere associated with the Customs Hall at Dover.

CUSTOMS OFFICER: Have you anything to declare, sir?

TEMPLE: No, nothing else.

CUSTOMS OFFICER: What about the briefcase – is it yours?

TEMPLE: Yes. It's full of papers – business documents. There's nothing else in it. I'll open it if you like.

CUSTOMS OFFICER: No, that's all right, Mr Temple. Thank you.

TEMPLE: Thank you. (*Aside*) Come along, Steve.

A pause.

STEVE: Did he open your briefcase?

TEMPLE: No.

STEVE: (*Casually*) Good. I put the earrings in there.

TEMPLE: Earrings? Which earrings?

STEVE: Why the ones I bought in … Oh, of course, I forgot to tell you.

TEMPLE: (*Alarmed*) What d'you mean – you forgot to tell me?

STEVE: (*Dismissing the matter*) It's nothing, Paul – don't fuss! (*Suddenly*) Ah, there's Charlie! (*Calling*) Charlie!

TEMPLE: By Timothy, Steve – you really are the limit!

CHARLIE: Good morning, Mrs T! Good morning, sir! I hope you 'ad a nice crossing.

TEMPLE: Yes. Very nice, thank you. Have you got the car?

CHARLIE: Yes, sir. It's all ready. Everything's oke – (*Corrects himself*) – on the beam!

TEMPLE: Yes, well, you can take this suitcase. No – the heavy one, Charlie!

CHARLIE: (*Innocently*) Oh, beg pardon, sir.

6

FADE background voices and noise.

CROSS FADE to the interior of a car. It is travelling at an average speed.

TEMPLE: Well, another half an hour and we'll be home.

STEVE: Yes, and I'm looking forward to it.

TEMPLE: So am I. It's nice to be home again. Are there any letters, Charlie?

CHARLIE: Dozens of 'em. All bills.

TEMPLE: I am surprised!

STEVE laughs.

A pause.

TEMPLE: (*Casually*) Did you see that placard, Steve?

STEVE: No.

TEMPLE: It's the third one I've seen. It just had the name Spencer on it and a large question mark.

STEVE: Spencer – and a question mark?

TEMPLE: Yes.

STEVE: I wonder what it means?

CHARLIE: (*Casually*) It's something to do with that murder case – the young girl that was found in Sloane Street.

TEMPLE: (*Curious*) What young girl?

CHARLIE: Oh, some actress or other. Dreisler I think her name was. Mary Dreisler.

TEMPLE: Mary Dreisler?

CHARLIE: Yes. I expect you'll hear all about it, Mr Temple.

STEVE: You can say that again!

MUSIC.

FADE UP the voices of SIR GRAHAM FORBES and DETECTIVE INSPECTOR VOSPER.

FORBES: … Yes, I agree with what you say, Vosper.

The door opens.

FORBES: On the other hand, we must remember that when the body was found … (*Looking up*) Yes, what is it, Sergeant?

SERGEANT: Mr Temple has arrived, sir.

FORBES: Oh, ask him in.

SERGEANT: Very good, sir.

The door closes.

VOSPER: (*Curious*) Did you send for Temple, Sir Graham?

FORBES: No, he phoned through this morning and made an appointment.

VOSPER: What is it he wants to see you about, sir – the Dreisler case?

FORBES: (*Irritated*) I don't know what he wants to see me about. What on earth makes you think he's interested in the Dreisler affair?

VOSPER: He saw Dreisler last night.

FORBES: (*Surprised*) Temple did?

VOSPER: Yes.

FORBES: Where?

VOSPER: At the Ritz Hotel.

FORBES: Is he a friend of Dreisler's?

VOSPER: I don't know: all I know is Mr Temple went to the Ritz and had a conversation with Dreisler which lasted about an hour. That was the second time he'd seen him in twenty-four hours.

FORBES: What do you mean?

VOSPER: The Temples have been abroad, they only got back on Wednesday.

FORBES: Yes, I know.

VOSPER: Dreisler was on the same train. I understand they had dinner together.

8

FORBES: Oh …

The SERGEANT enters.

SERGEANT: Mr Temple, sir.

FORBES: Come in, come in, Temple.

TEMPLE: Hello, Sir Graham! Good afternoon, Inspector.

VOSPER: Good afternoon, Temple!

FORBES: My word, you look well. I needn't ask whether you've had a good holiday.

TEMPLE: We had a wonderful time.

FORBES: How's Steve?

TEMPLE: Oh, she's fine.

FORBES: Well – sit down, Temple – sit down.

TEMPLE: Thank you.

A pause.

FORBES: Vosper tells me you're a friend of Rupert Dreisler's.

TEMPLE: Hardly a friend. I first met him in Paris several years ago, then he was on the train last Tuesday coming back from Austria and by coincidence Steve and I sat at the same table.

FORBES: I see.

TEMPLE: Look, Sir Graham. It's no good beating about the bush. I'm interested in this Dreisler case, that's why I'm here.

VOSPER: You saw Dreisler last night, Temple – at the Ritz Hotel.

TEMPLE: (*Smiling*) You seem to be very well informed, Inspector.

FORBES: What is it you want, Temple?

TEMPLE: Well – so far, I know very little about the case, Sir Graham. I want to know exactly what happened. Let me have the facts; assume I know nothing whatever about the murder.

9

FORBES:	(*Quietly*) Go on, Vosper.
VOSPER:	Well, Mary Dreisler was a student at the British School of Dramatic Art. She was a good-looking girl, talented, and I suppose no more sophisticated than the average girl these days. Although she hadn't a large circle of friends, she appears to have been reasonably popular and – so far as we can gather – she had no enemies. She lived in a flat at the top of a house in Old Brompton Yard.
FORBES:	Brompton Yard is a small mews just off Sloane Street.
TEMPLE:	I see.
VOSPER:	The house belongs to a widow – a Mrs Thornton. Well, on Monday night, the night of the murder, Mrs Thornton went out to a bridge party and apparently bumped into Mary just as she was leaving the house. According to Mrs Thornton, Mary seemed in quite good spirits and said she had a theatre date with a man called Peter Wallace. Well, to cut a long story short, Mary didn't keep that date. Wallace turned up at the theatre and waited for her until about a quarter to eight.
TEMPLE:	Go on …
VOSPER:	Mrs Thornton returned from her bridge party just after eleven; she heard no noise from the flat and she assumed, quite naturally, that Mary was still out with her boyfriend. The next morning when Mary didn't put in an appearance she went upstairs. Have you got the photograph, Sir Graham?
FORBES:	Yes, here it is.

10

VOSPER:	When Mrs Thornton opened the bedroom door, Temple … (*Passing the photograph*) This … is … what … she saw …

A moment.

VOSPER:	The girl was on the floor near the bed; you can see from the condition of the room that there must have been quite a struggle before she was strangled.

A tiny pause.

TEMPLE:	Who identified the body?
FORBES:	Mrs Thornton; this chap Peter Wallace who was practically engaged to Mary Dreisler, and another friend of hers called Judy Milton.
TEMPLE:	I see from the photograph that she was wearing a light-coloured dress; was she wearing this when Mrs Thornton saw her the night before?
FORBES:	Yes.
TEMPLE:	M'm. (*A moment*) What about the time factor?
FORBES:	The usual story, the medical people won't commit themselves. It might have happened almost any time between seven – which was when Mrs Thornton saw her – and midnight.
TEMPLE:	Motive?
FORBES:	That's just the point, there doesn't appear to be a motive.
TEMPLE:	Was anything missing?
VOSPER:	No, so far as we can tell, not a thing. You can rule out robbery, Temple. There was quite a bit of jewellery about the place and almost thirty pounds in her handbag.
TEMPLE:	I see. Well – go on, Inspector.
VOSPER:	I'm afraid that's all we can tell you.

11

FORBES:	There's the gramophone record.
TEMPLE:	What gramophone record?
VOSPER:	The morning Mrs Thornton discovered the body one or two letters arrived for Mary and also a parcel. The parcel contained a gramophone record and a note from someone who called himself Spencer. There was no address on the notepaper and the note, which had obviously been scribbled in a hurry, simply said: "Adored every minute of it. Love, Spencer."
TEMPLE:	(*Intrigued*) Adored every minute of it. Love, Spencer.
VOSPER:	Yes.
TEMPLE:	It sounds as if she'd lent this person Spencer the record and he was returning it.
VOSPER:	Yes, but the point is we can't find Spencer. We've checked at the BSDA and questioned most of Mary's friends and no-one's even heard of him.
TEMPLE:	What about Mrs Thornton?
FORBES:	No, she's never heard of him either.
TEMPLE:	What was the record?
VOSPER:	What do you mean?
TEMPLE:	What was it – a classical record or pop number?
VOSPER:	Oh – it was a number called "My Heart and Harry". I'd never heard of it.
FORBES:	Have you heard of it, Temple?
TEMPLE:	Yes, but you can't buy the record over here. The show's still running on Broadway and the tune hasn't been released yet.
FORBES:	Then how did Mary Dreisler get hold of a copy?

12

TEMPLE:	Probably through her father.
FORBES:	Yes.
VOSPER:	What happened last night, Temple – when you saw Dreisler?
TEMPLE:	Dreisler phoned and asked me to go round to the hotel. He sounded very excited over the phone and the first thing he did when I arrived was to hand me this note. (*He feels in his pocket*) Here it is.
VOSPER:	Thanks.
FORBES:	Read it out, Vosper.
VOSPER:	"Dear Mr Dreisler. If you would like to know why your daughter was murdered and who murdered her I suggest you make the acquaintance of Adrian Frost: ask him why he gave her the diamond brooch."
FORBES:	Well?
VOSPER:	That's all.
FORBES:	Isn't there a signature?
VOSPER:	No, there's no signature and no address.
TEMPLE:	Apparently the note was at the hotel when Dreisler arrived. He asked me to find out who Adrian Frost was and he also … asked me to investigate the case. I said that I would.
FORBES:	Go on, Temple …
TEMPLE:	I stayed talking to Dreisler about an hour and then returned to the flat. As soon as I opened the front door Steve greeted me with the news that a young man called Peter Wallace wanted to see me.

FADE OUT.

FADE IN.

STEVE:	Paul, there's a Mr Wallace wants to see you. He's in the drawing room.
TEMPLE:	Oh?
STEVE:	He's been here over an hour; he insisted on waiting.
TEMPLE:	Who is he, Steve – do you know?
STEVE:	He says he's a friend – or was a friend – of Mary Dreisler's. I haven't had much to say to him, I've been unpacking most of the time.
TEMPLE:	Yes, all right, Steve.

The sound of a door opening and closing.

TEMPLE:	Mr Wallace?
WALLACE:	(*A pleasant, middle-class voice*) Oh, good evening, sir.
TEMPLE:	I understand you want to see me?
WALLACE:	(*Nervously*) Yes, I … Mr Temple, I hope you don't think it's an impertinence my calling like this, but …
TEMPLE:	What is it you want to see me about?
WALLACE:	Are you investigating the Dreisler murder?
TEMPLE:	I'm not investigating anything at the moment. As a matter of fact, I've been abroad. I only got back this morning.
WALLACE:	Yes, I know, but there's a report in the evening paper that you're a friend of Mr Dreisler's and I thought perhaps …
TEMPLE:	You thought what, Mr Wallace?
WALLACE:	(*Still hesitant*) I thought that if you were investigating the case, I might be able to help you.
TEMPLE:	Well, let's assume for the moment that I am investigating it. How can you help me?
WALLACE:	I was very friendly with Mary Dreisler. In fact we were unofficially engaged.

14

TEMPLE:	Go on.
WALLACE:	For about a year we were terribly happy together. We used to go to dances and theatres and parties and things. And then suddenly – quite suddenly – Mary's attitude changed towards me.
TEMPLE:	How do you mean – changed?
WALLACE:	Well, she became rather cynical and bitter. She started criticising me, taking a dislike to – well – little things. The way I talked; the way I dressed; the way I walked into a restaurant. It seemed to me she was always comparing me with someone.
TEMPLE:	Who was she comparing you with? Have you any idea?
WALLACE:	(*Reluctantly*) Yes. A man called Adrian Frost.
TEMPLE:	Who's Adrian Frost?
WALLACE:	He was a friend of Mary's – a playwright. At least he calls himself a playwright. He's friendly with quite of lot of the BSDA students.
TEMPLE:	Are you at the BSDA, Mr Wallace?
WALLACE:	Good Lord, no! Do I look like an actor? I work for a firm of estate agents, Ratcliffe & Warner, Pelham Crescent.
TEMPLE:	Tell us, how did you meet Miss Dreisler in the first place?
WALLACE:	An actress friend of mine called Judy Milton took me to a Charity Matinee. Mary was playing one of the small parts and I – well – I got Judy to introduce me.
TEMPLE:	I see. Wallace, you said just now that if I were investigating this case, you might be able to help me.

WALLACE: Yes. (*Tensely*) Mr Temple, I know what I'm going to say may sound crazy! But I swear to you I'm not just saying it because I'm angry or embittered or anything like that.

TEMPLE: Go on.

WALLACE: I think Adrian Frost had some kind of influence – an evil influence – over Mary. I've no proof – no real proof – of what I'm saying, but – (*He hesitates*) – I think …

TEMPLE: What do you think?

WALLACE: I think directly, or indirectly, he was responsible for her murder.

TEMPLE: Is that why you sent the note to Mr Dreisler?

WALLACE: (*Puzzled*) What note?

TEMPLE: Someone sent Rupert Dreisler a note advising him to make the acquaintance of Adrian Frost. The note intimated that Frost was responsible for his daughter's death.

WALLACE: (*Surprised*) I didn't send that note.

TEMPLE: Then who did?

WALLACE: I don't know.

TEMPLE: Have you told the police about your suspicions? About your feelings about Adrian Frost?

WALLACE: Yes, but it's no earthly use talking to the police. I saw Inspector Vosper last night and all he did was ask me a lot of silly questions about a person I'd never heard of – someone called Spencer.

TEMPLE: Spencer?

WALLACE: Yes. Apparently, someone called Spencer sent Mary a gramophone record and the police can't account for it.

TEMPLE:	Wallace, tell me, what sort of a person is this Adrian Frost? To meet, I mean?
WALLACE:	He's good looking, well educated, perfect manners.
TEMPLE:	When did you first meet him?
WALLACE:	About six months ago. Judy Milton gave a cocktail party and Frost was one of the guests. I introduced him to Mary.
TEMPLE:	I see. You said just now he was a playwright, yet I've never heard of him.
WALLACE:	He calls himself a playwright, but I don't think he's written anything.
TEMPLE:	Is he well off?
WALLACE:	He appears to be. He's got a very nice flat in Regents Park.
TEMPLE:	Wallace, tell me, did Adrian Frost ever give Mary anything?
WALLACE:	Give her anything?
TEMPLE:	Yes. A ring – a pair of earrings – a brooch, perhaps?
WALLACE:	Not that I know of. (*Suddenly*) Wait a minute. About a month ago Mary suddenly acquired a diamond brooch. When I asked her where she got it from, she said her father had given it to her, but – I always had my doubts. (*A moment*) Why do you ask?
TEMPLE:	I wondered, that's all. Now, if you'll excuse me, Wallace, I've several things I must attend to.

FADE.

TEMPLE:	… Well, that's what happened last night, Sir Graham. Whether Wallace was telling the truth or not, I don't know.

17

FORBES:	What do you think, Vosper?
VOSPER:	In my opinion, he wasn't.
TEMPLE:	You think he did send Dreisler that note?
VOSPER:	Yes, I do. It's perfectly obvious that Wallace suspects Frost and he's determined to make us suspect him as well. That's why he sent the note to Dreisler. He knew that we'd hear about it.
TEMPLE:	(*Thoughtfully*) I'm not so sure about that. Have you met Frost?
VOSPER:	Yes, of course.
TEMPLE:	What's your opinion of him?
VOSPER:	I rather like him. He's a pleasant sort of chap, not exactly one of the world's workers, but at least he's not a crashing bore like Peter Wallace.
TEMPLE:	I wouldn't have called Wallace a bore, Inspector.
VOSPER:	(*Laughing*) You wait!
FORBES:	He rings Vosper twice a day to see if we're making any progress.
VOSPER:	He's read too many detective novels – that's his trouble.
TEMPLE:	What about this girl, Judy Milton?
FORBES:	Well, she's quite different from Adrian Frost, and Peter Wallace, too, for that matter. You'd never dream she was an actress.
TEMPLE:	Why do you say that?
FORBES:	Well, although she's a student at the BSDA, she's a very untheatrical type of girl. She doesn't even live in Town. She motors up every day from a cottage near Beaconsfield.
TEMPLE:	How old is she?
VOSPER:	About twenty-nine or thirty.

18

TEMPLE:	Was she very friendly with Mary Dreisler?
VOSPER:	Yes, I think so. She seemed very upset when we told her about the murder.
TEMPLE:	What about Peter Wallace? How did he take it?
VOSPER:	Well, he was very upset, of course, especially when we asked him to identify the body, but … (*He hesitates*) …
TEMPLE:	Go on, Inspector.
VOSPER:	(*Hesitantly*) I don't know. There's something rather odd about Peter Wallace. He looks a perfectly straightforward young man, the sort of chap who would be quite happy in stockbroking or an estate agent's office, but …
TEMPLE:	You're not happy about him?
VOSPER:	No, I'm not. Young men like that don't usually mix with girls like Mary Dreisler. They usually make friends with quite a different set of people. More the – well – (*He's lost for words*)
TEMPLE:	Conventional type?
VOSPER:	Exactly.
TEMPLE:	Umm. Tell me, did you talk to Judy Milton about the gramophone record? About the note from the person called Spencer?
VOSPER:	Yes, I told you, we've questioned several people about it.
TEMPLE:	What did Judy Milton say?
VOSPER:	She said she didn't know anything about the gramophone record, and she'd never heard of anyone called Spencer.
TEMPLE:	And Adrian Frost?
VOSPER:	He said exactly the same.
TEMPLE:	(*After a pause*) What sort of a person is this Mrs Thornton?
FORBES:	Mary Dreisler's landlady?

TEMPLE:	Yes.
FORBES:	Oh, she's a very nice woman, completely trustworthy.
TEMPLE:	How long had Mary been staying with her?
FORBES:	About nine or ten months.
VOSPER:	It's not quite accurate to say that Mary Dreisler was staying with her. The girl occupied the top part of the house.
FORBES:	Yes, it's more or less a self-contained flat – you know the sort of thing, Temple.
TEMPLE:	How much did she pay, do we know?
VOSPER:	I believe twenty guineas a week, but I'm not sure.
FORBES:	Mary had plenty of money. According to all accounts, her father made her a substantial allowance.
VOSPER:	He must have done. Dash it all, she paid twenty guineas a week for her flat; she dressed well; and she was even thinking of buying a car.
FORBES:	Yes.
TEMPLE:	Who told you about the car?
VOSPER:	We found a letter from a man called Brompton, a motor car salesman. They'd obviously been corresponding.
TEMPLE:	Brompton? C. S. Brompton?
VOSPER:	(*Surprised*) Yes, that's right.
FORBES:	Do you know him?
TEMPLE:	Yes, if it's the same man. He used to run a junk yard just outside Windsor. He was always mad on cars.
VOSPER:	Brompton. It isn't Clutch Brompton?
TEMPLE:	Yes, that's right.

FORBES: I remember Clutch Brompton. He very nearly got sent down four years ago for dangerous driving.

VOSPER: Yes, he'd have done a very nice stretch if it hadn't been for Temple.

TEMPLE: Clutch was innocent, although he had a police record. I saw the whole thing. The other fellow came out of a side turning like a streak of lightning. Anyway, you say he's been corresponding with Mary Dreisler?

VOSPER: Yes. Apparently, he was trying to sell her a car.

TEMPLE: Have you had a talk to him?

VOSPER: No, we didn't think it was important.

FORBES: Do you think it's important, Temple?

TEMPLE: No, I shouldn't think so. Anyway, leave it with me, I'll probably have a word with him. (*He rises*) Well, thank you, Sir Graham, for all the details. Goodbye, Inspector.

VOSPER: If anything else develops, I'll let you know.

TEMPLE: (*Faintly amused*) Thank you, Inspector, I'll do the same for you.

FADE OUT.

FADE IN on TEMPLE dialling a number on the telephone. After a moment we hear the number ringing out. STEVE enters.

STEVE: Paul, what on earth's going on? You must have made about fifteen phone calls in the last half hour.

TEMPLE: Eight, to be precise, darling. I'm trying to get hold of a chap called Clutch Brompton. Do you remember him?

STEVE: Yes, I do. A tough little man. He was had up for dangerous driving and you gave evidence.

21

TEMPLE: That's right. Well, apparently, he's in the motor car industry now and he tried to sell Mary Dreisler a car.

STEVE: Well?

TEMPLE: Well, I'd like to have a talk with him. I want to know what made him get in touch with Miss Dreisler in the first place.

STEVE: She probably answered an advertisement.

TEMPLE: Well, we'll see. Here, you take the phone, Steve. I know Clutch – he's more likely to be chatty if it's a woman speaking.

STEVE: Yes, all right, darling. What's the number?

TEMPLE: Putney 9301. It's a public house on the Upper Richmond Road. Whether he'll be there or not, I don't know. He used to go there a lot in the old days. Anyway, it's my last chance.

The receiver lifts at the other end. FRED NORSEN is a very tough Cockney in his late fifties.

FRED: (*On the phone*) Hello …

STEVE: Putney 9301?

FRED: That's right.

STEVE: I want to speak to Mr Brompton, please.

FRED: (*Aggressively*) Mr Brompton? You've got the wrong number, lady.

STEVE: Mr Clutch Brompton.

FRED: Oh, Clutch? Who is it calling?

STEVE: His sister.

FRED: (*Laughing*) Are you Marilyn, the cute little number he's always talking about?

STEVE: What d'you mean – cute little number?

FRED: (*Laughing*) Okay. I'll get him. Hold on.

A moment.

TEMPLE: What's happening?

STEVE: He's coming …

22

TEMPLE: All right, Steve, I'll take it.

A pause.

CLUTCH: (*Angrily*) Hello … is that you, Marilyn? Listen, I told you not to ring me, didn't I?

TEMPLE: Hello, Clutch, how are you?

CLUTCH: (*After a moment*) Who is that? Who's speaking?

TEMPLE: Paul Temple. You remember me, Clutch? – We met a long time ago.

CLUTCH: (*Bewildered*) Fred said it was Marilyn. He said it was Marilyn on the phone ...

TEMPLE: All right, Clutch, there's nothing to worry about. It was my wife.

CLUTCH: Oh! Well, what is it? What do you want?

TEMPLE: I want a little chat, Clutch. Just a friendly chat.

CLUTCH: Listen, I'm going straight now, Mr Temple. I'm in the motor car rack – business. Second-hand cars. Straight as a die, Mr Temple.

TEMPLE: (*Amused*) Yes, I know. That's what I want to talk to you about.

CLUTCH: (*After a moment*) What is it you want?

TEMPLE: You tried to sell a car to a girl called Mary Dreisler.

CLUTCH: Well?

TEMPLE: How did you get in touch with Miss Dreisler in the first place?

CLUTCH: That's my business.

TEMPLE: It's my business as well. Miss Dreisler was murdered. I'm investigating the murder.

CLUTCH: Look, Temple, you did me a favour once. Now I'm doing you one. Keep out of this Dreisler business. Don't be a damn fool. Keep out of it.

CLUTCH replaces the receiver.

TEMPLE: (*Quickly*) Clutch! Clutch, listen …

STEVE: What's happened?

23

TEMPLE: He rang off …

TEMPLE replaces the receiver.

STEVE: What did he say?

TEMPLE's thoughts are elsewhere.

STEVE: Paul, what did he say?

TEMPLE: Steve, what time is it?

STEVE: It's just gone seven.

TEMPLE: Tell Charlie to get the car, I'm going to see Brompton. I'll be back later, darling.

STEVE: I'll come with you.

TEMPLE: No. No, you stay here. Now, don't worry, I shan't be long, Steve.

FADE OUT.

FADE UP sounds of two men playing snooker.

FRED: You're rattled, Clutch, what's the matter with you tonight? You couldn't hit the side of a house.

CLUTCH: You're lucky, Fred, dead lucky.

FRED laughs.

CLUTCH: You've always been lucky at snooker.

CLUTCH throws down his cue.

FRED: That's a fiver you owe me. Now pick that cue up and I'll tell you what I'll do. (*He picks up some balls*) I'll play you a hundred up at billiards, give you a 30 start and the winner … (*He hesitates; looks up*) Looking for someone, mate?

TEMPLE: Yes, I'm looking for Mr Brompton.

FRED: Well, you haven't far to look. (*To CLUTCH*) Pal of yours, Clutch?

CLUTCH: (*A moment*) No. (*To TEMPLE; surly*) I'm Brompton. Who are you? What do you want?

TEMPLE: (*Pleasantly*) I understand you've got a car for sale. A 2.4 Dace.

CLUTCH: That's right.

24

TEMPLE:	Is that the car outside with trade plates?
CLUTCH:	Yes.
TEMPLE:	How many miles has it done?
CLUTCH:	Two thousand, genuine.
TEMPLE:	Do you mind if I take a look at it?
CLUTCH:	(*After a moment*) No, it's a pleasure. See you later, Fred.
FRED:	Okay. (*He continues to knock the balls about*)

FADE OUT.

FADE UP faint background noises of traffic.

CLUTCH:	(*Angrily*) Now what's the idea, Temple? I told you over the phone that I …
TEMPLE:	(*With authority*) Get in the car.
CLUTCH:	(*Surprised at TEMPLE's attitude*) What?
TEMPLE:	Get in the car. We can't talk here.
CLUTCH:	We've nothing to talk about. I told you over the phone that I …
TEMPLE:	Get in the car, Clutch.
CLUTCH:	(*A moment; then giving in*) Okay.

The car door opens and they get into the car.

CLUTCH:	Now what is it? What's on your mind?
TEMPLE:	Four years ago, I did you a favour, Clutch, a pretty big favour. If it hadn't been for me, you'd have …
CLUTCH:	I know. I know.
TEMPLE:	Do you remember what you said? You said, "Any time you want anything, Mr Temple – anything – just ask Clutch Brompton."
CLUTCH:	(*Worried*) Yes, and I meant it. Honest I did, Mr Temple.
TEMPLE:	Then, tell me, what made you get in touch with Mary Dreisler?

25

CLUTCH: She answered an advertisement of mine. She said she was interested in a car I had. As a matter of fact, it was this very car.

TEMPLE: What happened?

CLUTCH: I wrote to her. Gave her details but didn't even get a reply.

TEMPLE: Did you meet her?

CLUTCH: No, I told you I wrote to her. I didn't even talk to her on the blower.

TEMPLE: Clutch, what did you mean when you said keep out of this Dreisler business? If you'd never met Mary Dreisler …

CLUTCH: Temple, listen – I meet a lot of people in this racket, all sorts of people. Some of 'em can't keep their mouths shut.

TEMPLE: Well?

CLUTCH: According to what I've heard Mary Dreisler was mixed up with a pretty tough bunch. I – (*He hesitates*) – I wouldn't get too involved, if I were you.

TEMPLE: What do you mean – a pretty tough bunch? She was training to be an actress. She was a student at the BSDA.

CLUTCH: (*Dismissing the matter*) Okay, okay …

TEMPLE: Look, Clutch, you know something about this Dreisler affair. What is it?

CLUTCH: (*A moment*) If I tell you what I know, does that make us all square?

TEMPLE: What do you mean?

CLUTCH: I don't owe you a favour and you don't owe me one.

TEMPLE: Yes, Clutch, it makes us all square.

CLUTCH: Okay. (*He opens the car door and is about to get out*) Play the record, Mr Temple.

TEMPLE: (*Puzzled*) What record?

CLUTCH: "My Heart and Harry".

CLUTCH gets out of the car and slams the door behind him.

TEMPLE: (*Calling to CLUTCH*) Hi, Clutch, just a minute!

TEMPLE opens the car door.

CLUTCH: (*From the background, calling back to TEMPLE as he crosses the road*) No more questions, I'm going back to the pub.

There is the sound of an approaching car, racing down the road.

TEMPLE: (*As he gets out of the car; calling to CLUTCH*) Clutch, wait a second, I want to … Clutch, look out! Look out!!!!

The car races down, and deliberately knocks CLUTCH down. There is a scream from a woman bystander as the car races away: almost immediately the entire street comes to life with excited onlookers.

FADE UP of CLUTCH, groaning, in obvious pain.

Background of excited noises.

1st MAN: That was deliberate – it must 'ave been! He came round the corner like a flippin' rocket!

2nd MAN: He never even put his blinkin' brakes on!

GIRL: (*Excited; confused*) I got his number! I got his number all right … DLP … DLP 1 – 3 – Oh, dear – now what was it?

TEMPLE makes himself heard above the babble of voices.

TEMPLE: (*With authority*) Look, you over there! Get to a phone box – ring for an ambulance!

3rd MAN: (*Quickly*) Okay, mate!

TEMPLE: Tell them it's very urgent!

FADE UP of CLUTCH, still in pain.

TEMPLE: Here we are, Clutch – put your head on this coat …

CLUTCH:	(*Speaking with an obvious effort*) Mr Temple … I … I want to …
TEMPLE:	It's all right, Clutch, don't worry – we'll soon have a doctor here.
CLUTCH:	Mr Temple, don't forget what I told you … (*With a desperate effort to get the words out*) … Play … the … record …

MUSIC.

FADE UP of PAUL TEMPLE in a public telephone box.

TEMPLE:	(*On the phone*) This is Paul Temple. Put me through to Inspector Vosper, please. Extension 19.
SERGEANT:	(*On the other end of the phone*) One moment, sir.

We hear a click on the switchboard and then the receiver being lifted.

VOSPER:	(*On the other end of the phone*) Inspector Vosper, speaking.
TEMPLE:	Vosper? This is Temple.
VOSPER:	Oh, hello, Temple.
TEMPLE:	(*Urgently*) Vosper, listen. You remember that gramophone record you mentioned. The one that Mary Dreisler received?
VOSPER:	Yes.
TEMPLE:	Have you got it?
VOSPER:	(*Surprised*) What? The record?
TEMPLE:	Yes.
VOSPER:	No. I've got the note from Spencer, but the record's still at the flat.
TEMPLE:	Did you play the record?
VOSPER:	Why, no, of course not.
TEMPLE:	Well, pick it up and meet me at my place in half an hour.

28

VOSPER: What on earth do you want the record for?

TEMPLE: Meet me at my flat in half an hour.

VOSPER: (*Puzzled*) Yes. All right, Temple.

TEMPLE replaces the receiver.

FADE.

FADE UP of the sound of a doorbell ringing. The door opens.

TEMPLE: Hello, Steve. Where's Charlie?

STEVE: I've let him go out for the evening. He's been
           working awfully hard since we got back.

TEMPLE: Is Vosper here?

STEVE: Yes, he's in the study. Oh, and Paul, there's been
           three calls for you in the past hour, all from the
           same person.

TEMPLE: Oh? Who's that?

STEVE: A girl called Judy Milton. Apparently, she wants
           to …

TEMPLE: Judy Milton?

STEVE: Yes.

TEMPLE: What did she want – did she say?

STEVE: No, she absolutely insists on talking to you. I
           asked her each time if there was any message,
           but she just said she'd ring back.

TEMPLE: Yes, all right, Steve.

STEVE: Darling, what's Vosper doing here? Did you
           send for him?

TEMPLE: Yes, I did. Now, Steve, I want you to do
           something for me. Go into the drawing room and
           switch on the radiogram – we'll join you in a few
           minutes.

STEVE: The radiogram? Why on earth …

TEMPLE: (*Interrupting STEVE*) We'll join you later,
           darling.

A door opens.

TEMPLE enters his study. VOSPER rises from the armchair near the window.

TEMPLE: You beat me to it, Inspector. Sorry to have kept you waiting.

VOSPER: That's all right.

TEMPLE: Well, did you get the record?

VOSPER: No, I'm afraid I didn't.

TEMPLE: Oh. Why not?

VOSPER: Because apparently someone beat <u>me</u> to it.

TEMPLE: What do you mean?

VOSPER: According to Mrs Thornton someone called round last night and took the record away with him.

TEMPLE: Last night?

VOSPER: Yes.

TEMPLE: Well, who was it? Do you know?

VOSPER: It was Mr Dreisler. Mr Rupert Dreisler.

MUSIC.

END OF EPISODE ONE

EPISODE TWO

CONCERNING
JUDY MILTON

OPENING MUSIC.

FADE DOWN Music.

FADE UP the sound of a door opening.

TEMPLE: You beat me to it, Inspector. Sorry to have kept you waiting.

VOSPER: That's all right.

TEMPLE: Well, did you get the record?

VOSPER: No, I'm afraid I didn't.

TEMPLE: Oh. Why not?

VOSPER: Because apparently someone beat me to it.

TEMPLE: What do you mean?

VOSPER: According to Mrs Thornton someone called round last night and took the record away with him.

TEMPLE: Last night?

VOSPER: Yes.

TEMPLE: Well, who was it? Do you know?

VOSPER: It was Mr Dreisler. Mr Rupert Dreisler.

TEMPLE: Dreisler? You mean the girl's father?

VOSPER: Yes.

TEMPLE: But why should he want the record?

VOSPER: I don't know, Temple. Just at the moment I'm wondering why you want it.

TEMPLE: Someone – I can't tell you who – told me to get hold of the record. They said it might have a bearing on the Dreisler murder.

VOSPER: Who told you that?

TEMPLE: I've told you – I can't say who …

VOSPER: (*Interrupting* TEMPLE) Was it Clutch Brompton?

TEMPLE: (*A moment*) How did you know?

VOSPER: I heard about the car incident in Putney. Someone described the person who happened to

	be with Clutch at the time. I assumed you weren't talking about the weather, Temple.
TEMPLE:	Look, Inspector – if Clutch had said anything really important, I'd have told Sir Graham straight away.
VOSPER:	He told you about the record, Temple.
TEMPLE:	Yes, and I asked you to get hold of it for me. I could very easily have gone round to the flat myself.
VOSPER:	(*Relenting slightly*) Yes, I realise that. It's just that – well – this business is rather getting me down. We don't seem to be getting anywhere.
TEMPLE:	On the contrary, I think we're getting somewhere very fast.
VOSPER:	What do you mean?
TEMPLE:	If your daughter had been murdered, would you worry about a gramophone record?
VOSPER:	Not unless I thought it had some bearing on the case.
TEMPLE:	Exactly. The fact that Dreisler went round to the flat and collected the record shows that not only did he know about it but he obviously considered it of some importance.
VOSPER:	Yes. Can I use your phone?
TEMPLE:	Certainly. But are you going to phone Dreisler?
VOSPER:	Yes.
TEMPLE:	I wouldn't do that. If I were you, I'd drop in on him, Inspector. Don't you pass the Ritz on your way home?
VOSPER:	Yes, I do. Tell me, how well do you know Dreisler?
TEMPLE:	Not very well. I met him in Paris several years ago when he was producing Hamlet in modern dress. At the time there was some talk of him

	producing a play of mine, but nothing materialised.
VOSPER:	Is he a wealthy man?
TEMPLE:	He appears to be. He travels a great deal and apparently finances a lot of shows.
VOSPER:	In London?
TEMPLE:	No, mostly on the Continent.
VOSPER:	When Clutch Brompton mentioned the record, did he say anything about the note?
TEMPLE:	You mean the one Dreisler received about Adrian Frost?
VOSPER:	No, the one from Spencer that was sent to Mary Dreisler when the gramophone record was returned.
TEMPLE:	No. Clutch simply advised me to get hold of the record and to play it.
VOSPER:	He made no comment about the note – or anyone called Spencer?
TEMPLE:	No.
VOSPER:	I see. All right, Temple, I'll be in touch with you later.

The door opens and STEVE enters.

STEVE:	I've switched on the radiogram, Paul. I don't know whether you intend to …
TEMPLE:	The Inspector's leaving, Steve. I'll be with you in a minute.
STEVE:	(*Surprised*) Yes, all right, dear.
VOSPER:	Good night, Mrs Temple.
STEVE:	Good night, Inspector.
VOSPER:	(*To TEMPLE, as he goes out*) Will you be in all evening, Temple?
TEMPLE:	(*From the background*) Yes, I expect so.

The telephone rings.

| STEVE: | Shall I answer it, darling? |

TEMPLE: (*From the background*) Yes, please. I'll be back in a moment.

STEVE crosses and picks up the receiver.

STEVE: (*On the phone*) Hello!

JUDY: (*On the other end of the phone; a pleasant voice but at the moment rather tense*) Hello. Who is that, please?

STEVE: This is Mrs Temple speaking.

JUDY: Oh, this is Judy Milton again, Mrs Temple. Has your husband come in yet?

STEVE: Yes, he's here now. Hold on a moment.

TEMPLE returns.

STEVE: (*To TEMPLE*) It's that girl I told you about – Judy Milton.

TEMPLE: (*To STEVE*) I'll take it in the drawing room, Steve.

STEVE: (*On the phone*) Just a minute, Miss Milton – my husband's just coming.

JUDY: (*Tensely*) He won't be long, will he?

STEVE: No, of course not. He's coming now.

After a moment there is a click on the line as TEMPLE picks up the receiver in the drawing room.

TEMPLE: Hello?

JUDY: Mr Temple?

TEMPLE: Yes. What can I do for you, Miss Milton?

JUDY: I've got to see you. It's important. Terribly important. I must see you tonight.

TEMPLE: Well, what is it you want to see me about?

JUDY: About – about Mary Dreisler. There's something I've got to tell you, Mr Temple – please believe me, it really is important.

TEMPLE: All right, I'll see you, Miss Milton. You'd better take down my address. Have you got a piece of paper?

36

JUDY: (*Interrupting TEMPLE*) No, no, I don't want to come to London – not tonight – I don't think it would be wise. Could you – meet me somewhere?

TEMPLE: (*Faintly surprised*) Well, where would you suggest?

JUDY: I'm at Beaconsfield at the moment. I don't know whether you could come out here?

TEMPLE: (*Hesitantly*) Well …

JUDY: (*Urgently*) It is important, Mr Temple – please believe me.

TEMPLE: Very well. What's your address?

JUDY: Rosewood Cottage. It's actually through Beaconsfield on the road to Seer Green.

TEMPLE: I'll find it. I should be there in about an hour.

JUDY: Oh, and Mr Temple …

TEMPLE: Yes?

JUDY: Don't say anything to anyone about this … please …

TEMPLE: (*Noncommittally*) I'll see you in about an hour, Miss Milton.

TEMPLE replaces the telephone receiver.

FADE.

FADE UP the opening of a door.

TEMPLE: Were you listening, Steve?

STEVE: Yes, I was, and I don't like the sound of it. If you're going to see Miss Milton tonight, I'm coming with you.

TEMPLE: (*Thoughtfully*) Yes, all right. (*Suddenly*) Now, listen, Steve – I'm going down to the garage. While I get the car you write a note for Charlie telling him where we're going and if we're not back by midnight he's to get in touch with Sir Graham Forbes.

STEVE: Right

TEMPLE: What are you grinning at?

STEVE: Oh, I was just thinking – here we go again!

FADE OUT.

FADE UP sound of a car travelling at a moderate speed.

STEVE: Paul, we've been up and down this road half a dozen times.

TEMPLE: Well, she said it was on the main road to Seer Green.

STEVE: But there's isn't a cottage on this road. There's the large house on the corner and …

TEMPLE: We'll drive to the end and fork right. There's a phone box on the corner, I'll look her address up in the telephone box.

STEVE: Why on earth don't you ask somebody?

TEMPLE: Because there isn't anybody to ask. In any case, you know what always happens. (*In a broad Scots accent*) I'm afraid I don't know – I'm a stranger in these parts …

STEVE: (*Laughs; suddenly*) Here's someone, Paul. Now don't be silly, pull up, darling, and ask him.

The car draws to a standstill and TEMPLE winds down the car window.

TEMPLE: Excuse me – could you tell me where Rosewood Cottage is?

FROST: (*Surprised*) Rosewood Cottage? Why, yes, certainly. You drive to the end of the road and turn left. Then it's on the right-hand side about a hundred yards down.

TEMPLE: Oh, thank you very much.

FROST: The cottage stands well back from the road –
           you'll have to leave your car and walk across the
           field.

STEVE: Oh dear!

FROST: (*Smiling*) Well, it's not exactly a field – it's a sort
           of paddock.

TEMPLE: Well, thanks again.

FROST: (*Pleasantly*) Who is it you want? Miss Milton?

TEMPLE: Yes.

FROST: She's a friend of mine. I've just left her – well,
           about half an hour ago.

TEMPLE: (*Curious*) Oh?

FROST: Excuse me – your name isn't Temple, by any
           chance?

TEMPLE: Yes, it is.

FROST: Well, how extraordinary! Do you know, I thought
           I recognised you. (*Laughing*) I've just posted a
           letter to you, Mr Temple.

TEMPLE: You have?

FROST: Yes. Judy gave it to me. She asked me to post it
           for her. So I gather she's not expecting you.

TEMPLE: Well, as a matter of fact she is.

FROST: (*Puzzled*) Well, how extraordinary! I wonder why
           she gave me the letter. By the way, my name is
           Frost – Adrian Frost.

TEMPLE: Oh, I'm glad to meet you, Mr Frost. I understand
           you were a friend of Mary Dreisler's.

FROST: (*Hesitantly*) Yes, I knew Mary – we were quite
           good friends. Well, if you'll excuse me, I've got
           my car parked in a garage and I want to get there
           before they close.

TEMPLE: Yes, certainly. (*Suddenly*) Oh, Mr Frost, you've
           probably read in the newspapers – I'm rather
           interested in this Dreisler case.

FROST: Yes, I know.

TEMPLE: I wonder if you'd mind if I asked you a rather personal question?

FROST: (*With a little laugh*) Well, it rather depends on the question.

TEMPLE: Did you ever give Mary Dreisler a diamond brooch?

FROST: (*Obviously surprised by the question*) Yes, I did.

TEMPLE: Why?

FROST: Is that any concern of yours, Mr Temple?

TEMPLE: No, I admit it isn't – but I'd still like to know the answer.

FROST: I gave her the brooch on October 22nd – for a particular reason.

TEMPLE: What was that reason?

FROST: I suggest you make a point of finding out. Good night.

A pause.

TEMPLE changes gear and the car moves forward.

STEVE: (*As the car moves forward*) Well, I'm not exactly crazy about that young man.

TEMPLE: (*His thoughts elsewhere*) At least he wasn't a stranger in the district.

The car gathers speed.

FADE OUT.

FADE IN the sound of wind blowing across a deserted countryside. The sound of a persistent owl hooting is in the background.

FADE UP.

STEVE: (*Tired*) Paul, I just can't go any further, I'm exhausted.

TEMPLE: By Timothy, Steve, you really are the limit. It's only about a hundred yards from the car.

STEVE: In these shoes I feel as if I'd walked all the way from London.

TEMPLE: (*Laughing*) Come on, Steve – there's the cottage. Only another fifty yards.

STEVE: I like old thingummybob's idea of a paddock. It's more like Epson Downs.

TEMPLE: I'll bet this is lovely in the summer.

STEVE: Right now, give me Piccadilly Circus. Gosh, my feet are killing me!

TEMPLE: (*Laughing*) Come on!

FADE SCENE.

FADE UP of TEMPLE knocking on the door of the cottage.

STEVE: Isn't there a bell?

TEMPLE: My dear Steve, if there was a bell I should use it.

TEMPLE continues to knock on the door.

STEVE: I wonder why she doesn't answer.

TEMPLE: Perhaps she isn't in.

STEVE: Somebody's in. There's a light showing in the end room.

TEMPLE: Well, I'll try once again – then if there's no reply we'll go round the back.

TEMPLE knocks on the door.

There is a pause.

STEVE: It's very odd, Paul.

TEMPLE: It certainly is. You wouldn't think she could fail to hear us.

TEMPLE is interrupted by the unmistakable sound of a revolver shot coming from the inside of the cottage.

STEVE: (*Startled*) What was that?

TEMPLE: It sounded to me like a revolver shot from inside the cottage. Stand back, Steve, I'm going to try and force the door.

41

TEMPLE throws his weight against the door. He continues to do so until there is the sound of the lock breaking.

TEMPLE: (*Breathlessly*) That's done it! Now, you stay outside, darling, I shan't be long.

STEVE: No …

TEMPLE: Please do as I tell you – stay outside until I shout for you.

TEMPLE enters the cottage. There is a long pause during which we hear the sound of the wind again and the continuous hooting of the owl.

STEVE: (*Tensely; calling*) Paul, are you all right?

There is no reply.

STEVE: Paul!

There is another pause.

STEVE: (*Definitely alarmed*) Paul!

TEMPLE: (*Approaching*) It's all right, darling – it's all right.

STEVE joins TEMPLE in the hall of the cottage.

STEVE: What's happened?

TEMPLE: There's a girl in the kitchen – she's been shot. I think it's Judy Milton.

STEVE: Oh, Paul!

TEMPLE: (*Quickly*) No, don't go into the kitchen, Steve. I don't want you to see her.

STEVE: I suppose that was the shot we heard?

TEMPLE: Yes. She must have committed suicide. There's no one else in the cottage.

STEVE: D'you think anyone could have got out the back way while we …

TEMPLE: No, I don't think so, we'd have heard them.

STEVE: Paul, you're puzzled about something. What is it?

TEMPLE: Well, it looks like suicide. There's no one else in the cottage. We heard the shot and the revolver's in her hand and yet … I found this on the floor near the body.

STEVE: What is it?

A moment.

STEVE: Why, it's a catalogue of gramophone records!

TEMPLE: Yes. You see what someone's scribbled across it?

STEVE: (*Reading*) "Ask Spencer for … My Heart and Harry."

FADE OUT.

FADE IN the voice of SIR GRAHAM FORBES. He is puzzled and irritated.

FORBES: … Quite frankly, Temple, I just don't understand it.

TEMPLE: I'm not sure that I understand it myself, Sir Graham.

VOSPER: But surely there's only one possible explanation.

FORBES: What do you mean, Vosper?

VOSPER: Mr and Mrs Temple turned up at the cottage – they heard the revolver shot and Temple forced an entrance.

FORBES: Yes, we know that, but the point is Temple didn't see anyone.

VOSPER: He didn't see anyone for the very good reason there was no one in the cottage – except Miss Milton.

TEMPLE: In other words, you think Judy Milton committed suicide?

VOSPER: (*Sure of himself*) Of course she did.

TEMPLE: Then what about the catalogue I found? And the message about the gramophone record?

VOSPER: That doesn't mean anything – it certainly doesn't prove that she was murdered.

43

TEMPLE: I found the catalogue by the body, Inspector. There's no doubt in my mind at any rate, that it had been placed there by someone.

FORBES: I quite agree. How about the handwriting? Have you checked it, Vosper?

VOSPER: Yes, I had the report through about ten minutes ago, sir. Apparently, the words "Ask Spencer for My Heart and Harry" were written by the same person that wrote the note to Rupert Dreisler.

FORBES: You mean the note about Adrian Frost?

VOSPER: Yes.

FORBES: Could Miss Milton have written it? Have you checked her handwriting?

VOSPER: Yes, but it's not the same, sir. (*To TEMPLE*) Incidentally, Temple, what happened about that letter to you from Judy Milton – the one Adrian Frost said he'd posted.

TEMPLE: It didn't come by the first post, but of course it was rather late when he posted it.

FORBES: I can't quite see why she sent you a letter when she knew perfectly well that you were going to call on her.

TEMPLE: Yes, that's what I can't understand, Sir Graham.

VOSPER: Miss Milton must have telephoned you just after I left, Temple.

TEMPLE: Yes, she did. Which reminds me, Vosper, what happened after you left my flat? Did you call in at the Ritz?

VOSPER: Yes, I did.

TEMPLE: And did you see Dreisler?

VOSPER: Yes, I saw him and asked him about the gramophone record. He said he knew nothing about it. He hadn't even given it to his daughter in the first place. I told him that Mrs Thornton said she had seen him leave the flat with it and he said it was absolute nonsense.

TEMPLE: Had he been to the flat?

VOSPER: Oh, yes, he went to the flat all right. He admits that. He said he wanted to collect one or two things belonging to his daughter.

TEMPLE: Go on, Inspector.

VOSPER: Dreisler seemed to me to be telling the truth. So, I went back to Sloane Street and had another word with Mrs Thornton. She told me that she had seen Dreisler leave the flat with a brown paper parcel under his arm and she assumed that it was a gramophone record.

TEMPLE: Why should she do that?

VOSPER: Well, apparently, it looked like a gramophone record.

TEMPLE: I see.

FORBES: Did you search the flat again?

VOSPER: Yes, but I couldn't find the record, Sir Graham. Obviously, someone had taken it.

FORBES: (*Thoughtfully*) Ummm!

VOSPER: Of course, we may be wrong about the record. It may be just a red herring.

TEMPLE: And Spencer?

VOSPER: Well, he may be just a red herring, too. Perhaps he doesn't exist.

TEMPLE: I'd be inclined to agree with you, Vosper, if it wasn't for the fact that Clutch Brompton mentioned the record.

FORBES: What exactly did Brompton say, Temple?

TEMPLE: He simply advised me to get hold of the record and play it. Incidentally, how is Clutch?

VOSPER: He's still unconscious. I've been on to the hospital this morning, they don't hold out much hope I'm afraid.

TEMPLE: Oh, I'm sorry to hear that.

FORBES: I suppose you didn't see the driver of the car, Temple?

TEMPLE: Yes, I saw him, but he was wearing goggles. I'd never recognise him again.

FORBES: (*To VOSPER*) Have you traced the car?

VOSPER: Not yet, sir.

The door opens and a police sergeant enters.

SERGEANT: Excuse me, sir, a Mr Frost would like to see you.

FORBES: Mr Frost! Yes, all right, Sergeant, ask him in.

TEMPLE: He's obviously heard about Judy Milton.

VOSPER: Is it in the papers?

TEMPLE: Yes, there was a report in the Stop Press.

ADRIAN FROST enters. He is slightly on edge.

FROST: I'm sorry, interrupting you like this, but … (*He notices TEMPLE*) Oh, good morning, Mr Temple.

TEMPLE: Good morning.

FROST: Sir Graham, what's happened to Judy Milton? There's a report in my paper that she's committed suicide.

FORBES: Miss Milton's dead. Whether she's committed suicide or not, we don't know.

FROST: (*Confused*) What do you mean, exactly?

FORBES: We're not sure yet whether it was suicide or murder.

FROST: Murder?

FORBES: Yes.

A slight pause.

VOSPER:	We understand you saw Miss Milton last night, sir.
FROST:	Yes, I did. I was passing through Beaconsfield so I dropped in and had a drink with her.
VOSPER:	Was she a very old friend of yours, Mr Frost?
FROST:	Well, we've known one another for quite a little while, if that's what you mean.
TEMPLE:	Had you any special reason for calling on Miss Milton last night?
FROST:	Er – yes, I had, as a matter of fact.
TEMPLE:	What was that reason?
FROST:	I'd written the first act of a play and I wanted Judy to read it. She – she was awfully good at that sort of thing …
VOSPER:	What sort of thing, sir?
FROST:	Well – er – reading plays and giving one a candid criticism. It's a difficult thing to get, Inspector.
VOSPER:	Mr Temple tells me that when he saw you you were walking.
FROST:	Yes.
VOSPER:	Why was that?
FROST:	My car had gone wrong and I'd parked it in a garage.
VOSPER:	What was the name of the garage?
FROST:	(*Hesitantly*) I'm afraid I can't remember.
VOSPER:	Was it in Beaconsfield?
FROST:	(*Irritated*) Yes. Yes, I believe so.
FORBES:	Mr Frost, what time was it when you left the cottage?
FROST:	So far as I can remember about half past nine.
VOSPER:	Was Miss Milton in good spirits?
FROST:	Yes, certainly. She seemed quite bright.

FORBES: Did she tell you she was expecting Mr Temple?

FROST: No, she didn't. On the contrary, she gave me a letter for Mr Temple and asked me to post it.

TEMPLE: You did post it?

FROST: I did. Haven't you received it?

TEMPLE: Not yet, but there's still time. Frost, assuming for the moment that Miss Milton did not commit suicide – but was murdered.

FROST: Yes?

TEMPLE: Have you any idea who murdered her?

FROST: No, of course I haven't.

TEMPLE: And you can't suggest a motive?

FROST: No, I'm afraid I can't. The whole thing's a complete mystery to me, but then – so was this other terrible business with Mary Dreisler.

TEMPLE: (*After a moment*) Frost, have you got a gramophone?

FROST: (*Surprised*) A gramophone! Why, yes – yes, of course.

TEMPLE: Do you happen to have a record called "My Heart and Harry"?

FROST: No.

TEMPLE: Have you heard the record?

FROST: Yes. I heard it on the radio once.

TEMPLE: But you can't get the record over here, Mr Frost, – so how could you hear it on the radio?

FROST: On the short wave, Mr Temple, from New York.

TEMPLE: Oh, I see.

FROST: But what made you ask about "My Heart and Harry"?

TEMPLE: I wondered if you'd heard it, Mr Frost, that's all.

FADE.

FADE UP of ringing of phone bell. STEVE lifts the receiver.

STEVE: (*On the phone*) Hello? Who is that?

DREISLER: (*On the other end*) This is Rupert Dreisler. Could I speak to Mr Temple, please?

STEVE: Oh, I'm sorry, but my husband's out at the moment.

DREISLER: (*Rather perturbed*) When will he be back, Mrs Temple? Do you know?

In the background a door opens and closes.

STEVE: Well, I'm expecting him for lunch, but ... Oh, one moment, I think he's just arrived.

TEMPLE enters.

TEMPLE: Who is it, darling?

STEVE: It's Rupert Dreisler. He wants to talk to you. (*Handing TEMPLE the receiver*) He sounds rather worried.

TEMPLE: (*On the phone*) Hello? Paul Temple here.

DREISLER: Oh, Mr Temple, I've been intending to telephone you all morning but ...

TEMPLE: What can I do for you, Mr Dreisler?

DREISLER: Last night, a man called Vosper – I think he's a police Inspector – asked me a lot of questions about a gramophone record. I didn't understand him – my English, you know – is not always so good and ...

TEMPLE: What's on your mind, Mr Dreisler?

DREISLER: Well, after the Inspector left, I suddenly remembered that two or three years ago I gave my daughter an album of gramophone records – for a Christmas present, you know – and it occurred to me that perhaps the record he was talking about was in the album.

TEMPLE: Didn't the Inspector mention the title?

49

DREISLER: Yes, I think he said it was called "My Heart and Harry".

TEMPLE: That's right. It's a comparatively new number from a Broadway show. But surely you know that, Mr Dreisler?

DREISLER: (*With a nervous little laugh*) Why, yes – yes, of course – how stupid of me. I'm sorry to have bothered you.

TEMPLE: That's all right. By the way, I suppose you've heard about Miss Milton?

DREISLER: Miss Milton?

TEMPLE: Judy Milton – she was a friend of your daughter's.

DREISLER: No. Has something happened to Miss Milton?

TEMPLE: Yes – she died last night. It's my opinion she was murdered.

DREISLER: (*Shocked*) How dreadful! How ... absolutely dreadful. What are the police doing? What are they doing?

TEMPLE: They're making enquiries, Mr Dreisler. (*A moment*) Are you staying in London for long?

DREISLER: Yes, I'm staying for several weeks. I don't really feel I want to leave after what happened to Mary.

TEMPLE: Yes, I can understand that. Well, you know where I am, if you want me.

DREISLER: You're very kind. Thank you, Mr Temple. Goodbye.

TEMPLE: Goodbye.

TEMPLE replaces the receiver.

STEVE: What did he want, Paul?

TEMPLE: (*Thoughtfully*) I think he was rather puzzled why Vosper paid him a visit last night.

STEVE:	But he must have known that Mrs Thornton would notice the gramophone record.
TEMPLE:	It now transpires that he didn't take the record from the flat – at least he says he didn't.
STEVE:	But I thought Mrs Thornton said …
TEMPLE:	Apparently, all Mrs Thornton saw was a brown paper parcel that looked like a gramophone record. (*Looking up as the door opens*) Yes, Charlie?
CHARLIE:	The post, sir.
TEMPLE:	Thank you.
CHARLIE:	I think this is the letter you're expecting, sir. It's got a Beaconsfield postmark.
TEMPLE:	Oh, thank you, Charlie.
CHARLIE:	Will you be in to lunch, sir?
STEVE:	(*Impatiently*) Yes, Charlie, yes.
CHARLIE:	Okay, Mrs Temple.

TEMPLE opens the envelope.

STEVE:	(*Curious*) What does it say, Paul?
TEMPLE:	(*Reading*) "Dear Mr Temple, I have left a parcel in the cloakroom at the Neptune Club. I feel sure it will interest you. I suggest your wife picks it up. Yours sincerely, Judy Milton."
STEVE:	The Neptune Club? Isn't that the place we went to in Regent Street about a year ago?
TEMPLE:	That's right. It's run by a woman called Terry Gibson. She used to be an actress then she retired and bought this club in Regent Street. They say she's done awfully well with it.
STEVE:	(*Puzzled*) I wonder what it is, Paul. I wonder what she's left in the cloakroom?
TEMPLE:	Your guess it as good as mine, Steve. We'll go there tonight, darling. It's no good going

51

	round this afternoon. We'll only arouse suspicion.
STEVE:	Yes, all right. (*A moment*) Paul, do you think the person who murdered Mary Dreisler also murdered Judy Milton?
TEMPLE:	Yes, I do.
STEVE:	And yet … (*She hesitates*)
TEMPLE:	And yet – what?
STEVE:	And yet – Judy Milton couldn't have been murdered. You broke into the cottage the moment we heard the shot – if there'd been anyone there, you'd have seen them.
TEMPLE:	Yes, that's what puzzles me, Steve.

The door opens and Charlie enters.

CHARLIE:	Excuse me, Mrs Temple –
STEVE:	Yes, what it is, Charlie?
CHARLIE:	I'm having a spot of bother with the fridge. It's not working properly.
TEMPLE:	Well – what's the matter with it?
CHARLIE:	It's supposed to be automatic – you know – switches itself on and off. Well, it switched itself off about an hour ago and it hasn't switched on again.
STEVE:	Oh, well – give Taylor's a ring – Mayfair 8151.
CHARLIE:	Yes, Mrs Temple.
TEMPLE:	(*Suddenly very bright; excessively pleased with himself*) And thank you, Charlie, thank you very much.
CHARLIE:	(*Puzzled*) For what, sir?
TEMPLE:	For telling me about the fridge, Charlie.
CHARLIE:	(*Still bewildered*) Oh, not at all. It's a pleasure, Mr Temple.

CHARLIE goes out.

STEVE: Are you feeling all right, Paul?

TEMPLE: (*Amused*) Yes, I feel fine. Come along, let's have lunch.

STEVE: Paul, what are you grinning at?

TEMPLE: Come along, Steve!

FADE OUT.

FADE UP the noise of a car. The car draws to a standstill. The engine is switched off.

STEVE: Is that the Neptune Club over there?

TEMPLE: Yes, on the right. Now don't forget what I told you, Steve.

STEVE: Don't worry. I'll be all right.

TEMPLE: If you're longer than five minutes, I shall come and fetch you.

FADE OUT.

Slow FADE UP of background noises of the foyer of the Neptune Club. A dance orchestra can be heard playing in the background.

STEVE: Excuse me, where's the Ladies' Cloakroom?

TERRY: (*A well-spoken yet rather tough woman in the early fifties*) It's through that door over there on the left.

STEVE: Oh, thank you.

TERRY: It's Mrs Temple, isn't it?

STEVE: (*Surprised*) Yes.

TERRY: I thought I recognised you. I'm Terry Gibson.

STEVE: Oh, yes, of course, Miss Gibson. We met about a year ago.

TERRY: Yes, that's right. Is your husband joining you?

STEVE: (*Hesitantly*) Yes, he's just parking the car.

TERRY: Well, I hope you have a pleasant evening.

STEVE: Thank you.

TERRY: Have you reserved a table, Mrs Temple?
STEVE: Yes, I – I believe so.
TERRY: Well – see you later.
FADE DOWN background.
KATIE: (*A Cockney with a slight sing-song voice*)
            Good evening, madam – shall I take your
            coat?
STEVE: No, I'm not staying. I've just called to collect
            something.
KATIE: Oh? What is it, madam?
STEVE: I left a parcel here a few days ago.
KATIE: Have you got the ticket?
STEVE: No, I'm afraid I haven't. I don't think you
            gave me a ticket.
KATIE: We must have given you a ticket. We daren't
            breathe around here without a ticket.
STEVE: Well, I don't think you did …
KATIE: What name is it?
STEVE: Milton. Judy Milton.
KATIE: Well, now, wait a minute. Let's see if it's
            over here. (*A moment*) What sort of a parcel is
            it?
STEVE: Oh, just a – you know, an ordinary parcel.
KATIE: (*From the near background*) That's a great
            help, duckie, that is. (*Suddenly*) Now, wait a
            minute – is this it?
STEVE: (*Quietly*) Yes, that's it.
KATIE: It's a gramophone record by the looks of
            things.
STEVE: Yes, that's the one.
KATIE: Now, wait a minute. There's something
            written on this … (*She peers at the parcel*)
            Really! My eyes … I shall have to wear
            specs. I'm not a bit of use …

54

STEVE:	Don't worry, that's the parcel all right.
KATIE:	Yes, but I've got to make sure. Lord, if I gave it to the wrong person there'd be hell to pay with La Gibson and no mistake. What did you say your name was?
STEVE:	(*Nervously*) Judy Milton.
KATIE:	That's right. (*Reading*) "Miss Milton … To be called for." Well, here we are.
STEVE:	Thank you.
KATIE:	(*Accepting a tip*) Oh, thank you, Miss!

FADE SCENE.

FADE UP the noise of a crowded foyer.

TERRY:	Why, hello, are you leaving us so soon, Mrs Temple?
STEVE:	(*Taken by surprise*) I'm only going to look for my husband. I left my handbag in the car.
TERRY:	I'll send one of the boys for you.
STEVE:	No, no, I wouldn't dream of troubling you.
TERRY:	It's no trouble, I assure you.

PETER WALLACE enters. He doesn't immediately recognise STEVE.

WALLACE:	Good evening, Terry.
TERRY:	Good evening, Peter.

WALLACE stops, recognising STEVE.

WALLACE:	Why – it's Mrs Temple, isn't it?
STEVE:	Yes.
WALLACE:	Is your husband here?
STEVE:	(*Hesitantly*) He will be very shortly.
WALLACE:	(*Pleased*) Oh, good. I wanted to have a word with him. Curiously enough, I tried to get him on the phone about half an hour ago.
TERRY:	(*Curious*) You two know each other, then?
WALLACE:	(*Curtly*) Yes, we have met before.

STEVE: Well, if you'll excuse me …

WALLACE: No, don't go, Mrs Temple. Not for a moment, please. (*Dismissing TERRY GIBSON*) I'll see you later, Terry.

TERRY: (*After a moment*) Yes, all right, Peter.

TERRY GIBSON goes.

STEVE: What is it you want, Mr Wallace? I'm in rather a hurry.

WALLACE: Mrs Temple, does your husband know about this new development – about Judy Milton?

STEVE: Yes, he knows. We saw Miss Milton last night.

WALLACE: (*Surprised*) You did? Where?

STEVE: At Beaconsfield.

WALLACE: Why did you go out to Beaconsfield? Did Judy …

STEVE: (*Determined to break away*) Look, Mr Wallace, I can't stand and talk now. I'll get my husband to give you a ring.

WALLACE: But I thought you said your husband was joining you?

STEVE: (*As she leaves*) Good night, Mr Wallace.

WALLACE: Good night, Mrs Temple.

FADE OUT.

FADE UP the noise of Regent Street traffic and a car door opening.

TEMPLE: I was just coming to fetch you, Steve.

STEVE: It's a good job you didn't – you'd have got tied up with Peter Wallace.

TEMPLE: Yes, I saw him go into the club.

The car door closes as STEVE enters the car.

STEVE: I should have thought that place was too expensive for Mr Wallace.

TEMPLE: Well, I see you've got the parcel all right.

STEVE: Yes. And what do you think it is?

TEMPLE: Wait till I switch the light on.

TEMPLE switches on the interior car light.

TEMPLE: By Timothy!

STEVE: Yes, it's the record!

TEMPLE takes the parcel and rips off the brown paper.

STEVE: That's the one, isn't it, Paul?

TEMPLE: "My Heart and Harry" – yes, that's the one all right. Now, how on earth did Judy Milton get hold of it? And why did she leave it at the Neptune Club?

STEVE: And most important of all – what's on the record?

TEMPLE: Yes. Well, we'll find that out as soon as we get back to the flat.

TEMPLE presses the starter and the car engine starts.

FADE on the car driving away.

FADE UP on a doorbell ringing.

TEMPLE: What on earth's the matter with Charlie? Why doesn't he answer the door?

STEVE: Haven't you got your keys?

TEMPLE: I left them on the desk.

STEVE is searching her handbag.

STEVE: I don't know why it is, Paul, but you always leave your keys – well, I should have mine somewhere – Oh, here we are!

STEVE opens the door. TEMPLE and STEVE enter the flat.

TEMPLE: (*Calling*) Charlie! Charlie, where are you?

STEVE: He's probably gone to bed.

TEMPLE: It's my bet he's taken the night off and gone to the Palais.

STEVE: (*Calling*) Charlie! Are you in bed?

TEMPLE: Oh, come on, darling, let's go into the drawing room.
STEVE: I'll be with you in a minute. I'm just going to get a glass of … (*Suddenly*) Paul, wait a minute, listen.
TEMPLE: What is it?
STEVE: Did you hear something?
There is a slight pause. Then from the kitchen comes a definite groan of someone in pain.
TEMPLE: Yes, it's coming from the kitchen.
TEMPLE throws open the kitchen door and both TEMPLE and STEVE enter the kitchen.
STEVE: (*Alarmed*) Charlie!
TEMPLE: Get some brandy, Steve – quickly!
STEVE: Paul, what is it? What's happened?
TEMPLE: Darling, he's not lying on the floor for fun. Someone's knocked him out. Get the brandy.
STEVE: Yes, all right.
CHARLIE groans and attempts to raise himself from the floor.
CHARLIE: Is that … you … Mr Temple?
TEMPLE: Yes … what happened, Charlie?
CHARLIE: (*Still dazed*) The bell rang … I thought it was you and Mrs Temple … When I got to the door two men … Gosh, my head …
TEMPLE: Take it easy, you'll be all right.
CHARLIE: I felt such a fool. One minute I was standing in the doorway, the next … Gosh, my head feels like a sieve …
TEMPLE: You'll be all right in a minute, Charlie.
CHARLIE: Do you think I could have a drink?
TEMPLE: Yes, of course. Mrs Temple's getting you one … Now, if I were you, I should …
STEVE: Here's the brandy …
TEMPLE: Thanks.

TEMPLE pours the brandy into a glass.

TEMPLE: Now drink this, Charlie.

CHARLIE takes a long drink.

CHARLIE: (*A gasp*) That's better …

TEMPLE: Now, what exactly happened?

CHARLIE: Well, these two chaps I was telling you about knocked me out and dumped me in the kitchen. I 'eard a Dickens of a noise going on and then I passed out.

TEMPLE: What do you mean, a Dickens of a noise?

CHARLIE: I don't know. It sounded to me as if they were smashing the place to pieces.

STEVE: Paul …

TEMPLE: Yes?

STEVE: (*Significantly*) We can't play the record …

TEMPLE: What do you mean? Why can't we play it?

STEVE: They've smashed the radiogram.

MUSIC.

END OF EPISODE TWO

EPISODE THREE

INTRODUCING
PETE ROBERTS

OPENING MUSIC.
FADE DOWN MUSIC.
FADE UP.

TEMPLE: Now, what exactly happened?
CHARLIE: Well, these two chaps I was telling you about knocked me out and dumped me in the kitchen. I 'eard a Dickens of a noise going on and then I passed out.
TEMPLE: What do you mean, a Dickens of a noise?
CHARLIE: I don't know. It sounded to me as if they were smashing the place to pieces.
STEVE: Paul …
TEMPLE: Yes?
STEVE: (*Significantly*) We can't play the record …
TEMPLE: What do you mean? Why can't we play it?
STEVE: They've smashed the radiogram.
TEMPLE: They've – what?
STEVE: They've smashed the radiogram to pieces.
CHARLIE: Blimey! That must have been the noise I heard!
TEMPLE: But that's incredible, Steve! Why … Come along, Charlie, let's take a look.

FADE DOWN.

FADE UP TEMPLE, STEVE and CHARLIE entering the drawing room.
STEVE: Well, now do you believe me?
CHARLIE: (*Nonplussed*) They haven't touched a blessed thing except the radiogram – they must have been off their rockers!
TEMPLE: Charlie, do you think you'd recognise these men again?

CHARLIE: I don't know. I might recognise one of them
              … a tall, dark looking chap. Oooh! My head!
TEMPLE: Is it still hurting you?
CHARLIE: Well – it's not so bad as it was, but it's bad
              enough.
TEMPLE: You get to bed, Charlie. We'll deal with this
              mess.
CHARLIE: Yes, all right, Mr Temple.
STEVE: Good night, Charlie – and take some aspirin.
CHARLIE: Good night.
The door closes.
TEMPLE: Well, you're quite right, Steve. They certainly
              didn't intend us to play the record.
STEVE: Yes, but surely they must realise this is just a
              temporary setback. We can borrow a
              gramophone or take the record round to …
              (*She stops*)
TEMPLE: (*Quietly*) Are you thinking the same as I am?
STEVE: They're expecting us to go out again – to take
              the record somewhere.
TEMPLE: Yes. Steve, walk towards the door and put the
              light out.
STEVE: Why? What are you going to do?
TEMPLE: Do as I say, darling.
STEVE crosses the room and switches out the light.
TEMPLE draws back the curtain.
STEVE: What are you doing at the window?
TEMPLE: (*Quietly*) Just as I thought. There's someone
              watching the flat.
STEVE: Who is it? Do you know?
TEMPLE: No, I can't see clearly enough, but there's a
              man opposite and a taxi parked on the corner.
              (*He turns from the window*) Go into the study,

Steve, and ring Sir Graham. I'll be with you
in just a minute.

STEVE: Right.

FADE.

*FADE UP a number ringing out. A telephone receiver is
lifted.*

FORBES: (*On the other end of the phone*) Hello?

TEMPLE: Sir Graham?

FORBES: Yes.

TEMPLE: This is Temple.

FORBES: Oh, hello, Temple.

TEMPLE: Sir Graham, listen. I've got the record I spoke
                to Vosper about. Unfortunately, I can't play it
                – I'll explain why later. The point is this: I
                propose leaving the flat in about ten minutes.
                I'm almost certain someone will try to pick
                me up.

FORBES: Ten minutes. (*He looks at his watch*) I make it
                ten forty-five. Check?

TEMPLE: Check.

FORBES: Right, Temple. Don't worry – we know what
                to do.

TEMPLE: Thank you, Sir Graham.

TEMPLE replaces the receiver.

TEMPLE: Steve, get me a gramophone record – the
                same size as this.

STEVE: Paul, what are you going to do?

TEMPLE: (*Reassuringly*) I'm going to be a decoy,
                darling – but if I know Sir Graham, half
                Scotland Yard will be on my tail.

FADE.

FADE UP street noises. The sound of a taxi drawing to a standstill near the kerb. The driver of the taxi, ERIC LANSDALE, is a tough, middle-aged Cockney.

ERIC: Cab, sir?

TEMPLE: Oh, thank you. (*He opens the cab door*) Take me to 27 Welbourne Crescent.

ERIC: Yes, sir.

TEMPLE gets into the cab and closes the door. ERIC turns down his flag and the cab draws away.
FADE.

FADE UP the taxi travelling at a medium speed. TEMPLE slides back the windows and speaks to the driver.

TEMPLE: I said I wanted to go to Welbourne Crescent.

ERIC: Yes, I know.

TEMPLE: Well, that's in Knightsbridge.

ERIC: I know that, too.

TEMPLE: Well, what's the idea, bringing me into the Park?

ERIC: I'll tell you what the idea is.

The cab suddenly slows down to a standstill. ERIC gets out of the driver's seat and opens the cab door.

ERIC: Get out of the cab.

TEMPLE: I beg your pardon?

ERIC: You heard what I said – get out!

TEMPLE: Now, look here! I don't know who you think you're speaking to …

ERIC: I know who I'm speaking to, chummy. Your name's Temple.

TEMPLE: (*Apparently surprised*) How did you …

ERIC: Get out of the cab, Mr Temple, and give me the parcel you're carrying.

TEMPLE: Why do you want this parcel?

66

ERIC: Listen, chummy – this isn't Twenty Questions!
           Now do as I tell you and get out of the cab.

TEMPLE: And supposing I don't do as you tell me, Mr –
           whatever-your-name-is?

ERIC: Mr Temple, you see this revolver?

TEMPLE: I could hardly fail to see it. I trust it isn't as
           noisy as it looks.

ERIC: Give me that record!

TEMPLE: Certainly. Incidentally, I'm sorry to disappoint
           you but it's not the record you're expecting.

ERIC: What do you mean?

TEMPLE: Take a look at it. (*Suddenly; throwing the parcel*)
           Catch!

ERIC: (*Taken by surprise*) What the …

*TEMPLE leaps out of the cab and grabs ERIC's arm. There is
a brief struggle for the possession of the revolver.*

ERIC: Let go my arm … (*In obvious pain*) Leave go!

*In the background there is the sound of an approaching police
car.*

TEMPLE: Drop the revolver! Drop it!

ERIC drops the gun.

TEMPLE: Now, my pugilistic friend, what's this all about?
           Who put you up to this?

*The police car arrives on the scene. There is the sound of
voices and the opening and closing of the car doors.*

ERIC: (*Nervously*) I was told to pick you up – get the
           parcel – and take it to a house in Regents Park.

TEMPLE: Who told you to do that?

*FORBES arrives with VOSPER and several plain-clothes
men.*

FORBES: Temple, are you all right?

TEMPLE: Yes, I'm all right. But our friend here isn't in
           such good shape.

VOSPER: Take him down to the station – book him.

67

ERIC: (*Angrily*) What d'you mean – book him? You can't arrest me for …

VOSPER: (*Picking up the revolver*) Have you got a licence for this revolver?

ERIC: (*Surly*) No. No, I haven't. It isn't mine, anyway.

TEMPLE: Wait a minute, Vosper. (*To ERIC*) You said you were told to take the parcel to a house in Regents Park.

ERIC: (*Hesitantly*) Yes.

TEMPLE: Which house?

ERIC: A hundred and twenty-eight.

TEMPLE: Who told you this?

ERIC: I don't know. I can't remember his name.

VOSPER: No? But I've just remembered yours. You're Eric Lansdale, aren't you?

ERIC: (*Worried*) Yes.

VOSPER: I thought I'd seen you before somewhere. You used to be a friend of Sid Edwards.

ERIC: That's an 'ell of a time ago – when I lived in Brighton. I don't live there any more.

VOSPER: (*Significantly*) Neither does Sid Edwards.

FORBES: Don't you think you'd better tell us what this is all about?

ERIC: A fellow called Frost offered me fifty quid to pick up Mr Temple – pinch the parcel and take it to the house in Regents Park.

TEMPLE: When was this?

ERIC: About an hour ago. He telephoned me – said you'd be leaving the flat with a brown paper parcel.

FORBES: When did you first meet this man Frost?

ERIC: Oh, about two or three months ago.

FORBES: Where?

ERIC: At a pub called The Bronze Heart.

TEMPLE: Where's that?

ERIC: It's in Stepney.

TEMPLE: Did you meet him by appointment?

ERIC: (*Hesitantly*) No. I just bumped into him, and
            we got talking. I've – done one or two odd
            jobs for him since.

VOSPER: What sort of jobs?

ERIC: (*Nervously*) Just running about – messages –
            that sort of thing.

VOSPER: All right, Lansdale. Take him down to the
            station, Sergeant.

ERIC: What the 'ell are you talking about?

An angry and protesting ERIC is taken away.

SERGEANT: Come on now.

ERIC: (*Going off*) You can't do this to me just
            because I picked up somebody and … Take
            your hands off me!

ERIC and SERGEANT are now out of sound.

TEMPLE: I gather you've met Mr Lansdale before,
            Inspector?

VOSPER: Yes. He's a dangerous little devil. I wouldn't
            trust him as far as I could throw that cab.

FORBES: What about his story – do you believe it?

VOSPER: I don't know.

TEMPLE: (*Smiling*) I thought you liked Mr Frost,
            Inspector?

VOSPER: I do, but – anyway, let's see what he's got to
            say for himself.

FADE SCENE.

*FADE UP the voice of ADRIAN FROST. He is angry and
indignant.*

69

FROST:	I've heard some ridiculous stories in my time, but this really beats the lot. It really does, Inspector.
VOSPER:	I take it then that you've never heard of Eric Lansdale?
FROST:	Of course I've never heard of him. I have a large circle of friends, Inspector, but they don't include taxi drivers.
TEMPLE:	Have you heard of a public house called The Bronze Heart?
FROST:	(*Hesitating*) Yes.
TEMPLE:	Where is it?
FROST:	It's in Stepney.
FORBES:	Have you been there?
FROST:	Yes, I – went there about two months ago.
FORBES:	Why?
FROST:	(*Angrily*) Really, Sir Graham, what on earth has my visit to a pub in Stepney got to do with this Eric Lansdale, or whatever you call him?
FORBES:	Lansdale says that's where he met you.
FROST:	What? At the Bronze Heart?
FORBES:	Yes.
FROST:	But that's absurd!
TEMPLE:	Why did you go to Stepney?
FROST:	I went because … (*Still angry*) Dash it all, I don't see that it's any concern of yours.
TEMPLE:	(*Pleasantly*) It isn't. But if you don't tell us why you went there, we shall probably think the worst. Human nature being what it is, Mr Frost.
FROST:	Well, if you must know, that's precisely why I went there.
TEMPLE:	What do you mean?

FROST:	Human nature being what it is.
VOSPER:	I'm afraid I don't understand you.
TEMPLE:	You mean you went there just to see people, to study certain types?
FROST:	That's exactly what I mean.
FORBES:	But why should you do that?
FROST:	I'm writing a play. The whole of the second act takes place in the East End of London. I went down to Stepney to get – well – I suppose you'd call it local colour.
VOSPER:	That doesn't sound very convincing.
FROST:	I'm not trying to convince you, Inspector. I'm simply telling you the truth.
FORBES:	And you're quite sure that during your visit to Stepney you didn't meet Lansdale?
FROST:	I'm quite sure.
FORBES:	And you didn't ask Lansdale to get the record for you?
FROST:	I know nothing about the record other than what you've told me.
FORBES:	I see.
FROST:	Look, Sir Graham, you've either got to believe me or believe this other fellow. It's up to you.
FORBES:	Exactly. Good night, Mr Frost.
FROST:	(*Rather concerned*) Good night.
TEMPLE:	Good night, Frost.
FROST:	Good night, Temple. Good night, Inspector.
VOSPER:	Good night.

COMPLETE FADE.

FADE UP street noises. The sound of a stationary car ticking over.

FORBES:	We'd better take you back to your flat, Temple, then we can pick the record up and go on to Vosper's place. I take it you've got a gramophone, Vosper?
VOSPER:	Yes, sir.
FORBES:	Good. Well, that's all right, then.
TEMPLE:	(*Suddenly*) Wait a minute, I've left my gloves behind. I shan't be a second.

FADE ON sound of the car ticking over.

FADE UP of a door opening.

TEMPLE:	I'm sorry, Frost, but I think I left my gloves behind.
FROST:	Yes, you did. Here they are.
TEMPLE:	Oh, thank you.
FROST:	(*Amused*) What is it you want to ask me?
TEMPLE:	Ask you? What makes you think I want to ask you something?
FROST:	Your gloves! (*Shaking his head*) You didn't forget them.
TEMPLE:	Didn't I?
FROST:	No. (*Smiling*) What's on your mind, Temple?
TEMPLE:	Do you keep a diary?
FROST:	(*Surprised*) A diary? Why, yes, I do, as a matter of fact.
TEMPLE:	I thought so. Good night.
FROST:	(*Puzzled*) Good night.
TEMPLE:	(*Turning back; pleasantly*) Oh – er – my gloves …

FADE OUT.

FADE UP the sound of a doorbell ringing. Eventually the door is opened.

STEVE:	(*Surprised*) Why, hello, Mr Wallace.

WALLACE: Good evening, Mrs Temple. Is your husband in?

STEVE: No, I'm afraid he isn't at the moment.

WALLACE: Are you expecting him?

STEVE: Well – yes.

WALLACE: Mrs Temple, may I come in for a few minutes? There's something I want to tell you.

STEVE: (*Hesitantly*) Yes, all right, Mr Wallace.

WALLACE enters the hall, and they pass into the drawing room.

WALLACE: (*Entering the drawing room*) When I saw you at the Neptune Club, I was hoping you and your husband would join me for a drink.

STEVE: I only called to collect something – from the cloakroom.

WALLACE: Oh, I see. I was under a misapprehension, I thought your husband was with you.

STEVE: Is the Neptune a frequent haunt of yours?

WALLACE: I've been there once or twice with friends. It's quite pleasant and the food's good. Mrs Temple, when I saw your husband the other day I did rather a mean thing, I'm afraid.

STEVE: Did you?

WALLACE: Yes, I deliberately – quite deliberately – threw suspicion on Adrian Frost.

STEVE: I wouldn't say you threw suspicion on to him. You simply said he was a bad influence over Mary Dreisler and that in your opinion he was responsible for her death.

WALLACE: Yes – that's what I mean.

STEVE: You're entitled to your opinion, Mr Wallace, the same as anyone else.

WALLACE: Yes, I know, but –

STEVE: Have you changed your opinion then about Frost?

WALLACE: (*Embarrassed*) No, I haven't changed my opinion about Frost himself. I still think it's a pity Mary ever met him, but – well, let's face it, I was jealous of Frost. I always have been.

STEVE: Yes, I know. You told my husband that. But you also said that your jealousy had nothing whatever to do with your feelings about the murder.

WALLACE: Exactly. But on reflection, I don't think that was strictly true. I was jealous and I'm afraid I let my jealousy influence my – well – my better judgement.

STEVE: So you've come to the conclusion that Frost had nothing whatsoever to do with the murder?

WALLACE: Oh, I wouldn't say that, but –

STEVE: (*Irritated*) Well, what would you say, Mr Wallace?

WALLACE: Well, it's just that I wouldn't like to think that anything I'd said about Frost might have influenced your husband.

STEVE: My husband isn't very easily influenced. Now, if you'll excuse me –

WALLACE: Yes, of course, Mrs Temple. And thank you for seeing me. Oh, there is one other thing.

STEVE: Yes?

WALLACE: I don't know what Mr Temple thinks about this new development – the Judy Milton murder?

STEVE: It hasn't yet been established that she <u>was</u> murdered. Indeed, it looks very much like suicide.

WALLACE: Oh, I see.

STEVE: Still, what were you going to say?

WALLACE: I was going to say – if it <u>was</u> murder, and
             your husband thinks that the same person was
             responsible for both murders, then – it
             couldn't have been Frost.

STEVE: Why not?

WALLACE: He was a great friend of Judy's. He thought
             the world of her.

STEVE: Oh, did he? Well, thank you for calling, Mr
             Wallace. I'll tell my husband what you've
             told me.

WALLACE: Thank you, Mrs Temple. (*With a strange
             suggestion of friendliness*) You do
             understand, don't you?

STEVE: – Er – yes. Yes, I do indeed.

WALLACE: Thank you – you've been most kind.
             (*Crossing towards the door; pleasantly*) You
             needn't show me out, Mrs Temple, I can find
             my way.

FADE OUT.

*FADE UP of a key being inserted in a lock. The front door
opens. STEVE enters the hall.*

STEVE: Is that you, Paul?

TEMPLE: Yes, darling.

STEVE: Are you all right?

TEMPLE: (*Laughing*) Yes.

STEVE: What happened?

TEMPLE: I'll tell you later, Steve. Sir Graham's
             downstairs with Vosper – we're going round
             to the Inspector's to play the record.

STEVE: I'll get it for you. It's in the drawing room.

TEMPLE: How's Charlie?

75

STEVE:	Oh, he's much better. He's just had something to eat.

TEMPLE and STEVE enter the drawing room.

STEVE:	Here it is – this is the record.
TEMPLE:	Thank you, dear.
STEVE:	I'll get my coat.
TEMPLE:	There's no point in your coming, Steve.
STEVE:	That's what you think! I got the record! I want to know what's on it.
TEMPLE:	(*Laughing*) And so you shall the moment I get back.
STEVE:	(*Hesitantly*) Well …
TEMPLE:	You go to bed, darling, I'll be back in an hour or so.
STEVE:	I must confess I feel more like bed than anything else at the moment.
TEMPLE:	I'll see you later, dear.
STEVE:	Give my regards to Sir Graham and tell the Inspector he's quite right about Peter Wallace.
TEMPLE:	What do you mean?
STEVE:	Didn't Vosper say he was a crashing bore?
TEMPLE:	Yes.
STEVE:	Well, he is.
TEMPLE:	Why do you say that?
STEVE:	He was here ten minutes ago …
TEMPLE:	(*Surprised*) What! Wallace was here?
STEVE:	Yes. He said he wanted to see you – acted as if it was frightfully important. It turned out that he'd simply changed his mind about Adrian Frost.
TEMPLE:	How do you mean, changed his mind?
STEVE:	He said he was sorry if he gave you the impression that Frost murdered Mary

76

	Dreisler. He said his statement to you was inspired entirely by jealousy.
TEMPLE:	And he's now changed his opinion of Frost?
STEVE:	No, I don't think he's changed his opinion, but – well, he doesn't want to be responsible for suspicion falling on Frost.
TEMPLE:	Did Wallace give you the impression that he'd seen Adrian Frost – that pressure had been brought to bear on him?
STEVE:	Yes, I suppose he did, although I didn't think about it at the time. If you ask me, Wallace is as crazy as a coot.
TEMPLE:	Well, I'll see you later, Steve.
STEVE:	(*Calling*) Have you got your key?
TEMPLE:	(*From the background*) Yes. And don't answer the door, Steve. If the bell rings, let it ring.

FADE OUT.

FADE IN STEVE breathing heavily, asleep in bed. There is a slight creak as the door slowly opens. STEVE hears the noise and sits up in bed.

STEVE:	(*Frightened*) Who is it? Who's there?
TEMPLE:	It's all right, Steve, it's only me.
STEVE:	(*Relieved*) Oh dear! I was asleep.
TEMPLE:	I didn't want to disturb you.
STEVE:	What time is it?
TEMPLE:	About half past two.
STEVE:	Good heavens, as late as that? (*Suddenly*) Paul, what happened? Did you play the record?
TEMPLE:	Yes, we played it.
STEVE:	Well?

TEMPLE: We sat round the gramophone anticipating all
            sorts of things – and we heard a selection
            from Oklahoma.

STEVE: You heard – what?

TEMPLE: (*Laughing*) A selection from Oklahoma.

STEVE: But the label said …

TEMPLE: The label said "My Heart and Harry", but
            that's not what we heard. You should have
            seen Vosper's face.

STEVE: But, Paul, what does it mean?

TEMPLE: It means –

STEVE: (*Hanging on PAUL's words*) Yes?

TEMPLE: It means …

STEVE: Well?

TEMPLE: It means – I'm jolly tired and I'm going to
            bed.

STEVE: Now, look here, Paul, if you think I'm going
            to be fobbed off with …

TEMPLE: (*Still amused*) Good night, darling.

FADE OUT.

FADE UP TEMPLE and STEVE having breakfast.

TEMPLE: (*Calling*) More toast, Charlie.

CHARLIE: (*From the background*) Yes, Mr Temple,
            coming up!

STEVE: (*Irritated*) I do wish he wouldn't say
            "Coming up".

TEMPLE: (*Rather pleased with himself*) Why not? It's a
            perfectly good phrase. Darling, you haven't
            eaten your egg!

STEVE: I don't feel like eggs this morning.

TEMPLE: By Timothy, you are in a mood!

STEVE: Yes, I am. You haven't told me a thing about
            last night.

TEMPLE:	Yes, I have. I told you what happened in the Park; I told you about the record.
STEVE:	Yes, but you haven't explained anything.
TEMPLE:	What do you want me to explain?
STEVE:	Well, why should Judy Milton leave a gramophone record at the Neptune club? And why should the record have a label saying "My Heart and Harry" when …
TEMPLE:	(*Laughing*) When it was a selection from Oklahoma?
STEVE:	Exactly. (*A moment*) Well?
TEMPLE:	Well – what, Steve?
STEVE:	Well – explain …
TEMPLE:	(*His mouth is full; it is impossible to understand what he is saying*) Well, it's like this, darling: when Judy Milton …
STEVE:	(*Exasperated*) Paul, really, you are exasperating!

They laugh. CHARLIE enters.

CHARLIE:	Here's the fresh toast, sir.
TEMPLE:	Thank you, Charlie.
STEVE:	Is your head any better?
CHARLIE:	Yes, it's okay now, Mrs Temple, thank you.
STEVE:	Oh, good.

The doorbell rings.

TEMPLE:	See who that is, Charlie.
CHARLIE:	Yes, sir.
STEVE:	Are you expecting anyone?
TEMPLE:	It might be Vosper. I asked him to check on something for me.
STEVE:	Paul, seriously – what's your opinion of this Spencer Affair?
TEMPLE:	(*Quite seriously*) I think Mary Dreisler was mixed up in something – something quite

79

	different from – well – from studying to be an actress.
STEVE:	And you think that Judy Milton was mixed up in the same … (*Looking up*) Yes, Charlie?
CHARLIE:	There's a Miss Gibson at the door, sir. She says she'd like to see you if you can spare a moment.
TEMPLE:	Miss Gibson?
CHARLIE:	Yes, sir.
STEVE:	It must be Terry Gibson – the woman who runs the Neptune Club.
CHARLIE:	Yes, I think it is, Mrs Temple. She used to be on the stage. I recognise her.
TEMPLE:	All right, Charlie, ask her in.
CHARLIE:	Yes, sir.

CHARLIE goes out.

STEVE:	I wonder what she wants, Paul?
TEMPLE:	You saw her last night, didn't you?
STEVE:	Yes, I spoke to her. I was actually talking to her when Peter Wallace appeared.
TEMPLE:	Did she know Wallace?
STEVE:	Yes, I told you, they seemed to know one another quite well.

CHARLIE returns with TERRY GIBSON.

CHARLIE:	Miss Gibson, sir.
TEMPLE:	Thank you, Charlie.
STEVE:	(*Pleasantly*) Good morning, Miss Gibson.
TERRY:	Oh, dear, am I interrupting your breakfast? If I'd known, I shouldn't have dreamt of …
TEMPLE:	That's all right, Miss Gibson.
STEVE:	I'm afraid we're being terribly lazy this morning. We had rather a late night.
TEMPLE:	Would you care for some coffee?
TERRY:	No, thank you, Mr Temple.

STEVE: Do sit down.

TERRY: Thank you.

There is a tiny pause.

TEMPLE: Now, what can I do for you, Miss Gibson?

TERRY: Well, I think perhaps I'd better come straight to the point. I run the Neptune Club in Regent Street. I started it in 1961 and I've been doing extremely well with it ever since.

TEMPLE: Yes, I imagine you have.

TERRY: Now, the point is this, Mr Temple; I'm a businesswoman and I like to think I'm no fool.

TEMPLE: I'm sure you're no fool, Miss Gibson.

TERRY: I've done well with the Neptune Club because I've provided good food and good entertainment. Also, and believe me, this is very important, there's never been a breath of scandal attached to the Club. We have a first-class reputation and I want to keep it.

TEMPLE: I'm sure you do. But what has all this got to do with me?

TERRY: Mr Temple, you're investigating a murder case. Last night, Mrs Temple came to the club and collected something from the ladies' cloakroom. I don't know what that something was, but I do know that after she collected it, Mrs Temple was in a frantic hurry and left the Club immediately.

TEMPLE: Go on.

TERRY: She told the cloakroom attendant that her name was Milton – Judy Milton.

TEMPLE: Go on, Miss Gibson.

TERRY: Now I'm not interested in the parcel, Mr Temple; or in your wife's curious behaviour; but I am interested and perturbed at the thought   of   the Neptune receiving unfavourable publicity.

81

TEMPLE: Why should the Neptune Club receive unfavourable publicity – because my wife picked up a parcel from the cloakroom?

TERRY: As I said, Mrs Temple told Katie, the cloakroom attendant, that her name was Judy Milton. Judy Milton was found dead, presumably murdered, the night before last.

TEMPLE: Was Miss Milton a friend of yours?

TERRY: No.

TEMPLE: Then I fail to see why you should be perturbed in any way.

TERRY: I've told you why, Mr Temple. I don't want my Club to be associated with a murder case.

TEMPLE: Miss Gibson, you said just now that you hadn't any idea what was in the parcel my wife collected.

TERRY: That's true.

TEMPLE: But the cloakroom attendant knew what was in it – she told my wife that it looked like a gramophone record, which, indeed it was.

TERRY: (*Apparently surprised*) A gramophone record?

TEMPLE: Yes. (*A moment*) Miss Gibson, had you any other reason for calling to see me – other than your curiosity about the parcel?

TERRY: (*Hesitantly*) Yes.

TEMPLE: What was that reason?

TERRY: Well, when I read about the murder of Mary Dreisler, I suddenly realised that everyone associated with the murder had, at some time or another, visited the Neptune.

TEMPLE: Everyone?

TERRY: Well – Mary Dreisler frequently came with Peter Wallace. Then there was a young man called

82

	Adrian Frost. He was a friend of Mary Dreisler and he very often dropped into the cocktail bar.
TEMPLE:	And Judy Milton?
TERRY:	Yes, she came quite frequently at one time – but not so much recently.
STEVE:	And Mr Dreisler – did he visit the Neptune Club?
TERRY:	(*Hesitantly*) Rupert Dreisler only came once – that was about two months ago.
TEMPLE:	Was he alone?
TERRY:	Yes. He came to see a cabaret artist I'd engaged, a man called Pete Roberts.
TEMPLE:	(*Interested*) Oh, yes, I seem to remember reading something about Roberts.
TERRY:	There was quite a lot in the newspapers about him. That's probably why Dreisler came. A lot of the theatre people came to see Pete.
STEVE:	Didn't you spot Roberts in a seaside concert party and offer him …
TERRY:	There were so many stories about how I spotted poor old Pete. The fact of the matter is, I dropped into a pub one night and Pete was at the bar singing his head off. He was as drunk as an owl, but my word, what a voice – I'd never heard anything like it.
STEVE:	What happened?
TERRY:	I gave him a six weeks contract at the Neptune. He was terrific the first night – got wonderful notices. After that he was never sober. I stuck it for three weeks and then gave him the sack.
STEVE:	What's he doing now?
TERRY:	The last I heard of him he was working in a pub in Stepney.
TEMPLE:	What was the name of the pub? Do you know?

TERRY: No, I'm afraid I don't.

TEMPLE: Was it The Bronze Heart?

TERRY: (*Surprised*) Yes – yes, now you come to mention it, I believe it was.

TEMPLE: Miss Gibson, you say Rupert Dreisler saw Pete Roberts. Did he talk to him at all?

TERRY: Yes, I introduced them to each other – they had a long talk together.

TEMPLE: What about, do you know?

TERRY: Well, from what Pete told me, Dreisler wanted to take him to America.

TEMPLE: What was Pete's reaction?

TERRY: He didn't seem very keen on the idea, but you could never tell with Pete. It's always the same with a dipso. They never get worked up about anything. My word, if anyone had a chance, Pete had it – he could have been a star by now.

TEMPLE: Why did he drink? Do you know?

TERRY: (*Surprised at the question*) Why?

TEMPLE: Yes.

TERRY: Well, I don't know – I suppose he just liked it.

TEMPLE: (*His thoughts apparently elsewhere*) There's usually a reason, Miss Gibson.

FADE OUT.

FADE UP background noises of a crowded bar of a public house.

1st MAN: … So I said to this chap with the fancy waistcoat, if you think I'm going to pay fifteen bob for a haircut, you've got another think coming, Sweeny! Here's four and a tanner!

84

2nd MAN:	And what did he say?
1st MAN:	What could he say? He'd already cut it.

FADE DOWN the voices to the background.

TEMPLE:	Good evening.
WARREN:	(*A tough Cockney*) Good evening, sir.
TEMPLE:	Are you the landlord?
WARREN:	Yes. Warren's the name.
TEMPLE:	Well, my name's Temple – Paul Temple.
WARREN:	Oh, yes. Yes, I've heard of you, Mr Temple. What can I get you?
TEMPLE:	Well, eventually you can get me a whisky and soda, and one for yourself, too, if you feel like joining me.
WARREN:	Thank you, sir.
TEMPLE:	But first of all – I'm looking for a man called Pete Roberts. Can you help me?
WARREN:	Yes, he works here.
TEMPLE:	Is this his night off?
WARREN:	Not officially.
TEMPLE:	What does that mean?
WARREN:	When he feels like a night off, he just takes it. Has one on the house, as you might say. This is one of those.
TEMPLE:	Oh, I see.
WARREN:	He may be down later – if he feels he can manage the stairs.
TEMPLE:	Oh – he lives here, then?
WARREN:	That's right. He's got a room on the top floor. You can go up and see him if you like, but I doubt if you'll get much out of him.
TEMPLE:	Thanks – I'll try. On the top floor, you said?
WARREN:	That's right. It's the door facing the window. Is Pete a friend of yours?
TEMPLE:	No, he's a friend of a friend of mine.

WARREN:	Oh, I see.
TEMPLE:	How long has he been working for you, Mr Warren?
WARREN:	About six weeks.
TEMPLE:	Is he still on the bottle?
WARREN:	He's hardly ever off it. He's a lovely chap when he's sober, too. Got a smashing voice, you know. Talk about that pop singer – Vince what's-his-name? – Pete wraps him up, absolutely wraps him up.
TEMPLE:	Yes, so I've heard. See you later.
WALLACE:	Okay. And tell Pete if he can stand I can do with him down here.

FADE OUT.

After a moment there is the sound of a door opening.

TEMPLE:	(*Pleasantly*) May I come in?

PETE ROBERTS is lying on the bed. He is a man of about thirty-two or three and has a slight North Country accent.

PETE:	(*Obviously the worse for drink, but not actually drunk*) Who are you?
TEMPLE:	Are you Pete Roberts?
PETE:	That's right. What do you want?
TEMPLE:	I want to have a talk with you. Can I sit down?
PETE:	If you can find a chair. What do you want to talk about – the weather?
TEMPLE:	No, not the weather, Mr Roberts.
PETE:	Don't call me Mr Roberts. Call me Pete. Everybody calls me Pete. (*With a touch of sentiment*) Everybody. Would you like a drink?
TEMPLE:	No. But I'll buy you one – later.
PETE:	Okay, I'll hold you to it. I'll hold you to it, Mr – er – what did you say your name was?

TEMPLE: I didn't – but it's Temple.

PETE: Temple? Name's famil – famil – (*He gives up*) Do you write books?

TEMPLE: Yes.

PETE: I thought so. Once read a book of yours. (*A moment*) Didn't like it. (*Almost a suggestion of tears*) Just didn't like it.

TEMPLE: Pete, you remember when you worked at the Neptune Club?

PETE: Yes.

TEMPLE: You met a man called Rupert Dreisler.

PETE: That's right.

TEMPLE: What did Mr Dreisler talk to you about?

PETE: (*His thought elsewhere*) Who?

TEMPLE: Mr Dreisler.

PETE: What did he talk about?

TEMPLE: Yes.

PETE: Don't remember. Don't even remember Mr Dreisler.

TEMPLE: Yes, you do. He was an Austrian. A squat, dumpy little man.

PETE: Oh, that's right. Funny accent. (*Amused*) Couldn't understand half of what he said.

TEMPLE: What did he talk about, Pete?

PETE: Who?

TEMPLE: (*Patiently*) Mr Dreisler.

PETE: I expect he offered me a job. Wanted to make a star out of me. They all wanted to make a star out of me. (*Depressed; near to tears again*) It was no use. I told them it was no use. Booze, I said, just booze. That's all I want to do. 'S'all I ever want to do. (*Looking up*) What did you say your name was? Temple?

87

TEMPLE: Pete, what happened the night you met Rupert
            Dreisler? Now, tell me about it? What actually
            happened?
PETE: (*After a moment; fade on this speech*) I was
            singing a song ... (*Angry at the thought of what
            happened*) There was the usual racket going on
            from the waiters ... The clatter of dishes ...
            babble of voices ... I told Terry about it. I used
            to tell her night after night ... Can't sing with
            this racket going on, Terry, I used to say.   Just
            can't sing ... just can't sing, old girl ...

COMPLETE FADE.

*FADE UP a dance orchestra and PETE singing a number in
the crowded restaurant of the Neptune Club. The song
finishes and there is a storm of appreciative applause. The
applause gradually dies down.*
TERRY: Well done, Pete. You're on form tonight.
PETE: (*Irritated, but sober*) So were the blasted waiters.
            I never heard such a noise. Terry, you'll have to
            do something about it. I can't sing with that
            racket going on the whole time.
TERRY: I've told them, Pete, but it's impossible to keep
            the room dead quiet.
PETE: Well, you'll have to do something about it. I
            really can't go on like this, Terry. Tell Harry to
            bring a bottle of Scotch to my dressing room.
TERRY: Pete – wait a minute – there's someone I want
            you to meet.
PETE: What? Tonight?
TERRY: Yes. It's a man called Dreisler. He's an
            impresario.
PETE: I've never heard of him. Tell Harry to bring the
            Scotch up straight away.

TERRY:	No, Pete, wait a minute. Dreisler's an important man. He's presented a lot of well-known artists both here and in America.
PETE:	So what? I'm an important artist.
TERRY:	Yes, I know that, Pete, but I think you ought to … (*She breaks off*)
DREISLER:	Having trouble with the young man, Terry?
TERRY:	Pete, this is the gentleman I was telling you about.
DREISLER:	Glad to meet you, Mr Roberts, isn't it?
PETE:	(*Truculently*) It is.
DREISLER:	(*Pleasantly*) I've a bottle of Scotch on my table, Mr Roberts. I doubt whether I shall finish it myself. Would you care to join me?
PETE:	(*Hesitating*) Well – for a few minutes, perhaps.
DREISLER:	(*Smiling at TERRY*) We'll see you later, Terry.

The dance orchestra starts to play. People start dancing again.

FADE the orchestra and noise of the dancers to the distant background.

FADE IN RUPERT DREISLER's voice.

DREISLER:	… Well, there you are, Pete, that's the proposition.
PETE:	But I don't see that it is a proposition. All you've asked me to do is to give an audition. I can give anyone an audition.
DREISLER:	I don't think you've understood me, Pete. This show I'm producing is a Broadway show. It's going to cost a great deal of money. In New York, musicals – well, they just cost the earth. Now I think you could play the lead in this production. You've got a wonderful voice and the right kind of personality, but …

PETE: It's the "but" I don't like.

DREISLER: But I've got to convince other people that you can play the lead. In order to convince them, you'll have to agree to an audition.

PETE: (*About to leave the table*) I don't like auditions. If you want me, okay – if you don't want me, that's okay too.

DREISLER: No, Pete, wait a minute. Supposing you don't give an audition, that you make a record for us – a special record? How about that?

PETE: Where would I make the record? In London or in New York?

DREISLER: Why, in London, of course. But leave that to me. I'll fix it up. All you've got to do is to go along to the recording studio.

PETE: Well – I've no objection to that, I suppose.

DREISLER: But you've got to sing a particular number. I'll let you have a copy of this first thing tomorrow morning.

PETE: (*Indifferent*) Okay. Okay.

DREISLER: As soon as you've made the record, I'll fly it out to New York. Will one afternoon this week suit you for the recording?

PETE: Yes – I should prefer the afternoon, I'm not so hot in the morning.

DREISLER: I can understand that. (*He rises*) Well, I'll say good night, Pete.

PETE: (*Surprised*) Oh. Oh, good night, Mr Dreisler.

There is a pause.

DREISLER: (*Casually; turning*) Oh, by the way – the song I want you to sing …

PETE: (*Pouring himself a drink*) Yes?

DREISLER: It's called "My Heart and Harry".

MUSIC.

END OF EPISODE THREE

EPISODE FOUR

THAT OLD INTUITION

OPENING MUSIC.
FADE DOWN MUSIC.

FADE UP background noises and dance orchestra in the restaurant at the Neptune club.
FADE to appropriate background.

DREISLER: … you've got to sing a particular number. I'll let you have a copy of this first thing tomorrow morning.

PETE: (*Indifferent*) Okay. Okay.

DREISLER: As soon as you've made the record, I'll fly it out to New York. Will one afternoon this week suit you for the recording?

PETE: Yes – I should prefer the afternoon, I'm not so hot in the morning.

DREISLER: I can understand that. (*He rises*) Well, I'll say good night, Pete.

PETE: (*Surprised*) Oh. Oh, good night, Mr Dreisler.

There is a pause.

DREISLER: (*Casually; turning*) Oh, by the way – the song I want you to sing …

PETE: (*Pouring himself a drink*) Yes?

DREISLER: It's called "My Heart and Harry".

PETE: "My Heart and Harry"? That's a new one on me.

DREISLER: It's a big hit in America, that's why I picked it. I want my American associates to hear you sing it.

PETE: (*A shrug*) It makes no difference to me. "My Heart and Harry" – "Annie Laurie" – I sing 'em all the same way.

DREISLER: (*Amused*) Good night, Pete.

PETE: If you're going to send me the song, you'd better have my address.

DREISLER: No, I'll send it to you here, care of Terry
                Gibson. I'll let you know later where the
                recording studios are.
PETE: Righto. Good night.
DREISLER: Good night.

*FADE UP the background noises and sound of the dance
orchestra. TERRY GIBSON arrives at the table.*

TERRY: Well, what did the great impresario want?
PETE: (*Rather unfriendly*) As if you don't know.
TERRY: I don't know. He just said he wanted to talk to
                you – said he had a proposition.
PETE: Well, he has.
TERRY: Pete, why the chip on your shoulder the
                whole time? You're making more money now
                than you've ever made. If you behave
                yourself and play your cards right, you'll be a
                star. It's my bet that within a year …
PETE: Who wants to be a star? (*Repenting slightly*)
                Terry, be a good girl, leave me alone.
TERRY: Look, Pete, I don't like taking advice, and I
                don't like giving it, but I'm going to give you
                some; lay off the drink, because if you don't
                …
PETE: (*Calling a waiter*) Harry, take the lead out of
                your pants and bring me a bottle of Scotch …

FADE OUT.

FADE IN PAUL TEMPLE's voice.

TEMPLE: … Well, go on, Pete – what happened? Did
                he deliver the song?
PETE: Yes, he delivered it. I rehearsed for four days
                and then went out to a lousy recording studio
                at Putney. Why I had to go to Putney, I don't
                know – should have thought there were plenty

	of studios in London. Look, why are you interested in me? What do you want to know about all this for?
TEMPLE:	I'm investigating the murder of Mary Dreisler. I think you might be able to help me.
PETE:	How can I help you? (*Near to tears*) I can't even help myself.
TEMPLE:	Look, Pete, we'll go downstairs in a minute and have a drink, but first there's several things I want to know. When you went out to the recording studios, what happened exactly?
PETE:	Whadya think happened? I just sang the song. I sang the song and they recorded it.
TEMPLE:	Did they play it back to you?
PETE:	No.
TEMPLE:	Why not?
PETE:	I don't know why not. I wasn't interested. The pubs were open, and I wanted to get out of the crumby joint.
TEMPLE:	What did they call this recording studio? Can you remember?
PETE:	Yes. It was called The Disc Recording Company. It's in a basement in the Upper Richmond Road. A young fellow runs it. He's the whole works.
TEMPLE:	So you just made the record and left the studios?
PETE:	That's right.
TEMPLE:	Did Dreisler contact you again?
PETE:	Yes, he telephoned me the next day and asked me how I'd got on. (*With a note of contempt in his voice*) That was the last I heard of him. Haven't heard a ruddy word since.

97

PAUL TEMPLE: All right, Pete. Now let's go downstairs. I'll buy you that drink.

PETE rises from the bed. It is an effort, but he finally manages it.

PETE: (*Holding on to TEMPLE's arm*) Mr Temple, I like you. I really like you. I like everything about you. And one thing in particular, I like very, very much.

TEMPLE: (*Amused in spite of himself*) What's that, Pete?

PETE: You haven't once said – "Pull yourself together, old man."

FADE OUT.

FADE UP the background noises associated with the entrance hall of the Ritz Hotel.

RECEPTIONIST: Good evening, sir.

TEMPLE: Good evening. Could you tell me whether Mr Dreisler is in the hotel?

RECEPTIONIST: I believe he is, sir. I'll ring his room. What name shall I say?

TEMPLE: Temple.

RECEPTIONIST: Thank you, Mr Temple.

TEMPLE: (*Suddenly, moving from the reception desk*) Oh, excuse me, I'll be back in a moment. (*Raising his voice in order to attract someone's attention*) Frost!

FROST: (*Surprised*) Oh, hello, Temple!

TEMPLE: (*Pleasantly*) I thought I recognised you coming out of the lift.

FROST: Yes, I've just been to see – a friend of mine.

TEMPLE:	I'm rather glad I bumped into you, Frost. I was going to give you a ring, as a matter of fact.
FROST:	Oh, really?
TEMPLE:	Yes, I wanted to ask you if you'd ever met a man called Pete Roberts?
FROST:	Pete Roberts? Yes, I've met him. He's a singer – at least, he is when he's sober.
TEMPLE:	Where did you meet him? At the Bronze Heart?
FROST:	(*Apparently puzzled*) The Bronze Heart?
TEMPLE:	Yes. The pub – in Stepney.
FROST:	Good Lord, no! I met him at the Neptune Club. Terry Gibson introduced us. What makes you think we met at the Bronze Heart?
TEMPLE:	Roberts works there.
FROST:	(*Apparently very surprised*) Does he?
TEMPLE:	Yes.
FROST:	Well, I never knew that. My word, he must have come down in the world.
TEMPLE:	I'm afraid he has.
FROST:	Well, if you'd excuse me, Temple … (*Suddenly*) Oh, by the way, when you mentioned my diary the other night, I'm afraid I didn't realise what you were talking about. Now I understand.
PAUL TEMPLE:	(*Smiling*) Do you?
FROST:	Yes, I do. (*Significantly*) You will be pleased to know I've – taken the necessary steps. Good night, Temple.
PAUL TEMPLE:	Good night.

The RECEPTIONIST joins TEMPLE.

RECEPTIONIST: Mr Dreisler is in his room, sir. Suite 29, on the first floor.

TEMPLE: Thank you.

FADE UP of the background noises.
Slow FADE DOWN.

FADE UP TEMPLE knocking on the door of Suite 29.
The door is opened by RUPERT DREISLER.

DREISLER: (*Embarrassed and faintly effusive*) Come in, Mr Temple! This is a pleasant surprise.

TEMPLE: I was passing the hotel, so I thought I'd drop in and have a chat with you, Mr Dreisler.

DREISLER: Yes, of course – by all means. I'm delighted to see you.

They pass through the hall into the drawing room.

DREISLER: I hope you haven't left Mrs Temple downstairs.

TEMPLE: No, I'm alone this evening.

DREISLER: Can I offer you a drink? A whisky and soda, perhaps? Or …

TEMPLE: Not at the moment, thank you – if you don't mind.

DREISLER: (*Anxiously*) Is there any news? Tell me – have you discovered anything?

TEMPLE: Yes, I've discovered quite a few things, Mr Dreisler – that's why I thought it would be a good idea if we had a little chat.

DREISLER: By all means. But tell me, please – what is it you have found out? Do you know who murdered my daughter?

TEMPLE: (*Rather vaguely*) I have my suspicions. But suspicions unfortunately … (*Quite*

100

	suddenly) I understand you saw Mr Frost this evening?
DREISLER:	(*Taken aback by the question*) Why yes. He left just a few moments ago.
TEMPLE:	Did he ask to see you?
DREISLER:	(*Hesitantly*) No. On the contrary. I asked to see him.
TEMPLE:	Why?
DREISLER:	(*Uncomfortably*) I'm afraid you're going to be annoyed with me, Mr Temple, when I tell you why.
TEMPLE:	Why should I be annoyed?
DREISLER:	Because there's something I haven't told you.
TEMPLE:	Go on.
DREISLER:	Last night I received a telephone call. I don't know who it was from. A man's voice – a voice I didn't recognise – said, "Have you asked Mr Frost about the brooch? When you know why he gave your daughter the brooch, you'll know who murdered her."
TEMPLE:	Go on, Mr Dreisler.
DREISLER:	Before I could ask the man who he was, or what he meant, he rang off. I was going to telephone you and then …
TEMPLE:	You decided to see Mr Frost yourself?
DREISLER:	Yes. I do hope you're not annoyed, Mr Temple.
TEMPLE:	No, I'm not annoyed. But you did ask me to investigate the case and I can't really help you, Mr Dreisler, if you don't tell me everything.

DREISLER:	Yes, I know. I know I did the wrong thing and I apologise.
TEMPLE:	What did you say to Frost?
DREISLER:	I was perfectly frank with him. I told him about the note I'd received, and the telephone call.
TEMPLE:	And what did he say?
DREISLER:	He said he knew about the note, you'd already mentioned it.
TEMPLE:	And the telephone call?
DREISLER:	He couldn't account for it.
TEMPLE:	And what about the brooch?
DREISLER:	I didn't have to ask him about the brooch. I knew that he'd given her one, because I found it in her dressing table. As a matter of fact, that's one of the reasons why I sent for him.
TEMPLE:	What do you mean?
DREISLER:	I gave the brooch back to Frost. It was worth a great deal of money, and I thought – well – since Mary was dead it was better to return it …
TEMPLE:	Did you ask him why he gave your daughter the brooch in the first place?
DREISLER:	No. No, I did not. Young people today, they're not – well, times have changed. I like Frost. In spite of the message I received and the telephone call, I don't think he murdered my daughter. On the contrary, I think he was very fond of her.
TEMPLE:	I see. (*A moment*) Dreisler, the last time we met I asked you about a gramophone record. A number called "My Heart and Harry".
DREISLER:	Yes?

TEMPLE:	Why didn't you tell me the truth about that record?
DREISLER:	The truth? I don't understand. What do you mean?
TEMPLE:	Why didn't you tell me about your visit to the Neptune Club? About Pete Roberts?
DREISLER:	Why should I? What has that got to do with ... (*Suddenly*) Who told you about Pete Roberts – Terry Gibson?
TEMPLE:	Yes.
DREISLER:	But why should Terry Gibson tell you about Pete Roberts? What has Roberts got to do with all this?
TEMPLE:	Didn't you ask Roberts to make a record for you?
DREISLER:	Yes, I did.
TEMPLE:	A record of "My Heart and Harry"?
DREISLER:	Is that what Terry Gibson told you?
TEMPLE:	No. Roberts told me himself.
DREISLER:	But that's nonsense! Absolute nonsense!
TEMPLE:	Supposing you tell me your version of the story, Mr Dreisler.
DREISLER:	(*Angrily*) What do you mean? My version? There's only one version! (*After a moment, calmer*) About two months ago, when I was in London, I had a message from Terry Gibson. I used to know Terry in the old days when she was on the stage. She told me that she'd discovered a new singer, a man called Pete Roberts, and that he was absolutely wonderful. Well, I've heard that story so many times, I was not optimistic. However, one night I called at the Neptune Club and it didn't take me five minutes to realise that

Terry was right. Pete Roberts was a real discovery. He had a wonderful voice, and he knew exactly how to put a number over. After his act, I had a talk to him. I told him I was interested in his future, and I asked him to make a special recording for me.

TEMPLE: Why?

DREISLER: I wanted to send the record to America, to an associate of mine.

TEMPLE: Go on.

DREISLER: Well, a couple of days later he went down to a recording studio in Putney.

TEMPLE: Why Putney? Aren't there recording studios in the West End?

DREISLER: Yes, of course, but – (*Smiling*) Business is business. I happen to own the one in Putney.

TEMPLE: Oh, I see.

DREISLER: Anyway, to cut a long story short, the record was no good. The young man who runs the Putney business telephoned me and said that Roberts just didn't bother – in fact, he was half tight – could hardly stand in front of the microphone.

TEMPLE: I see.

DREISLER: After that I made a few enquiries and discovered that Roberts was completely unreliable – aggressive and nearly always drunk. (*A shrug*) I decided to forget the whole business.

TEMPLE: When you saw Pete Roberts and asked him to make the record, did you suggest that he should sing a particular song?

DREISLER: No, I didn't. I told him to please himself.

TEMPLE:	You definitely didn't ask him to sing "My Heart and Harry"?
DREISLER:	No, I didn't. Is that what he told you?
TEMPLE:	Yes. He said you actually sent him a copy of the song, and that he rehearsed for four days.
DREISLER:	But that's untrue! Quite untrue, I assure you, Mr Temple. (*Thoughtfully*) Now why did he tell you that? And why did he pick on that particular number?
TEMPLE:	I don't know why.
DREISLER:	Mr Temple, I assure you I've told you the truth about this business – the whole truth.
TEMPLE:	I understand from Inspector Vosper that after your daughter died you went to her flat and collected some of her things?
DREISLER:	Yes. Yes, I did. But there was no gramophone record, I assure you.
TEMPLE:	Did you ever see the record?
DREISLER:	No, I didn't. Speaking personally, I have no real proof that it exists. But, of course, I'm prepared to take Inspector Vosper's word for it, that it does.
TEMPLE:	Did your daughter leave any letters? Diaries – notebooks – that kind of thing?
DREISLER:	No, I don't think so. I certainly didn't find any.
TEMPLE:	All right, Mr Dreisler. Thank you very much. Oh, there's just one other thing.
DREISLER:	Yes?
TEMPLE:	Were you in London last October?
DREISLER:	(*Surprised*) Last October? Yes. Yes, I was.
TEMPLE:	On the 22nd?
DREISLER:	(*Thoughtfully*) No, on the 22nd I was in Paris. I arrived in Paris on the 16th and flew back to

	Vienna on November 3rd or the 4th. I'm not sure which.
TEMPLE:	Thank you.
DREISLER:	Why do you ask?
TEMPLE:	Does the date October the 22nd mean anything to you?
DREISLER:	No … (*Puzzled*) No, I don't think so. Should it?
TEMPLE:	It was on October the 22nd that Frost gave your daughter the diamond brooch.
DREISLER:	Oh.
TEMPLE:	It was a <u>diamond</u> brooch, Mr Dreisler?
DREISLER:	(*Still puzzled*) Yes. Yes, it was.
TEMPLE:	I thought so. Good night.
DREISLER:	(*Obviously bewildered*) Good night, Mr Temple.

FADE OUT.

FADE UP a door opening.

CHARLIE:	Good evening, Mr Temple!
TEMPLE:	Hello, Charlie.
CHARLIE:	Let me take your hat and coat, sir.
TEMPLE:	(*Obviously tired*) Thank you, Charlie. By the way, what's that ladder doing downstairs? In the hall near the staircase.
CHARLIE:	It belongs to the people in the flat below, sir – they're moving in on Saturday.
TEMPLE:	Oh, I see.
CHARLIE:	(*A private joke*) Mrs Temple's in the drawing room, sir, with Sir Graham.
TEMPLE:	With Sir Graham? How long's he been here?
CHARLIE:	Since eight o'clock, sir.
TEMPLE:	Eight o'clock?
CHARLIE:	Yes, sir. He came to dinner.

TEMPLE:	(*Obviously taken aback*) He came to dinner? ... By Timothy, Charlie! I ...
CHARLIE:	You forgot!
TEMPLE:	I certainly did.
CHARLIE:	(*With emphasis*) Mrs Temple's in the drawing room, sir.

TEMPLE opens the drawing room door and enters.

STEVE:	... You mean that the actual shot – the shot that killed Judy Milton ...
FORBES:	... Was fired before you and your husband arrived on the scene. You see, what actually happened ... Oh, here you are, Temple!
TEMPLE:	Sir Graham, I'm most terribly sorry!
STEVE:	Paul, really!

FORBES laughs.

TEMPLE:	Darling, I absolutely – utterly – completely – forgot all about it.
STEVE:	Of course you forgot all about it – you don't have to tell us that!
FORBES:	It's been a most enjoyable evening, anyway.
STEVE:	Thank you, Sir Graham. But, Paul, where on earth have you been? You went out at five o'clock.
TEMPLE:	(*Tired*) Oh, I've been all over the place, Steve. I've seen Dreisler, Pete Roberts ...
FORBES:	Pete Roberts – the man Terry Gibson told you about?
TEMPLE:	That's right. Did Steve tell you about Terry Gibson?
FORBES:	Yes, we've just been talking about her.
STEVE:	(*From the background*) You don't deserve a drink, Paul, but you look as if you need one. Would you like a whisky and soda?
TEMPLE:	By Timothy, yes!

FORBES: (*Drawing near to TEMPLE, slightly more confidential*) I had a message from Vosper this morning. You were right about Judy Milton.

TEMPLE: (*Immediately interested*) Oh? Did Vosper do what I suggested?

FORBES: Yes. And we found it. It was fitted into a cupboard. Quite an ingenious little weapon. It had a time switch and everything, just as you suspected.

TEMPLE: Oh, good. I was beginning to get worried.

FORBES: What made you think of it?

TEMPLE: Curiously enough it was something Charlie said about our fridge. He complained about … (*Accepting the drink from STEVE*) Oh, thank you, darling.

STEVE: (*Significantly*) Paul … Sir Graham's got something to tell you about Clutch Brompton.

TEMPLE: How is Clutch?

FORBES: He's in a pretty bad way I'm afraid. Frankly, I don't think there's much hope.

TEMPLE: Oh dear. I'm sorry to hear that. I suppose you haven't found the car yet? The one that ran him down?

FORBES: No, I'm afraid not.

TEMPLE: Has Vosper seen Clutch since the accident?

FORBES: Yes, he's seen him once or twice, but he won't talk to Vosper. He won't talk to any of us.

STEVE: He wants to see you, Paul.

TEMPLE: Clutch does?

FORBES: Yes. One of the doctors telephoned me and said he'd been asking for you. I'd like you to see him, Temple.

TEMPLE: Why, yes. By all means, Sir Graham.

FORBES: I was hoping we might have gone along to the hospital this evening after dinner, but …

TEMPLE: That's all right, Sir Graham, there's still time.

STEVE: Paul, have you had anything to eat this evening?

TEMPLE: Yes, darling – sandwiches. Masses of sandwiches. (*To FORBES*) I'll just finish this drink, Sir Graham, and then I'm with you.

FORBES: What time do you make it, Steve?

STEVE: It's just gone 10.15, Sir Graham.

FORBES: I promised I'd phone Vosper and let him know whether we were going or not.

TEMPLE: Use the one in the study, Sir Graham – Oh, and incidentally, would you ask Vosper to do something for me?

FORBES: Why, yes, certainly.

TEMPLE: Ask him to find out whether Mary Dreisler had a passport, and if she had, ask him to check on the number of times she used it.

FORBES: (*Curious*) Is it urgent?

TEMPLE: No, but I'd like to know, Sir Graham.

FORBES: All right, Temple, I'll ask him.

SIR GRAHAM leaves the drawing room.

There is the sound of the door opening and shutting.

TEMPLE: Darling, I'm sorry about tonight.

STEVE: Oh, that's all right. But I really wondered what on earth had happened to you. What did you think of Pete Roberts?

TEMPLE: Oh, he's quite a character.

STEVE: Was he sober?

TEMPLE: No. I doubt whether he's ever completely sober.

STEVE: Is he good looking?

TEMPLE: Yes, I suppose you'd call him good looking. Why?

STEVE:	I wondered, that's all.
TEMPLE:	What do you mean – you wondered? You must have had a reason for asking whether he was good looking or not.
STEVE:	When Terry Gibson told us about him, I got the impression that she – well, that she was probably in love with him. I wondered whether he was good looking, that's all.
TEMPLE:	In love with him? Terry Gibson! Do you know, I never thought of that!
STEVE:	You can't think of everything, darling!
TEMPLE:	Steve …
STEVE:	Yes?
TEMPLE:	I've made one or two rather curious discoveries during the past two or three days, and – well, frankly, dear, I'm worried.
STEVE:	You look worried. I was only saying to Sir Graham this evening, it's the first time I've ever seen you …
TEMPLE:	I'm worried about you!
STEVE:	No! What do you mean?
TEMPLE:	You know what happened to Mary Dreisler – to Judy Milton.
STEVE:	But, Paul, they were involved in this business. I'm not involved in it. At least, not in the same way.
TEMPLE:	The person who murdered Mary Dreisler, the person behind the affair – call him Spencer if you like – is pretty ruthless. He's not going to take any chances, Steve. If, by getting at you, he can force me out of this case, then he'll do it.
STEVE:	Nonsense! You've been up against a pretty tough bunch before, Paul. It isn't the first time that …

TEMPLE: Look, Steve, this man's ruthless, and he's desperate. Also, he's got a lot to lose. I want you to take care, darling.

STEVE: (*Realising that TEMPLE is serious*) Yes, of course.

TEMPLE: If I telephone you at any time, just because it sounds like me, don't take it for granted that it is. Fall back on that Charlie routine. You know – the one we had while I was on the Gilbert case.

STEVE: (*Amused*) I say "Where's Charlie fishing?" and you say …

TEMPLE: "In the Thames". If I don't say "In the Thames" …

STEVE: I shall assume that it isn't my excessively cautious husband.

TEMPLE: No, I'm serious, darling.

STEVE: All right, Paul. I shan't forget.

The door opens and SIR GRAHAM FORBES returns.

FORBES: I've spoken to Vosper about the passport. He's looking into it, Temple.

TEMPLE: Oh, thank you, Sir Graham. Well, I'm ready now. Have you a car handy?

FORBES: Yes, it's waiting.

TEMPLE: Good night, darling. I shan't be long.

STEVE: Good night, Sir Graham.

FORBES: Good night, Steve. And thank you for a most enjoyable evening. You must invite me again sometime when your husband's out.

STEVE: (*Laughs*) Yes, all right, Sir Graham. (*To TEMPLE*) I'll wait up for you, Paul.

FADE OUT.

FADE IN of a door opening.

NURSE: Will you come this way, please, Mr Temple?

TEMPLE: Thank you, Sister.

FORBES: I'll wait here for you.

TEMPLE: Yes, all right, Sir Graham.

TEMPLE goes out into the corridor with the NURSE.

TEMPLE: How is Brompton?

NURSE: He seems a little better this evening, but I'm afraid he's very ill, Mr Temple. Normally, we wouldn't allow visitors, but he's been asking for you most persistently.

TEMPLE: I see.

The NURSE and TEMPLE pass down the corridor.

A second door is opened.

NURSE: This way, sir. (*Quietly*) Don't stay too long.

TEMPLE: No, of course not.

FADE UP CLUTCH BROMPTON. He is breathing heavily and is obviously very ill.

TEMPLE: Hello, Clutch.

CLUTCH: (*Weakly*) Who is that?

TEMPLE: It's Temple. I understand you want to see me.

CLUTCH: Oh hello, Mr Temple. I'm glad you've come ... I've been asking for you.

TEMPLE: Yes, I know you have, Clutch. How do you feel?

CLUTCH: I feel a little better tonight ... I wanted to see you because ... Mr Temple, you remember the car that ... ran me down?

TEMPLE: Yes.

CLUTCH: (*With an effort*) I ... saw the driver ...

TEMPLE: Yes, I know you did.

CLUTCH: I shouldn't tell you this. I hate people who can't keep their mouths shut but ...

TEMPLE: Look, this is a murder case, Clutch. It's not a case of petty larceny. It's your duty to talk.

CLUTCH: Yes, I know. That's what they keep telling
             me, but …

TEMPLE: Who was it, Clutch? Who was driving the
             car?

CLUTCH: It was a man called Lansdale – Eric Lansdale.

TEMPLE: Lansdale? But the police have already got
             Lansdale – they picked him up last night.

CLUTCH: (*Surprised*) They did?

TEMPLE: Yes. He was driving a taxi. He thought I had a
             gramophone record that my wife … But go
             on, Clutch. Tell me about Lansdale.

CLUTCH: He's just a stooge – a rough-neck. He'll do
             anything for money. But he won't talk, Mr
             Temple, because – he's frightened …
             Lansdale works for a man called Spencer …
             That's the man you've got to find …

TEMPLE: Have you met Spencer? Do you know him?

CLUTCH: No, but I know all about him … because …
             (*He is obviously in pain*)

TEMPLE: You're in pain, Clutch. I'll fetch the Sister.

CLUTCH: No … no, wait … please, Mr Temple … (*Still
             in pain, but determined to talk*) Temple,
             listen. There's a bungalow on the river … on
             an island near Henley.

TEMPLE: On an island?

CLUTCH: Yes. It's called Salex Island. It's about five or
             six acres. Spencer bought the land about two
             years ago. That stretch of river is always
             deserted in the winter. That's why he … (*He
             is unable to continue*)

The NURSE arrives at the bedside.

NURSE: I'm sorry, Mr Temple, I'll have to give him
             an injection.

TEMPLE: (*Rising*) Yes, of course.

113

Start FADING on the following dialogue.

TEMPLE: Thank you, Clutch, I'll see you again. And good luck.

CLUTCH: (*With an effort*) Thank you for coming.

TEMPLE: It's all right, Sister. I can find my way out.

COMPLETE FADE.

FADE IN of a piano being played. The sound of the piano continues for some little time. Then a door opens.

CHARLIE: Oh, excuse me, Mrs Temple.

STEVE: (*At the piano*) Yes, what is it, Charlie?

CHARLIE: I was wondering if I'd left any glasses in here.

STEVE: Yes, there's two on the table over there. But don't bother with them tonight, Charlie. You can go to bed. I can see to the glasses.

CHARLIE: No, that's all right, Mrs Temple. I can easily …

CHARLIE is interrupted by the ringing of the telephone.

CHARLIE: Shall I take it, Mrs Temple?

STEVE: Yes, please.

CHARLIE crosses and lifts the telephone receiver.

CHARLIE: … Hello?

We hear a man's voice on the other end of the line. It sounds remarkably like PAUL TEMPLE.

VOICE: Hello?

CHARLIE: Who is that?

VOICE: Who do you think it is, Charlie?

CHARLIE: Oh, I'm sorry, Mr Temple! (*To STEVE*) It's Mr Temple. (*With a laugh*) I didn't recognise his voice.

STEVE crosses and takes the receiver from CHARLIE.

STEVE: Hello, Paul!

VOICE: Steve, I'm at the hospital. I've just seen Clutch Brompton. Now listen, darling. I want

114

STEVE: you to get the car out and come down here straight away.

STEVE: (*Surprised*) What – now?

VOICE: Yes, it's urgent. I'll tell you all about it when I … I say, this is a terrible line – Can you hear me?

STEVE: Yes, I can hear you. You want me to get the car and pick you up straight away.

VOICE: That's right, Steve. I'll be waiting for you in the main entrance.

STEVE: It's the North Middlesex Hospital, isn't it?

VOICE: Yes, that's it. The main entrance is in Portland Street. (*A sudden thought*) Oh, and Steve – pack a suitcase and tell Charlie we're going to be out of town for two or three days.

STEVE: (*Surprised*) Oh? Where are we going, Paul?

VOICE: I'll tell you when I see you, dear.

STEVE: Yes, all right. I'll be with you as soon as I can …

VOICE: Wait a minute. Haven't you forgotten something?

STEVE: (*Suddenly remembering*) Oh, good Lord, yes!

VOICE: By George, Steve, you really are the limit.

STEVE: Where's Charlie fishing?

VOICE: In the Thames.

STEVE: (*Laughing*) I'll be with you in about twenty minutes.

STEVE replaces the telephone receiver.

STEVE: Charlie! Go into the box room and get me a suitcase – one of the leather ones.

CHARLIE: Yes, Mrs Temple.

STEVE: And when you've done that, go down to the garage and fetch the car.

CHARLIE: Okey-dokey.

STEVE: We shall probably be away for two or three days, Charlie, so I want you to … Now, what are you smiling at?

CHARLIE: (*Grinning*) By Timothy, as Mr Temple would say, never a dull moment!

STEVE: (*Laughs, then a sudden thought occurs to her, and she stops laughing*) Yes …

CHARLIE: What is it, Mrs Temple?

STEVE: I was just thinking, Charlie. That's exactly what he <u>didn't</u> say.

CHARLIE: What do you mean?

STEVE: He said "By George" – not "By Timothy". "By George, Steve, you really are the limit."

CHARLIE: "By George"? That doesn't sound like Mr Temple.

STEVE: No, but it was. It must have been because I said … (*Reassuring herself*) Well, it must have been!

CHARLIE: I'll get the suitcase.

STEVE: No, wait a minute. When you gave me the phone you said … "It's Mr Temple, I didn't recognise his voice."

CHARLIE: Well, I didn't – not at first – it was a bad line.

STEVE: Yes, of course, that's it! He probably didn't say "By George" anyway. Get the suitcase, Charlie.

CHARLIE: Okay, Mrs Temple.

STEVE: No – no, wait a minute. I've got a funny feeling about that phone call. A sort of intuition.

CHARLIE: Well, you know what Mr Temple thinks about your intuitions.

STEVE: Never mind what Mr Temple thinks! Get the phone book and look up the North Middlesex Hospital. I'm ringing back.

CHARLIE: (*Wearily*) Okay.

START FADE.

CHARLIE: The North Middlesex.

STEVE: That's right – it's in Portland Street.

COMPLETE FADE.

FADE In the voice of SIR GRAHAM.

FORBES: … Salex Island? I've never heard of it. You say it's near Henley?

TEMPLE: That's what he said. I rather imagine it's not far from Belton's Lock.

FORBES: I'll get the Maidenhead people on to this straight away.

TEMPLE: No, please don't do that, Sir Graham. What I'd like you to do is this: ask Vosper to make a few discreet enquiries. Tell him to find out who the land belongs to, and whether the bungalow is occupied. Once I've got some definite information I'll go down there and take a quiet look at the place.

FORBES: Right. Well, I suppose we'd better be making a move. I expect the Sister wants to use her office.

TEMPLE: Yes. You needn't run me back to the flat, Sir Graham.

FORBES: You know, this is a curious business, Temple. When I first heard about the Dreisler murder, I was firmly convinced it was the conventional murder case. Love motivation. Jealousy. You know the kind of thing. Now I don't think so. I think Mary Dreisler was

117

	mixed up in something bigger than that. Something much bigger.
TEMPLE:	And you think the fact that she was a drama student …
FORBES:	… Was just a coincidence.
TEMPLE:	I agree with you, Sir Graham. On the other hand we mustn't lose sight of the fact …

The door opens and the SISTER enters.

SISTER:	Excuse me.
FORBES:	(*Pleasantly*) Oh, sorry, Sister. Did you think we were never going?
SISTER:	No, no, don't let me disturb you – but there's a telephone call for Mr Temple.
TEMPLE:	For me?
SISTER:	Yes, I asked them to put it through here …

As the SISTER speaks the telephone bell rings and she crosses and picks up the receiver.

SISTER:	(*On the phone*) Is this Mr Temple's call?
OPERATOR:	(*On the other end*) Yes – one moment please.
SISTER:	(*Offering TEMPLE the receiver*) Here you are, sir.
TEMPLE:	Oh, thank you.

The SISTER leaves the office. The sound of the door closing. A slight pause.

FORBES:	Were you expecting a call?
TEMPLE:	No, I can't imagine who it is, unless … (*Suddenly; on the phone*) Hello?
STEVE:	(*On the other end*) Hello – is that you, Paul?
TEMPLE:	Yes. Hello, Steve! What is it, darling? Is anything the matter?
STEVE:	Paul, you are expecting me, aren't you?
TEMPLE:	Expecting you?
STEVE:	Yes – at the hospital.
TEMPLE:	Why, no!

118

STEVE: Paul, didn't you telephone me about five minutes ago?

TEMPLE: No, of course I didn't! Steve, what happened? Tell me exactly what happened.

FORBES: Is Steve all right?

TEMPLE: Yes – yes, she's all right, Sir Graham. (*On the phone*) Go on, Steve.

STEVE: Well, I had a phone call. It sounded exactly like you ... You said "Pack a suitcase, get the car, and meet me at the hospital" ...

TEMPLE: But, Steve, didn't you do what I told you? Didn't you say ...

STEVE: Yes, I did – that's the extraordinary thing! I said – "Where's Charlie fishing?" – and you said ... at least the voice said ... "In the Thames."

TEMPLE: All right. Now listen, Steve. Don't leave the flat – don't answer the door. I'll be with you in fifteen minutes.

TEMPLE replaces the receiver.

FORBES: What is it, Temple?

TEMPLE: Get your hat, Sir Graham.

FADE OUT.

FADE IN the voices of STEVE, TEMPLE, and SIR GRAHAM FORBES.

TEMPLE: ... Well, whichever way you look at it, Sir Graham, Steve was lucky – confoundedly lucky ...

FORBES: ... I agree, Temple, but the point is, how the devil did he know what to say when Steve said ...

STEVE: I don't know why you both keep on saying I was lucky. It was intuition – pure intuition!

TEMPLE: You and your intuition, Steve. If you hadn't
             suddenly decided to ring the hospital …
STEVE: Darling, don't be obstinate. That <u>was</u> intuition!
TEMPLE: All right, Steve. Anyway, whatever it was, I'm
             all for it.
FORBES: Steve, I know we've asked you this at least half a
             dozen times – but what exactly did he say?
STEVE: He said, "Pack a suitcase, get the car, and meet
             me at the hospital."
FORBES: M'm …
STEVE: Paul, what do you think they intended to do? –
             Pick me up?
TEMPLE: Yes, I should imagine so, unless …
STEVE: Unless what?
FORBES: Are you thinking the same as I am, Temple?
TEMPLE: The car?
FORBES: Yes.
STEVE: The car? – What do you mean?
FORBES: Where do you keep your car, Temple?
TEMPLE: In a garage in Sloane Mews.
FORBES: Is there anyone there?
TEMPLE: Yes. Most of the time. It's a fairly large garage.
             They do a lot of repair work. Come along, Sir
             Graham, we'll go down there and have a word
             with them.

START FADE.

TEMPLE: Don't leave the flat, Steve – we'll be back in
             about ten minutes.
STEVE: (*Thoughtfully*) Yes, all right, Paul.

FADE OUT.

FADE IN background noises of a fairly large garage.
TOM FOSTER, a middle-aged mechanic, is working on a
repair job.

120

TEMPLE: Good evening, Tom.

TOM: Oh, hello, Mr Temple! (*To FORBES*) Good evening, sir.

FORBES: Good evening.

TEMPLE: Working late tonight, Tom?

TOM: Yes, this is supposed to be out by ten o'clock tomorrow morning. You wouldn't think so to look at it, would you?

TEMPLE: (*Laughing*) You certainly wouldn't.

TOM: It's a Fred Karno job this, and no mistake.

TEMPLE: Tom, has anyone called this evening – to look at my car?

TOM: Yes, a gentleman called just after you brought it in, Mr Temple. I'm surprised you're thinking of changing it, sir. That's the last thing I'd do if it was mine.

TEMPLE: Is that what he said – that I was thinking of changing it?

TOM: Why, yes – that's why he wanted to have a look at it.

FORBES: What did he say exactly?

TOM: (*Puzzled*) Well, he asked me which was Mr Temple's car. He said he wanted to have a look at it because there was some talk of a part exchange.

FORBES: Did he look at it?

TOM: Yes, he had the bonnet up and everything. I left him to get on with it, sir.

FORBES: What was he like, this man?

TOM: Oh, about thirty – pleasant enough. Bit of a fancy dresser. Berkeley Square type, I suppose.

TEMPLE: Had he anything with him?

TOM: What do you mean, sir?

TEMPLE: Well, did he carry anything. A briefcase or …

121

TOM: Yes, he had a case, sir. I hope I did the right
                thing, Mr Temple. He looked respectable
                enough, and he said he only wanted to have a
                look at the car.

TEMPLE: Yes, that's all right, Tom. Where is the car?

TOM: It's in Bay 22 on the first floor, sir. I had to
                put it up there because we were rather busy
                down here and I didn't want …

*TOM is interrupted by a sudden and violent explosion. A
time-bomb device has exploded in TEMPLE's car on the first
floor above. Windows are shattered and part of the ceiling
collapses.*

TOM: (*Dazed*) My God – what was that!

TEMPLE: Are you all right, Sir Graham?

FORBES: (*Dazed*) Yes, but something hit me on the
                shoulder and …

TOM: You're covered in plaster, sir. Holy mackerel!
                Just look at the ceiling! What was it? Was it
                the boiler room?

*There is a background of excited voices. People are attracted
to the garage by the explosion.*

TEMPLE: No, it wasn't the boiler room, Tom! Come on,
                Sir Graham – let's go upstairs!

FADE ON the sound of approaching voices.

*FADE UP the sound of the garage lift ascending. The lift
stops. The metal doors of the lift slide open.*

TOM: Mr Temple! Just look at that wall! And the
                window – and your car!

TEMPLE: I am looking at it!

FORBES: Is that your car, Temple?

TEMPLE: (*Significantly*) It was! By Timothy, Sir
                Graham – we can laugh at Steve's intuition

but … She might have been driving that car
…

FADE OUT.

FADE UP of a front door opening and TEMPLE and FORBES entering the flat. TEMPLE closes the door.

TEMPLE: (*Calling*) Steve! We're back! Go into the drawing room, Sir Graham, I'll join you in a moment.

FORBES: Do you mind if I help myself to a drink?

TEMPLE: I was just going to suggest it. Have a large scotch and soda.

FORBES: I'm not so sure about the soda just at the moment.

TEMPLE laughs.
START FADE.

TEMPLE: (*Passing into another room, calling*) Steve … Steve, darling!

COMPLETE FADE.

FADE UP SIR GRAHAM helping himself to a drink. The sound of liquid being poured, soda water, ice, etc.
TEMPLE enters.

FORBES: I've taken you at your word and helped myself to the largest … Temple, what is it? What's happened?

TEMPLE: I've been all over the flat, Sir Graham. Charlie isn't here – and there's no sign of Steve …

MUSIC.

END OF EPISODE FOUR

EPISODE FIVE

A SURPRISE FOR PETE ROBERTS

OPENING MUSIC.
FADE DOWN MUSIC.

FADE UP SIR GRAHAM helping himself to a drink. The sound of liquid being poured, soda water, ice, etc.
TEMPLE enters.

FORBES: I've taken you at your word and helped myself to the largest … Temple, what is it? What's happened?

TEMPLE: I've been all over the flat, Sir Graham. Charlie isn't here – and there's no sign of Steve …

FORBES: But we've only been out of the flat ten minutes!

TEMPLE: Yes, I know.

FORBES: Do you think they heard the explosion and went down to the garage?

TEMPLE: I suppose that is possible. But surely we'd have …

FORBES: What is it, Temple? What are you staring at?

TEMPLE: Look at this piece of wire, Sir Graham – near the radiator. I've never noticed it before.

TEMPLE pulls the wire from behind the radiator.

TEMPLE: By Timothy …

FORBES: (*Moving in*) What is it?

TEMPLE: This place is wired – there's a small microphone behind the radiator. Somebody must have been listening to every word …

FORBES: But where does it lead to? Where does the wire go?

In the background, there is the sound of the front door closing and STEVE's voice talking to CHARLIE.

TEMPLE: (*Following the wire*) Wait a minute! (*He continues to pull wire from behind the*

	radiator) It looks to me as if it goes through …
FORBES:	Here's Steve!
STEVE:	(*Rather excited*) So you found it, Paul!
TEMPLE:	Darling, where on earth have you been?
FORBES:	(*To STEVE*) Steve, did you find this? – The microphone, I mean?
STEVE:	Yes, I pulled the wire out. I've been downstairs. The wire leads through the French windows into the flat below.
TEMPLE:	But how on earth did you find it?
STEVE:	Well, I just couldn't understand how that man on the phone knew what to say – about Charlie fishing, I mean. So after you and Sir Graham went down to the garage, I started to search the flat. I thought there might be a microphone somewhere. It seemed the only possible explanation.
FORBES:	Who has the flat down below?
TEMPLE:	It's empty. The new people are moving in at the end of the week.
FORBES:	Do you know them?
TEMPLE:	No, but it's my bet they've nothing to do with this.
STEVE:	Charlie says that people have been coming and going the whole week. Electricians, decorators …
FORBES:	Yes, but someone must have been in here as well – otherwise they couldn't have fitted the microphone …
TEMPLE:	Someone's been in here all right!
FORBES:	What do you mean?

TEMPLE: This thing was fitted while we were at the Neptune Club. When Charlie was knocked out and the gramophone smashed.

STEVE: Yes, of course. I ought to have thought of that.

FORBES: (*Laughing*) You seem to have done pretty well, Steve. (*Moving towards the door*) I'll get on to Vosper straight away. He can check with the …

TEMPLE: (*Stopping FORBES*) Sir Graham …!

FORBES: Yes?

TEMPLE: (*Smiling; quietly*) You've poured yourself a very large whisky and soda – if you don't drink it, I will.

MUSIC.

FADE UP TEMPLE and STEVE having breakfast the following morning.

TEMPLE: More toast, darling?

STEVE: No, thanks.

TEMPLE laughs.

STEVE: What's amusing you?

TEMPLE: Listen to this … (*Reading from a newspaper*) "The car, which was slightly damaged, belonged to Mr Paul Temple …" Slightly damaged! By Timothy! It was blown to smithereens!

STEVE: What are you going to do about a car, Paul?

TEMPLE: I've hired one for the time being. Incidentally, Steve, I … (*He hesitates*) I may be going away for two or three days.

STEVE: Going away? Where?

TEMPLE: Well – I want to take a look at that place I was telling you about. Salex Island. If I just

	go down for the day it's going to look pretty obvious. On the other hand, if I take two or three days off and go fishing …
STEVE:	Listen, Mr T! If you're going on any fishing expedition, I'm going with you!
TEMPLE:	Now look, Steve! The best thing you can do … (*He looks up*) Yes – what is it, Charlie?
CHARLIE:	Inspector Vosper, sir.
TEMPLE:	Oh – come in, Vosper.
VOSPER:	Good morning. Good morning, Mrs Temple.
STEVE:	Good morning, Inspector. Would you like a cup of coffee?
VOSPER:	(*Hesitantly*) Well –
STEVE:	Black or white?
VOSPER:	White, please.

STEVE pours the coffee.

TEMPLE:	Sit down, Inspector.
VOSPER:	I understand you had quite a night last night.
TEMPLE:	Well, I've had worse, Inspector – but not much worse!
VOSPER:	Well, I've checked on the flat below. The new tenants are called Belford. Sir Charles and Lady Belford – he's a retired diplomat. There's nothing there. I'm quite sure the Belfords know nothing about the microphone.
TEMPLE:	Yes, I quite agree.
VOSPER:	Someone obviously planted the thing the night your man was knocked out, and they've been slipping into the flat downstairs for an hour or two ever since.
TEMPLE:	Yes, that's what I think, Vosper.
STEVE:	Your coffee, Inspector.
VOSPER:	Thank you, Mrs Temple.
STEVE:	Help yourself to sugar.

TEMPLE: Sir Graham tells me you've solved the Judy Milton mystery.

VOSPER: Well, thanks to you, Temple. What gave you the idea?

TEMPLE: Something Charlie said about the fridge automatically switching itself off and on. It suddenly made me think that there might be a concealed revolver with a time switch.

VOSPER: There was. We found it in a cupboard underneath the stairs. The time switch was put into action when you pressed the door bell.

STEVE: So the shot we heard didn't kill Judy Milton?

VOSPER: No, Mrs Temple. This thing went off under the stairs. Your husband broke into the cottage and found Judy Milton dead – shot – with the revolver in her hand. Naturally, you both thought the shot you heard had killed her.

STEVE: Which was precisely what we were intended to think.

TEMPLE: Yes.

VOSPER: The murderer was probably miles away by the time the revolver went off.

STEVE: This Mr Spencer – if you can call him Spencer – seems to think of everything.

VOSPER: Well, he thinks of a great deal, Mrs Temple.

TEMPLE: What about the passport?

VOSPER: (*Curious*) Ah, yes. Why did you want to know about Mary Dreisler's passport?

TEMPLE: It was just a thought. Had she a passport?

VOSPER: (*Not convinced by TEMPLE's casualness*) Oh, yes, she'd got one all right. (*He takes a paper from his pocket*) She'd been abroad about fifteen times in the last two or three years …

STEVE: Surely that's rather a lot, Inspector?

VOSPER: Well, I understand she frequently went to meet her father.

TEMPLE: Where?

VOSPER: Oh, in Paris, Vienna, Rome – all over the place.

TEMPLE: What about the date I mentioned?

VOSPER: Yes, I'm coming to that. October the 22nd. She was in Paris on the morning of the 22nd and flew back to London the same day.

TEMPLE: (*Pleased*) Thank you, Vosper.

VOSPER: (*Curious*) Is that what you wanted?

TEMPLE: That's what I wanted, Inspector.

VOSPER: Now, the other point – the place Clutch Brompton mentioned.

TEMPLE: Salex Island.

VOSPER: Yes. I've been on to the Maidenhead people …

TEMPLE: But I particularly asked Sir Graham …

VOSPER: (*Stopping TEMPLE*) It's all right, Temple. Inspector Webb at Maidenhead is a very good friend of mine. Don't worry. My enquiries were quite off the record – he won't say a word.

TEMPLE: Well, I hope not, Inspector.

VOSPER: Salex Island is a plot of land in the middle of the Thames. It's in a deserted stretch of the river about two miles from Henley and about a mile from Belton's Lock.

TEMPLE: How big?

VOSPER: Oh, five or six acres. There's a bungalow on the island. It was built just before the war. The whole place, the bungalow, land and everything was sold privately about three years ago.

TEMPLE: Who was it sold to?

VOSPER: Well, that's it – there seems to be a bit of a mystery about it. A chap called Lester bought the

132

place, but so far as I can gather very few people have ever seen him.

STEVE: Doesn't he ever go down there?

VOSPER: Not in the summer. I understand from Webb that he's been down there once or twice in the winter – which seems rather curious.

STEVE: Who looks after the bungalow?

VOSPER: A caretaker chap. I've just been checking on him.

TEMPLE: Well?

VOSPER: He's got a police record. A pretty bad one, too. Larceny, robbery with violence …

TEMPLE: M'm …

STEVE: Spencer … Lester … There's not a lot of difference.

VOSPER: That's what I thought, Mrs Temple. Well, I'd better be making a move.

TEMPLE: Thank you, Inspector, for the information.

VOSPER: Not at all. Oh, and Temple –

TEMPLE: Yes?

VOSPER: I think I know what's at the back of your mind, take care …

MUSIC.

STEVE: … Now are you sure you've got everything, Paul?

TEMPLE: I think so. Fishing tackle – suitcase – binoculars … Yes, I'm ready, darling. You can take the case down to the car, Charlie.

CHARLIE: Yes, Mr Temple. What if there are any messages, sir? Where can I get in touch with you?

TEMPLE: You can't. I'll ring you, Charlie. Probably some time tonight.

CHARLIE: Okey-dokey.

133

In the background the telephone can be heard ringing.

STEVE: That's the phone – shall I take it?

TEMPLE: No, you go down to the car, Steve. I'll join you.

STEVE: Don't be long.

START FADE.

STEVE: No, it's all right, Charlie, I can carry the hat-box
…

FADE UP TEMPLE lifting the phone receiver.

TEMPLE: (*On the phone*) Hello?

FROST: (*On the other end*) Is that Paul Temple?

TEMPLE: Yes.

FROST: Oh, this is Adrian Frost.

TEMPLE: Good afternoon, Frost.

FROST: (*Nervously, rather lost for words*) Temple, I've just been reading about – about what happened last night.

TEMPLE: Last night?

FROST: Yes, the explosion …

TEMPLE: (*Smiling to himself*) Oh yes – the explosion.

FROST: That must have happened soon after you left the Ritz?

TEMPLE: Yes, it did. (*A slight pause*) Is that why you telephoned?

FROST: (*Still rather at a loss for words*) Well, I was so amazed when I read about it, I thought that I ought to … I hope Mrs Temple's all right?

TEMPLE: Yes, she's fine. Fortunately, she wasn't with me … when it happened.

FROST: Oh. Oh, well that's a good thing. (*A moment*) I understand you saw Mr Dreisler last night.

TEMPLE: (*Still smiling*) Yes, I did.

FROST: I saw him too. He probably told you.

TEMPLE: I believe he did mention it.

134

FROST: He gave me the brooch back. The one I gave to
            Mary.
TEMPLE: Yes, I know.
FROST: (*Nervously, deciding to close the conversation*)
            Well, I just thought I'd make sure that you and
            Mrs Temple were all right.
TEMPLE: That was very kind of you.
FROST: Not at all.
TEMPLE: (*Stopping FROST from ringing off*) Oh, by the
            way …
FROST: Yes?
TEMPLE: The first time we met, at Beaconsfield – when I
            asked you about the brooch …
FROST: I'm afraid I was rude, frightfully rude. I've
            regretted it ever since.
TEMPLE: That's all right. If I remember rightly you said,
            "I gave Mary the brooch for a particular reason.
            I suggest you find out the reason, Mr Temple."
FROST: Yes.
TEMPLE: Well, I think I've found it.
FROST: Oh, have you?
TEMPLE: Yes. I suggest you gave it to her because –
            because you were under a misapprehension.
FROST: (*On edge*) What do you mean – a
            misapprehension?
TEMPLE: Goodbye, Frost. Thank you for ringing.
TEMPLE replaces the receiver.
MUSIC.

FADE UP the sound of a car travelling at an average speed.
STEVE: How long are we going to stay in Henley, Paul?
TEMPLE: Two or three days – four, if necessary.
STEVE: Have you booked a room?

135

TEMPLE:	Yes, I phoned this morning. We're not staying at the hotel. We're staying at a small pub by the river.
STEVE:	Oh? – Why's that?
TEMPLE:	Well, I've stayed at this place before. It's awfully good, and I don't think we shall be quite as conspicuous.
STEVE:	Is it far from Salex Island?
TEMPLE:	About a mile, I think.
STEVE:	Paul, oughtn't you to have turned to the left by the hospital.
TEMPLE:	Yes, but we're going to the Neptune first. I want to have a word with Terry Gibson.
STEVE:	Will she be there at this time of the day?
TEMPLE:	I imagine so. She's got an office there. Anyway, we'll see.
STEVE:	What do you want to see her about?
TEMPLE:	About Pete Roberts and his meeting with Dreisler. I want to know who was telling the truth.
STEVE:	Well, if you want my opinion, I think Pete Roberts was. I think Dreisler did ask him to go to Putney and make the record.
TEMPLE:	Dreisler admits that. He simply says that he didn't ask him to sing the song "My Heart and Harry".
STEVE:	Yes, well, I've got a funny sort of feeling about Mr Dreisler.
TEMPLE:	(*Laughing*) Here we go again …
STEVE:	No, I'm serious, darling.
TEMPLE:	I'm sure you are.
START FADE.	
STEVE:	You can laugh, but if it hadn't been for my intuition …

TEMPLE: I know, I know, Steve!
FADE traffic noises and the sound of the car.

FADE IN the sound of a piano. A jazz PIANIST is rehearsing at the Neptune Club. He suddenly stops playing.
TEMPLE: Excuse me, I'm looking for Miss Gibson.
PIANIST: She's probably in her office.
TEMPLE: Where is that?
PIANIST: You see that door, on the balcony?
TEMPLE: Yes.
PIANIST: You go through there, and there's another door marked "Private". That's it.
TEMPLE: Thanks.
PIANIST: You're welcome!
The PIANIST starts to play the piano again.
FADE OUT.

FADE ON TERRY GIBSON's voice. She is on the telephone.
TERRY: … (*Obviously worried*) I don't like it – it's far too drastic and it's unnecessary. Besides, even if we get rid of Pete it doesn't mean to say that … (*She suddenly breaks off as the office door opens and TEMPLE enters; she is annoyed*) What is it? What do you … (*Recognising TEMPLE*) Oh, oh, hello … Come in, Mr Temple! (*Quietly; on the phone*) I'll ring you back. (*She replaces the receiver*)
TEMPLE: Forgive me for intruding, Miss Gibson, I didn't realise …
TERRY: (*Regaining her composure*) Come in, Mr Temple – come in.
TEMPLE: I thought this was your secretary's office. Otherwise …

TERRY: That's all right. I was just giving my Head
            Waiter a piece of my mind – not that it'll make
            the slightest difference. Don't open a nightclub,
            unless you adore having staff trouble.

TEMPLE: (*Laughs*) I've troubles of my own at the
            moment. Miss Gibson, I saw Pete Roberts last
            night, and he told me about his interview with
            Rupert Dreisler.

TERRY: Yes?

TEMPLE: I understand you saw Pete immediately after
            the interview.

TERRY: Yes, I did. I went to his table just after Dreisler
            left. Do sit down.

TEMPLE: No, no, I won't keep you. Pete Roberts told me
            that Dreisler asked him to make a special
            recording so that he could take it to America.

TERRY: Yes, that's true.

TEMPLE: He said that Dreisler insisted on him singing a
            song called "My Heart and Harry".

TERRY: Well?

TEMPLE: Well – is that true, Miss Gibson?

TERRY: (*Hesitantly*) Yes, I believe it is.

TEMPLE: You believe it is?

TERRY: Well, I can't be absolutely certain. I've only
            got Pete's word for it – the same as you.

TEMPLE: But Pete did tell you …

TERRY: He told me that Dreisler wanted him to make a
            record. A record of the song you've just
            mentioned.

TEMPLE: Thank you, Miss Gibson, that's all I want to
            know. Sorry to have been such a nuisance.

TERRY: Mr Temple …

TEMPLE: Yes?

TERRY: Why are you interested in this song – "My Heart
            and Harry"?
TEMPLE: (*Smiling*) Would you like to know why, Miss
            Gibson? Would you really like to know?
TERRY: (*Puzzled by TEMPLE's manner*) Yes, I would.
TEMPLE: Because I'm always interested in … red herrings.
MUSIC.

*FADE UP the sound of a car which is travelling in London
traffic. TEMPLE is driving.*
There is a pause.
STEVE: You're very quiet.
TEMPLE: Am I?
STEVE: You've hardly said a word since you left Terry
            Gibson.
TEMPLE: Yes, I know. Sorry, darling.
STEVE: Paul, has this case beaten you?
TEMPLE: (*A little laugh*) No, Steve, no.
STEVE: But you're puzzled, aren't you?
TEMPLE: Just a little bit.
STEVE: You know, while you were in the Neptune Club
            talking to Terry Gibson, I started thinking.
TEMPLE: (*Half listening*) Did you?
STEVE: Yes, I did. I made a note – a mental note – of all
            the suspects in this case. And they're a pretty
            curious bunch. Now take Rupert Dreisler.
            International impresario, father of the dead girl.
            But if you asked me to name one   show   he's
            presented, either here or on Broadway, I couldn't
            do it. And then Adrian Frost. He's a playwright –
            at least, he says he is – but he doesn't write any
            plays. And Pete Wallace – well, he's really
            crackers – absolutely up the wall.
TEMPLE laughs.

139

STEVE: Well, he is, isn't he? And the curious thing is, you know, that all these people have one thing in … (*Suddenly*) Paul, where on earth are you going? You turn left here, darling.

TEMPLE: It's all right, Steve. I know where I'm going.

STEVE: But this isn't the way to Henley.

TEMPLE: I know. I've just remembered, I've got another call to make.

STEVE: Another call? Where are we going now?

TEMPLE: To Stepney to see Pete Roberts. There's something I've got to tell him.

STEVE: Well – why not telephone him?

TEMPLE: No, I don't want to do that.

STEVE: Why not?

TEMPLE: Well, what I want to say to him isn't quite the sort of thing you'd say on the telephone.

STEVE: What do you mean? What are you going to tell him?

TEMPLE: (*Almost casually*) I'm going to tell him – I think he's going to be murdered …

MUSIC.

FADE IN noises associated with the general cleaning of the bar parlour. Music comes from a radio in the background.

WARREN: (*Irritably*) We're closed. Didn't you see the notice on the door?

TEMPLE: Yes, I saw it.

WARREN: Well, it isn't there for fun.

TEMPLE: Is Pete Roberts in?

WARREN: Yes, he's upstairs, but you can't … (*Coming from behind the bar, recognising TEMPLE*) Oh, I'm sorry, I didn't recognise you, Mr Temple.

TEMPLE: That's all right.

WARREN: (*Calling to someone in the background*) Put some more lights on, George – you can't see a blessed thing in here.

TEMPLE: You say Pete's in his room?

WARREN: Well, he was half an hour ago, but he's in and out all the time these days. Like a blinking jack-in-the-box. Shall I give him a shout?

TEMPLE: No, I'll go upstairs and see him. Oh, is there a phone upstairs?

WARREN: No, there's only the one in the corridor. Through that door on the right.

TEMPLE: Well, I want to make a phone call. Don't let Pete go out without my seeing him.

WARREN: Okay. If he comes down I'll tell him you're here.

TEMPLE: Thanks.

FADE background noises and the sound of the radio.

FADE UP the sound of a telephone ringing and a receiver being lifted at the other end.

MAN: (*On the other end of the phone*) Scotland Yard …

TEMPLE: (*On the phone*) Put me through to Inspector Vosper please.

MAN: Who is speaking?

TEMPLE: Paul Temple.

MAN: Thank you, sir.

We hear a click on the line as VOSPER picks up the receiver in his office.

VOSPER: (*On the other end of the phone*) Hello?

TEMPLE: Hello, Vosper. This is Temple.

VOSPER: (*Surprised*) Oh, hello – I thought you were out of Town?

TEMPLE: We're on our way, Vosper. But listen, something's happened – something important.

VOSPER: What is it?

TEMPLE: There are two things I want you to do. One is a little unorthodox, but I'm afraid you've got to do it.

VOSPER: Don't worry! If it's going to help us, we'll do it.

TEMPLE: Get onto the telephone exchange and ask them to check on all the calls at the Neptune Club. I want a list of all calls since ten o'clock this morning. It's important.

VOSPER: Right – I'll see to that.

TEMPLE: The other thing is this: I think we're going to hear from Spencer again. Unless I'm mistaken there's going to be another murder.

VOSPER: Are you sure, Temple?

TEMPLE: I'm pretty sure. I know who they're after, and I want you to play safe and pick him up. It doesn't matter what the charge is. Pick him up, Vosper.

START FADE.

VOSPER: Yes, but listen, Temple, we can't just arrest someone because you say so …

TEMPLE: Inspector, this is what I want you to do …

COMPLETE FADE.

FADE IN noises of the bar parlour and music from the radio set.

FADE DOWN to background.

WARREN: He's still upstairs, Mr Temple.

TEMPLE: Thanks. I'll go up.

WARREN: You know the room – the door facing the stairs.

TEMPLE: Yes. Thank you.

FADE noises of the bar parlour and the radio.

FADE UP TEMPLE knocking on the door of PETE's room. There is a pause.

TEMPLE knocks again. There is no reply. TEMPLE tries the door handle, but the door is locked. He knocks again. Suddenly, the door is unlocked and thrown open.

PETE: (*Annoyed*) What's the big idea? Can't a chap have a ruddy shave without … (*Recognising TEMPLE*) Oh, hello? What do you want?

TEMPLE: I want to see you, Pete. Can I come in?

PETE: (*Not very friendly*) Yes, if you want to.

TEMPLE enters the room. The door closes.

PETE: You'll have to sit on the bed. I'll get this soap off my face.

TEMPLE: No, that's all right. You carry on. It won't take me a couple of minutes to say what I've got to say anyway.

PETE continues shaving. During the following dialogue we hear the water tap being turned on and off in the wash-hand basin.

TEMPLE: (*Pleasantly*) Do you usually shave in the afternoon?

PETE: I don't usually shave at all – not if I can help it. What is it you want?

TEMPLE: Pete, you remember the last time we met – we talked about Terry Gibson and Rupert Dreisler?

PETE: Yes.

TEMPLE: You said that Dreisler asked you to sing a song – "My Heart and Harry".

PETE: That's right. I sang the ruddy thing.

TEMPLE: Do you know why I was interested in that song?

PETE: (*Apparently disinterested*) No. Haven't a clue.

TEMPLE: I was interested in it because I believe – and Scotland Yard believe – that the man who murdered Mary Dreisler sent her a gramophone

143

record – a record of, presumably, "My Heart and Harry".

PETE: Whadya mean – presumably?

TEMPLE: Well, the label said "My Heart and Harry", but since we didn't have a chance of playing it we don't actually know what was on the record.

PETE: Well, what's all this got to do with me? (*Suddenly*) Look, I didn't send Mary Dreisler the record, if that's what you're thinking.

TEMPLE: No, that's not what I'm thinking. The man who sent the record called himself Spencer. It's my belief that he murdered Mary Dreisler and Judy Milton. It's also my belief that he's going to – murder you.

PETE: Are you kidding?

TEMPLE: No, I'm not kidding.

PETE: But why the hell should he murder me?

TEMPLE: I don't know why. I was hoping you'd be able to tell me.

PETE: But I don't know anything about this chap Spencer. Except what I've read in the newspapers. (*Suddenly, drawing closer to TEMPLE*) Look, what put this crazy idea into your head? What makes you think he's after me?

TEMPLE: Something I – overheard. (*Concluding the interview*) Anyway, I thought you ought to know about it. Watch your step.

PETE: (*Obviously shaken*) Just a minute. Just a minute, chum. Whadya mean? Something you overheard – where?

TEMPLE: I overheard part of a telephone conversation. I'm not prepared to tell you where I overheard it, or who was speaking, but – your name was mentioned.

144

PETE: But I don't understand this. Why pick on me? Why should this chap Spencer want to do me in?

TEMPLE: I don't know, Pete. But don't under-rate him – and remember what I said – watch your step …

MUSIC.

FADE UP the bedroom door opening.

STEVE: At last! I thought you were never coming.

The door closes.

TEMPLE: Sorry to have been so long, dear. Have you unpacked?

STEVE: Ages ago.

TEMPLE: Oh, good.

STEVE: My dear Paul, it's nearly half past seven. You went out at five o'clock.

TEMPLE: Yes, I know.

STEVE: (*Imitating TEMPLE*) "Shan't be long, dear. Just popping into the village for half an hour."

TEMPLE: (*Laughing*) I was looking for someone – it took me longer than I thought.

STEVE: Who were you looking for?

TEMPLE: A man I know. He runs a boat-building firm. I wanted to hire a boat and I didn't want to go to the obvious people.

STEVE: Oh, I see. Did you get one?

TEMPLE: Yes, he's fixed me up all right. I've told him we'll pick it up later.

STEVE: Tonight?

TEMPLE: Yes. Come on, we'd better go down and have some dinner.

STEVE: (*Smiling*) Paul, I've got some news for you.

TEMPLE: What do you mean?

STEVE: Who do you think had lunch here today?

TEMPLE: I don't know. Who?

145

STEVE: Mr Dreisler.

TEMPLE: Dreisler?

STEVE: Yes.

TEMPLE: How do you know?

STEVE: I saw him.

TEMPLE: What? Where did you see him?

STEVE: Well, while I was unpacking, I suddenly noticed that I wasn't wearing my sapphire ring. I flew into a panic, dashed downstairs, and telephoned Charlie.

TEMPLE: And the ring, as usual, was in the bathroom.

STEVE: (*Laughing*) Yes.

TEMPLE: Well, go on.

STEVE: Anyway, when I came out of the telephone box, I saw Rupert Dreisler. He was standing on his own near the reception desk.

START FADE.

STEVE: Although he didn't take any notice of me I was sure that he'd seen me, so I made a point of going up to him …

COMPLETE FADE.

FADE IN STEVE's voice addressing RUPERT DREISLER.

STEVE: … It is Mr Dreisler, isn't it?

DREISLER: (*Apparently surprised*) Yes.

STEVE: Mrs Temple …

DREISLER: Oh, hello, Mrs Temple. I didn't recognise you. Are you staying down here?

STEVE: Yes, we've just arrived. My husband wanted to get away from Town for two or three days.

DREISLER: I see.

STEVE: But what are you doing here, Mr Dreisler? I thought you were staying at the Ritz.

DREISLER: I am. I had an appointment in Henley this morning and I dropped in here for lunch. (*Smiling; pleasantly*) Is that the correct phrase – "dropped in here"?

STEVE: Yes, that's the correct phrase. You must have had a very good lunch. It's nearly five o'clock.

DREISLER: I had coffee in the lounge and fell asleep. When you are my age that's the sort of thing that happens to you.

STEVE: It happens to you at any age!

They both laugh.

A slight pause.

DREISLER: Well, if you'll excuse me, my car is waiting.

STEVE: Yes, of course.

DREISLER: (*Hesitantly*) Oh, Mrs Temple …

STEVE: Yes?

DREISLER: I hope that doesn't mean that he's ill, or anything?

STEVE: No, no, he's not ill.

DREISLER: You see, I asked him to make certain investigations for me. He said that he would.

STEVE: Yes, I know.

DREISLER: But perhaps I am asking too many questions. Perhaps that is why your husband is down here, because … (*Waiting for STEVE to answer*)

STEVE: (*Politely*) Because?

DREISLER: Because he has discovered something – something which necessitated a visit to Henley-on-Thames?

STEVE: Well, if he has, he hasn't told me anything about it. (*With a disarming little laugh*) But then, of course, he doesn't tell me everything. Goodbye, Mr Dreisler.

DREISLER: Goodbye, Mrs Temple. I hope we shall meet again.

STEVE: I hope so.

DREISLER: Perhaps you and your husband would have dinner with me one evening when you return to Town …

FADE OUT.

FADE UP STEVE's voice.

STEVE: … I watched him go outside. A few minutes later he drove away.

TEMPLE: Was there anyone else in the car?

STEVE: Just a chauffeur.

TEMPLE: Did you recognise the chauffeur?

STEVE: No, I'd never seen him before.

TEMPLE: M'm. All right, Steve – let's go and have some dinner. Oh, by the way, I suppose you didn't ask Charlie if there were any messages?

STEVE: Yes, I did. There's nothing important.

TEMPLE: Oh, good.

STEVE: (*Remembering*) Oh, Peter Wallace telephoned – but then he's always telephoning.

TEMPLE: What time was this?

STEVE: Oh, just after we left. He told Charlie his flat has been broken into, or something like that. When Charlie said we were out he said he'd ring back later. He seems an extraordinary young man. I can't imagine what Mary Dreisler saw in him.

TEMPLE: There's something you've overlooked, darling. (*A pause*) We never knew Mary Dreisler.

MUSIC.

FADE UP the sound of a small motor launch on the river. The sound of the launch is heard for a little while before STEVE speaks.

STEVE: It's a wonderfully clear night, Paul. Just look at that moon.

TEMPLE: A little too clear for my liking.

A pause.

STEVE: How far is this island – we seem to have been going for hours.

TEMPLE: You never were a very good judge of time, darling. We've been going exactly forty-five minutes.

STEVE: Oh, nonsense!

TEMPLE: It's true. We left the boathouse at nine o'clock, and it's now … (*He stops speaking and peers ahead*)

STEVE: What is it?

TEMPLE: I think we're coming to it, Steve – it should be just round the bend.

STEVE: Mind your head! Watch that branch!

There is the sound of tree branches brushing against the side of the boat.

TEMPLE: There we are … That's Salex Island!

STEVE: (*Peering ahead*) What a strange looking place …

TEMPLE: It doesn't look very inviting, does it, in spite of the moonlight.

STEVE: It certainly doesn't.

There is a slight pause.

The sound of the launch continues.

STEVE: How big is it supposed to be?

TEMPLE: About five or six acres.

STEVE: It looks bigger than that.

TEMPLE: I can't see the bungalow.

149

STEVE: It's not surprising. You can't see anything – the place is an absolute wilderness.

TEMPLE: By Timothy, Steve! What a hide-out! You could stay here for weeks, and no one would be any the wiser.

STEVE: What are you going to do, Paul – now we're here?

TEMPLE: We'll sail right round the island and take a good look at it.

STEVE: (*A little nervously*) And then what?

TEMPLE: And then we'll – take another good look! (*With a little laugh*) Darling, I did tell you to stay at home, didn't I?

STEVE: That's a great help!

FADE UP the sound of the motor launch.

A pause.

STEVE: You still can't see the bungalow …

TEMPLE: It must be somewhere behind those trees.

STEVE: What are you doing?

TEMPLE: I'm switching the motor off. We're going in …

STEVE: What do you mean – going in?

TEMPLE: I'm going to take a look round, Steve. I shan't be long.

STEVE: Do you think that's wise?

TEMPLE: It'll be all right, darling – don't worry.

TEMPLE switches the motor off. The boat drifts slowly along.

A pause.

Background of night noises. Sound of a distant owl. Water can be heard lapping against the side of the boat. With a dull thud the boat strikes land.

TEMPLE: Here we are, Steve – pass me that rope, darling. That's it …

STEVE: What are you doing?

TEMPLE: I want to tie it to that tree if I can …

150

TEMPLE leans forward and throws a rope around a tree. He pulls on the rope.

TEMPLE: Ah, that's it …

STEVE: The water looks awfully deep, Paul.

TEMPLE: Yes, I think it is just round here. Now listen, Steve – I'm going up to the bungalow. I want you to stay in the boat and …

STEVE: (*Interrupting TEMPLE*) Paul! Listen!

In the distant background can be heard the barking of a dog. The barking continues for a moment or two, then stops.

TEMPLE: That's coming from the bungalow. Well, if there's a dog there's probably someone there.

STEVE: Have you got the torch?

TEMPLE: Yes. I'll be back in five or ten minutes, I promise you.

TEMPLE climbs out of the boat on to the bank and the noise of the water increases as he does so.

STEVE: All right?

TEMPLE: Yes, I'm fine.

STEVE: Take care.

TEMPLE: I shan't be long, I promise you, darling.

STEVE: All right, Paul.

FADE on the sound of water lapping against the boat.

FADE UP TEMPLE forcing his way through the thick grass and woodland. After a moment, the dog starts barking again. It is now much nearer. TEMPLE continues towards the bungalow, and the noise of the dog grows much louder. It stops barking, and then suddenly from the background we hear a loud, terrified scream from STEVE. TEMPLE stops dead. STEVE's voice can be heard calling from the background. She is obviously desperately frightened.

STEVE: (*Shouting*) Paul! Paul, come back! Paul!

TEMPLE turns and rushes back towards the boat.

151

TEMPLE: I'm coming – it's all right, Steve. I'm coming!
FADE OUT.
FADE UP the noise of water lapping against the boat. STEVE is still frightened and calling for TEMPLE. He arrives, out of breath and obviously alarmed.
TEMPLE: Steve, what is it? Are you all right?
STEVE: Paul, just after you left I ... saw something ...
TEMPLE: What do you mean, dear – you saw something?
STEVE: I saw something in the water ... a body ... a man's body ... It came up to the surface ... It floated on the surface!
TEMPLE: Steve, are you sure?
STEVE: Yes, I'm quite sure.
TEMPLE: Where was this? Where did you see the body?
STEVE: Just – just down there. Near that dinghy.
TEMPLE: Hold this torch ...
TEMPLE kneels down and puts his arm in the water. He gropes his way, feeling for the body.
TEMPLE: Is this the spot?
STEVE: Yes.
A pause.
TEMPLE: I can't find anything ...
STEVE: Paul, I swear I saw it ...
TEMPLE: Wait a moment!
STEVE: What is it? (*Almost a cry of alarm*) Paul, what is it?
TEMPLE: Switch the torch on.
The torch is switched on and there is a gasp from STEVE.
TEMPLE: You were right, Steve.
STEVE: It's Peter Wallace!
MUSIC.

END OF EPISODE FIVE

EPISODE SIX

HOME AGAIN!

OPENING MUSIC.

FADE DOWN MUSIC.

FADE UP the sound of TEMPLE swishing his arm through the water in search of the body seen by STEVE.

TEMPLE: Where was this? Where did you see the body?

STEVE: Just – just down there. Near that dinghy.

TEMPLE: Hold this torch …

TEMPLE kneels down and puts his arm in the water. He gropes his way, feeling for the body.

TEMPLE: Is this the spot?

STEVE: Yes.

A pause.

TEMPLE: I can't find anything …

STEVE: Paul, I swear I saw it …

TEMPLE: Wait a moment!

STEVE: What is it? (*Almost a cry of alarm*) Paul, what is it?

TEMPLE: Switch the torch on.

The torch is switched on and there is a gasp from STEVE.

TEMPLE: You were right, Steve.

STEVE: It's Peter Wallace!

TEMPLE: Yes, it's Peter Wallace …

STEVE: Is he – dead?

A moment.

TEMPLE: Yes … I'm afraid you'll have to give me a hand, Steve – we've got to get him into the boat.

STEVE: Yes, all right.

TEMPLE and STEVE take hold of WALLACE and endeavour to lift him out of the water.

STEVE: (*Breathlessly*) We'll never do it, Paul. He's … too … heavy …

TEMPLE: We've got to … Wait a minute …

155

TEMPLE leans forward and takes a firm grip on WALLACE.

TEMPLE: ... Now you hold on to me, Steve ... that's it ...
Pull, Steve ... harder ...

TEMPLE and STEVE are slowly pulling the body out of the water. The body is gradually pulled out of the water and into the boat.

TEMPLE: That's done it.

TEMPLE and STEVE relax, utterly exhausted.

There is a pause.

STEVE: Paul ...

TEMPLE: Yes.

STEVE: Were you surprised – when you recognised him?

TEMPLE: No.

STEVE: I didn't think you were. I could tell by your expression that you knew ...

TEMPLE: Don't talk, dear – not for a moment.

There is a pause.

In the distant background the dog starts to bark again.

STEVE: How long do you think he'd been in the water?

TEMPLE: Not very long. About half an hour perhaps.

STEVE: What are you going to do?

TEMPLE: I'd still like to take a look at that bungalow, Steve.

STEVE: Paul, I can't stay here, not with ...

TEMPLE: Yes, all right, dear. We'll go up to the bungalow together.

STEVE: Don't you think it would be better if we went back to Henley?

TEMPLE: We will in a few minutes, Steve – but just let's take a look at the place now we're here.

STEVE: Yes, all right.

TEMPLE and STEVE climb off the boat onto land.

FADE.

156

FADE UP of TEMPLE and STEVE moving through thick undergrowth towards the bungalow.

STEVE: There's the bungalow …

TEMPLE: Yes …

STEVE: I don't see any sign of the dog.

TEMPLE: No.

STEVE: It doesn't look as if anyone lives here.

TEMPLE: They obviously don't. I should imagine this place is only used once in a blue moon.

TEMPLE and STEVE approach the bungalow and ascend the wooden terrace surrounding the building.

STEVE: Paul, what are you going to say if there's anyone here?

TEMPLE: I'm going to ask them about Peter Wallace. Wallace must have been up here, otherwise … (*He stops*)

STEVE: What is it?

TEMPLE: The door's open … (*Raising his voice; calling*) Hello, there! Anybody at home?

A pause.

STEVE: I've got a funny feeling. I – I think someone's watching me.

TEMPLE: Yes, I know what you mean.

TEMPLE slowly pushes open the door.

TEMPLE: Let's take a look inside …

The door is pushed open, and TEMPLE and STEVE enter the bungalow. There is the sound of footsteps on the wooden floor. They speak softly, not wishing to be overheard.

TEMPLE: This place hasn't been looked after very well …

STEVE: Doesn't it smell musty …

TEMPLE: The whole place could do with a coat of paint.

STEVE: Have you got the torch, Paul – there's a room in here.

TEMPLE: Probably the lounge …

157

TEMPLE and STEVE pass from the hall to the lounge.

STEVE: … Yes, this is the lounge, by the look of things.

TEMPLE: (*Surprised*) Is that a filing cabinet over there?

STEVE: It looks like it …

TEMPLE crosses to the cabinet and opens one of the steel drawers.

STEVE: Funny having a steel filing cabinet in a drawing room.

TEMPLE: Yes, but I don't think anyone really lives here. It's my bet the bungalow is used more or less as a meeting place – a sort of hide-out.

STEVE: Is there anything in the file?

TEMPLE: No. It's been emptied … (*Examining the file*) In rather a hurry, too, I should imagine.

STEVE: Paul, there's something on the floor.

TEMPLE: Where?

STEVE: Near the file – a piece of paper …

TEMPLE: Oh, yes. (*He picks it up*)

STEVE: What is it?

TEMPLE: It looks like a menu card … You hold the torch, Steve. I can see it better then.

A moment.

STEVE: It's not a menu exactly …

TEMPLE: No, it's one of those cards you sometimes find in restaurants – you know, advertising the cabaret, that sort of thing …

STEVE: What does it say? (*Reading*) La Mediterranee.

TEMPLE: La Mediterranee. Boulevard St Germain, Paris … Pauline and Michelle … your favourite dancers …

STEVE: Pauline and Michelle – your favourite dancers. Etienne Gastoux – first class prestidigateur …

TEMPLE: Why on earth don't they just say conjurer?

STEVE: (*Without thinking, with a French pronunciation*) And Pierre Roberts, baritone.

TEMPLE: Pierre Roberts!

STEVE: Pete Roberts!

TEMPLE: Yes.

STEVE: Is there a date on that card?

TEMPLE: (*A moment*) No. I can't see one.

STEVE: That's a serious coincidence, isn't it, Paul?

TEMPLE: It is!

STEVE: I wonder what sort of a place this is – La Mediterranee.

TEMPLE: It sounds like a nightclub.

STEVE: Have you heard of it?

TEMPLE: No, I haven't, but that doesn't mean anything. There are hundreds of them in Paris.

STEVE: It's rather odd that card should have been left behind …

TEMPLE: Yes. The person who cleared the file either dropped it or …

STEVE: Or it was planted deliberately, and you were meant to find it.

TEMPLE: Yes … Let's go back into the hall. There must be another room on the other side.

STEVE: Do you want the torch?

TEMPLE: No, you keep it …

TEMPLE and STEVE leave the lounge and return to the hall.

STEVE: There's another door over there. It's probably the dining room …

TEMPLE: Steve, wait a minute!

STEVE: What is it?

TEMPLE: (*Softly*) There's someone outside, on the verandah …

STEVE: Are you sure?

TEMPLE: Yes, I'm sure I heard …

159

As TEMPLE speaks the front door is slammed and a key quickly turns in the lock. Almost immediately there is the sound of footsteps and the noise of a dog barking.

STEVE: What was that?

Quick FADE DOWN of the footsteps and the dog barking during the following dialogue.

TEMPLE: (*Quickly crossing to the front door*) It's the front door! Someone was watching us – they've locked us in!

STEVE: Locked us in!

TEMPLE: Yes …

STEVE: (*Rather frightened*) What are we going to do?

TEMPLE: (*Feeling the door handle*) We've got to get out, that's all there is to it! Steve, shine the light on the door. On the <u>door</u>, darling.

TEMPLE starts throwing his weight against the door.

STEVE: Are you trying to break the lock?

TEMPLE: Yes.

STEVE: Do you think you can do it?

TEMPLE: I think so – it's not very strong.

After a determined onslaught the lock begins to give way.

STEVE: It's giving way.

The lock finally breaks, and TEMPLE pushes open the door.

STEVE: That's done it!

TEMPLE: Yes, but stay where you are, Steve.

STEVE: Where are you going?

TEMPLE: I'll be back in a minute!

STEVE: Paul! I'd rather …

TEMPLE: Darling, please do as I tell you!

TEMPLE goes out on to the balcony.

There is a pause.

The sound of a distant owl hooting in the background is heard. From far away we can hear the dog barking.

TEMPLE: (*Calling*) Come on, Steve – it's all right now.

STEVE joins TEMPLE on the balcony.

STEVE: Has he gone?

TEMPLE: Yes.

STEVE: Who was it – do you know?

TEMPLE: I've a pretty shrewd idea. We were darned fools to walk into the place like that. I ought to have realised that he would … (*He stops*)

STEVE: What is it?

TEMPLE: Listen!

From the distant background we hear the motor launch starting and gradually moving away from the island.

STEVE: (*Alarmed*) It's the boat!

TEMPLE: Yes, I know! That's what I was afraid of!

START FADE.

STEVE: You mean he's taken the boat?

TEMPLE: Yes. (*Quickly*) Come on, Steve!

CROSS FADE to the sound of the boat going down the river.
FADE the sound of the boat completely.

FADE UP the sound of TEMPLE and STEVE groping their way through the grass and undergrowth to the river.

STEVE: (*Alarmed*) Paul, he <u>has</u> taken it! The boat's gone! Look!

TEMPLE: Yes.

STEVE: And Wallace – has he taken the body?

TEMPLE: Yes, unless he's dumped it in the river again.

STEVE: (*Obviously shaken*) What are we going to do?

TEMPLE: There's only one thing we can do – we'll have to use that dinghy.

STEVE: (*Dubiously*) It doesn't look very safe.

TEMPLE: Well, we've either got to use it or stay here until someone passes by …

STEVE: But that may not be for hours!

161

TEMPLE: Exactly. (*A decision*) Let's have a look at the dinghy.

TEMPLE climbs down the bank and examines the dinghy which is in the water.

STEVE: (*After a moment*) What's it like?

TEMPLE: (*Hesitantly*) Well – it's not leaking …

STEVE: That's something! Are there any oars?

TEMPLE: There's a sort of paddle thing.

STEVE joins TEMPLE by the dinghy.

STEVE: It doesn't seem very safe! Do you think we can both get in it?

TEMPLE: Yes, of course we can.

STEVE: I don't like it very much.

TEMPLE: It's not exactly the "Queen Mary"! But we haven't got much choice, have we?

STEVE: You get in first – and see what happens.

TEMPLE: Yes, all right.

TEMPLE climbs into the dinghy. It sways slightly then steadies itself.

STEVE: All right?

TEMPLE: It's steadier than it looks. Come on – give me your hand.

STEVE climbs into the dinghy.

TEMPLE: Steady! (*A moment*) That's it – sit down …

STEVE: How do we steer?

TEMPLE: There's a rudder on your left … No, on your left, Steve …

STEVE: What – this?

TEMPLE: That's it. (*A moment*) Ready?

STEVE: Yes.

TEMPLE: Right … Off we go!

TEMPLE puts the paddle into the water.

STEVE: Don't go too fast!

TEMPLE: You needn't worry about that!

The dinghy starts to move.

STEVE: How far is it across?

TEMPLE: About two hundred yards I should imagine, no
              more. (*Passing*) By Timothy, this is going to be
              pretty hard going!

STEVE: Steady, Paul! We're rocking about, rather!

TEMPLE: It's all right, Steve …

TEMPLE continues paddling the dinghy.

FADE On the sound of water.

FADE UP TEMPLE and STEVE in the dinghy.

STEVE: There's some reeds just ahead of you, Paul …

TEMPLE: Yes, I know – I can feel them …

STEVE: We'd better not get caught in them, otherwise
              we're …

TEMPLE: We've got to go through them, darling – there's no
              other way.

STEVE: I didn't notice them before.

TEMPLE: Yes, I did. There's a lot of them near the bank.
              We shall have to be careful that …

*As TEMPLE speaks, in the background there is the sound of a
revolver shot and a bullet striking across the surface of the
water.*

STEVE: (*Alarmed*) What was that?

*There is a second revolver shot and again the bullet hits the
water.*

STEVE: (*Frightened*) Paul!

TEMPLE: Someone's firing at me!

*There is another shot. The bullet hits the water near the
dinghy.*

STEVE: That nearly hit the boat!

TEMPLE: Steve, we've got to get out of this dinghy!

STEVE: What do you mean?

TEMPLE: We're a sitting target, he can't help but hit us!

STEVE: But what are we going to do?

TEMPLE: I don't think it's very deep here, Steve. I'm going
           to turn the boat over! Make for those reeds, the
           bank's about thirty yards on the other side …

*Another revolver shot is heard and this time the bullet hits the
dinghy.*

STEVE: That hit the dinghy!

TEMPLE: Yes! We can't stay here, Steve – ready?

STEVE: Yes!

TEMPLE: (*Turning the dinghy over*) Over we go!

*TEMPLE turns the dinghy over and both he and STEVE fall
into the river. They start swimming towards the bank and the
reeds.*

FADE OUT.

FADE UP.

TEMPLE: … Make for those weeds, Steve! Get behind them!

STEVE: Yes … Yes, all right. Who – who do you think it
           is? Do you think it's the same man?

TEMPLE: Don't talk, Steve.

TEMPLE and STEVE reach the weeds.

TEMPLE: (*Softly*) All right?

STEVE: Yes … It's quite shallow just here …

There is another shot. The bullet strikes the water.

*A flock of wild geese rise from the reeds and pass overhead.
In the distant background there is the sound of a motorboat.*

STEVE: Paul, do you hear that? It's the motorboat …

TEMPLE: Yes, I think he's searching for us. (*Anxiously*)
           Keep your head down, Steve – don't let him see
           you …

STEVE: Thank goodness you saw these weeds …

TEMPLE: We're only about thirty or forty yards from the
           bank, as soon as he … Keep still, Steve!

FADE UP the sound of the motorboat. It draws gradually nearer and nearer.

STEVE: (*Softy; tensely*) He's passing …

TEMPLE: Sssh!

The boat passes the weeds and then slowly continues down the river.

STEVE: Did you see who it was?

TEMPLE: No. I had to keep my head down or he'd have spotted me …

STEVE: Do you think he's gone?

TEMPLE: We'll give him five minutes – then we'll make for the bank.

STEVE: (*Shivering*) Yes, all right.

TEMPLE: Do you think you can hold on for another five minutes?

STEVE: Yes … Yes, of course.

MUSIC.

FADE UP TEMPLE and STEVE having breakfast.

STEVE: More coffee?

TEMPLE: No, thanks, dear. Steve, I'm awfully sorry about last night.

STEVE: (*With a little laugh; but obviously still tired*) Oh, nonsense.

TEMPLE: It was entirely my fault.

STEVE: I always thought moonlight bathing was over-rated – now I'm sure of it!

TEMPLE: I had to turn the dinghy over, Steve. If we'd stayed in it, he'd have hit us. As it is, I don't know how the devil he missed …

STEVE: I was terrified he was going to come back again.

TEMPLE: So was I. (*A moment*) You didn't sleep very well, did you?

165

STEVE: I'm afraid I didn't. When I was in that wretched river, I kept saying to myself – Oh, if I was only at home and in bed! Then when I get to bed, I just couldn't get to sleep!

TEMPLE: Anyway, it's good to be home again.

STEVE: It certainly is! Now aren't you glad we didn't stay at Henley, but came straight home?

TEMPLE: Yes. (*Smiling*) I couldn't very well argue with you, after all you'd been through.

CHARLIE: (*Quietly, to STEVE*) Would you like a kipper, Mrs Temple?

STEVE: I should <u>loathe</u> a kipper, Charlie! I never want to see another fish as long as I live!

CHARLIE: Well, would you like me to do you a nice little omelette or something?

STEVE: I wouldn't like you to do me a nice little anything. Thank you.

TEMPLE laughs.

STEVE: What time is it?

TEMPLE: It's just gone eleven. You were late this morning, remember.

STEVE: Is it surprising? Incidentally, what have you been up to, Paul? Charlie tells me you went for a walk.

TEMPLE: Yes, I did. I went round to the hospital and had another talk to Clutch Brompton.

STEVE: Oh. How is he?

TEMPLE: He's very much better. They've tried a new drug on him, and it looks as if it's going to work.

STEVE: Oh, good.

TEMPLE: I had quite an interesting talk to Mr Brompton. At last, I'm beginning to see daylight.

STEVE: Well, that's more than I am.

166

TEMPLE: (*Amused*) Drink your coffee, darling.

A pause.

STEVE: (*Seriously*) Paul … You thought Wallace was going to be murdered, didn't you?

TEMPLE: Yes. I tried to stop it. I even told Vosper to arrest him so that he'd be out of danger.

STEVE: Paul, what's this all about? Why was Mary Dreisler murdered?

TEMPLE: Well, according to Clutch Brompton, Mary Dreisler belonged to a small group who made a living – and a very good living – out of smuggling precious stones.

STEVE: Precious stones?

TEMPLE: Yes. Principally stolen diamonds. They were brought into this country from the Continent and handed over to a fence. The fence, who called himself – or herself – Spencer, was the leader of the group. It was this person who murdered Mary Dreisler.

STEVE: And was Clutch Brompton a member of this group?

TEMPLE: No. But sometimes the group had to employ a certain number of outsiders. They couldn't always bring the stuff over themselves. Clutch was one of the outsiders.

STEVE: I see.

TEMPLE: Unfortunately for Clutch he became too friendly with Mary Dreisler.

STEVE: What do you mean?

TEMPLE: Mary Dreisler told him about a record she made. A record which was … (*Looking up at CHARLIE*) Yes, what is it?

CHARLIE: Inspector Vosper would like to see you, sir.

TEMPLE: Yes, show him in, Charlie.

STEVE: (*Curious*) Go on, Paul. What about this record? What did Mary Dreisler …

TEMPLE: (*Rising from the table*) Later, Steve – later. (*Greeting Vosper*) Hello, Inspector – how are you?

VOSPER: Very depressed!

TEMPLE: Oh, really – why?

VOSPER: Well, I feel I've let you down.

TEMPLE: That's nonsense – I'm sure you did everything you could, Vosper.

VOSPER: We just couldn't find him – we seemed to miss him by five or ten minutes every time. It was the same story everywhere we went.

STEVE: Are you talking about Peter Wallace?

TEMPLE: Yes, darling. (*To VOSPER*) What's the latest news?

VOSPER: We haven't found the body yet. The Maidenhead people are dragging the river.

TEMPLE: They'll find it. It's bound to be there.

VOSPER: Why do you think Wallace went down to Henley?

TEMPLE: Obviously someone sent him a message and he fell for it. (*After a moment*) I saw Clutch Brompton this morning.

VOSPER: Yes, so I believe. Incidentally, Sir Graham tells me that you want to see Eric Lansdale.

TEMPLE: Yes, I do. Can you arrange it?

VOSPER: I've already done so. Twelve o'clock?

TEMPLE: That'll do nicely.

STEVE: Lansdale? Isn't he the man who picked you up in the taxi and demanded the record?

TEMPLE: Yes, darling.

The telephone rings.

STEVE: But why do you want to see Eric Lansdale? I should have thought …

168

TEMPLE: Just a moment, dear.

TEMPLE lifts the receiver.

TEMPLE: (*On the phone*) Hello … Paul Temple speaking.

FORBES: (*On the other end of the line*) Temple? This is Forbes.

TEMPLE: Oh, hello, Sir Graham.

FORBES: Is Vosper with you?

TEMPLE: Yes. Would you like to speak to him?

FORBES: No, you can give him a message. Tell him we've found Wallace. The body was in a backwater about fifty yards from Belton's Lock.

TEMPLE: Our friend must have dumped him there soon after he left us.

FORBES: Yes.

TEMPLE: What about the bungalow, Sir Graham?

FORBES: I've just been talking to the Maidenhead people about it. Apparently, it's hardly been used – it was obviously a meeting place of some kind – a hide-out.

TEMPLE: Yes, that's what I thought.

FORBES: I take it you haven't seen Lansdale yet?

TEMPLE: No, I'm seeing him at twelve o'clock. I'll ring you later, Sir Graham.

FORBES: Right. Goodbye, Temple.

TEMPLE: Goodbye.

TEMPLE replaces the receiver.

START FADE.

VOSPER: Have they found Wallace?

TEMPLE: Yes, they found the body near Belton's Lock.

FADE OUT.

FADE UP of a door opening. There is background noise of a typewriter and several voices.

TEMPLE: Good morning, Sergeant.

SERGEANT: Good morning, sir.

TEMPLE: My name is Temple. I understand Inspector Vosper telephoned you …

SERGEANT: Oh, yes, sir. You want to see Lansdale.

TEMPLE: That's right.

SERGEANT: I'll get someone to take you down straight away, sir. (*Raising his voice*) Johnson!

The typewriter stops; JOHNSON crosses to the SERGEANT's desk.

JOHNSON: Yes, Sergeant?

SERGEANT: This is Mr Temple. Take him down to No 18 – Lansdale.

JOHNSON: Yes, Sergeant. (*To TEMPLE*) This way, Mr Temple.

START FADE.

TEMPLE: Thank you, Sergeant. I'll see you later.

SERGEANT: I shall be here, sir.

COMPLETE FADE.

FADE UP of a key being inserted in a steel prison cell door. The door is opened.

JOHNSON: You've got a visitor, Lansdale.

LANSDALE: What do you want? I didn't ask to see you.

TEMPLE: (*Pleasantly*) I know you didn't. (*To JOHNSON*) Thank you, Officer.

The door closes.

LANSDALE: You heard what I said – what do you want?

TEMPLE: I want to ask you something, Lansdale. Do you mind if I sit down?

LANSDALE: You should have telephoned my secretary for an appointment, or sent me a cable. Telegraphic address: Luxurious, London …

170

TEMPLE:	You've got yourself to blame for the mess you're in, no one else, Lansdale. Now, if you've got any sense …
LANSDALE:	Now, look, chum, don't start that "we can do a deal" stuff, because we can't. I'm in this chicken coop for picking you up and making a damn nuisance of myself. That's all – nothing else.
TEMPLE:	You picked me up for a particular reason – you picked me up because a man called Spencer …
LANSDALE:	(*Angrily*) I don't know anything about Spencer. I've told Vosper that and I'm telling you it. Now get out – leave me alone!
TEMPLE:	You work for Spencer. Spencer is a fence. It's my bet that …
LANSDALE:	Look, chum, I've told you, I know nothing about Spencer. Now will you do as I …
TEMPLE:	(*With authority; taking LANSDALE by surprise*) Lansdale, you remember the day you went to Henley, the day you went to Salex Island …
LANSDALE:	(*Without thinking*) Yes. (*Suddenly*) I don't know what you're talking about. I've never heard of Salex Island.
TEMPLE:	(*With sarcasm*) You've never heard of it, but apparently, you've been there.
LANSDALE:	I haven't been there. I made a mistake. I thought you were talking about something else. Now, listen, Temple, I don't have to stand for this. You've no right to come down here and ask me a lot of questions.
TEMPLE:	Lansdale, do you know Clutch Brompton?
LANSDALE:	(*After a moment*) I've heard of him.

TEMPLE:	He's very ill – he's in hospital.
LANSDALE:	Yes, I know.
TEMPLE:	Clutch is an old friend of mine. I saw him this morning.
LANSDALE:	Well?
TEMPLE:	He told me about Mary Dreisler. He told me about the group of people, headed by Spencer, who makes a living out of smuggling precious stones from the Continent.
LANSDALE:	Clutch talks too much, if you ask me.
TEMPLE:	He said you were a member of that group …
LANSDALE:	That's a lie! That's a lie and Clutch Brompton knows it!
TEMPLE:	But you work for Spencer – you were working for Spencer the night you picked me up.
LANSDALE:	That's different.
TEMPLE:	How is it different?
LANSDALE:	(*Hesitantly*) Spencer employs a lot of people – outsiders – you don't have to be a member of the group. Clutch knows that. He was an outsider. So was I.
TEMPLE:	Did you ever meet Spencer?
LANSDALE:	No.
TEMPLE:	Well, how did he contact you?
LANSDALE:	Through someone else.
TEMPLE:	Who – for instance?
LANSDALE:	I've told you who. I told you the night I picked you up.
TEMPLE:	You said it was Frost.
LANSDALE:	It was Frost. He telephoned me and said he wanted the record.
TEMPLE:	That's not what Mr Frost says.

LANSDALE: Then he's lying.

TEMPLE: Lansdale, when I saw Clutch this morning, he
            told me …

LANSDALE: I'm not interested in what Clutch told you. If
            Clutch wants to shoot his big mouth off that's
            his business and not mine. Now get out, and
            leave me alone.

TEMPLE: (*A moment*) All right. (*He hesitates*) Oh, er –
            did you know Peter Wallace, by any chance?

LANSDALE: No, I've never heard of him. Why?

START FADE.

TEMPLE: … He was murdered last night. I thought
            perhaps you might be interested, that's all.

COMPLETE FADE.

FADE UP the voice of the SERGEANT.

SERGEANT: Oh, are you leaving, Mr Temple?

TEMPLE: Yes, goodbye, Sergeant.

SERGEANT: Was everything satisfactory, sir?

TEMPLE: Yes, thank you. (*A sudden thought*) Oh, by
            the way, Sergeant – did Lansdale have much
            money on him, when he was picked up, I
            mean?

SERGEANT: Oh, about twenty-two or three pounds if I
            remember correctly, sir. Not counting the
            foreign money.

TEMPLE: Foreign money?

SERGEANT: There were six thousand French francs in his
            wallet.

TEMPLE: Oh. Have you got the wallet?

SERGENT: Yes, I've got all his stuff here in an envelope.
            Would you like to see it?

TEMPLE: Yes, I would, Sergeant.

The SERGEANT opens a drawer and empties the contents of an envelope on to a desk.

SERGEANT: Here we are, sir … wallet … pocketknife … cigarette lighter … packet of cigarettes … ball pen … Hello, what's this? Looks like a toothpick …

TEMPLE: Let me have a look at that, Sergeant.

SERGEANT: Yes, it's a toothpick. You know the kind, sir, wrapped in cellophane. You pick them up in restaurants …

TEMPLE: Yes. That's why I want to have a look at it.

A moment.

TEMPLE: (*Reading*) La Mediterranee, Boulevard St Germain, Paris.

SERGEANT: (*With a laugh*) Paris! And they say crime doesn't pay!

TEMPLE: (*Pleased with himself*) Here you are – thank you, Sergeant!

SERGEANT: (*Surprised*) Don't you want to see the wallet, sir?

TEMPLE: No, thanks, I'll take it as read. Goodbye!

SERGEANT: (*Puzzled*) Goodbye, Mr Temple.

MUSIC.

FADE UP noises associated with a bar parlour.

TEMPLE: Good evening. Is Pete Roberts about?

WARREN: (*Turning*) Oh, hello, Mr Temple! Yes, I think he's up in his room …

TEMPLE: May I go up?

WARREN: Yes, certainly. Wait a minute – here he is! (*Calling*) Pete! (*To TEMPLE*) He's spotted you. He's coming down. Can I get you anything, sir?

TEMPLE: Yes, I'll have a whisky and soda. Will you join
            me?
WARREN: Later in the evening, if I may, sir.
TEMPLE: Hello, Pete …
PETE: Do you want to see me?
TEMPLE: Yes, but first let me buy you a drink.
PETE: (*To WARREN*) The usual.
WARREN: Righto, Pete!
TEMPLE: We'll sit over there in the corner …
WARREN: Okay. I'll bring the drinks over to you.
FADE DOWN on the background noises.
PETE: What is it you want this time?
TEMPLE: What makes you think I want anything?
PETE: Well, you didn't visit Stepney just for the
            pleasure of my company, I'm sure of that.
TEMPLE: Pete, have you heard of a place called La
            Mediterranee?
PETE: Yes, it's a nightclub – in Paris.
TEMPLE: That's right. Have you been there?
PETE: Yes, sure. I've appeared there in cabaret.
TEMPLE: When was this?
PETE: Oh, about six months ago.
TEMPLE: How long were you there?
PETE: Well – I was booked for three weeks, but I only
            stayed for four nights.
TEMPLE: Why was that?
PETE: Oh, I had a disagreement with the management
            and … Well, I just couldn't stick the joint. One
            night I got tight and – well, you know what
            happened, it's the usual story.
TEMPLE: You certainly throw your opportunities away,
            don't you, Pete?
PETE: Yes, and I'm just beginning to realise what a
            damn fool I've been.

TEMPLE: Why do you say that?
PETE: I had a letter this morning. Not a very friendly one, I'm afraid.
TEMPLE: A letter?
PETE: Dear Sir, the Commissioners of Inland Revenue regret to inform you …
TEMPLE: Oh! How much do you owe them?
PETE: Four thousand quid. Now where am I going to get four thousand quid from? (*Angrily*) And don't say "You must have earned it" because if there's anything that gets my goat …
TEMPLE: I wasn't going to say that. I was going to say your only chance is to sober up and start work again.
PETE: Yes, I know. I've been thinking about that.

WARREN arrives at the table with the drinks.

WARREN: Whisky and soda, Mr Temple.
TEMPLE: Thank you.
WARREN: Here you are, Pete.
PETE: Thanks.
TEMPLE: (*Raising his glass*) Skoal!
PETE: Cheers.

They drink.

There is a slight pause.

TEMPLE: What sort of a place is this La Meditererranee?
PETE: Oh, typical Paris nightclub. Floor show – champagne – everything overheated – and I mean everything.
TEMPLE: How did you get the booking – through an agent?
PETE: No, a chap called Reynaud dropped into the Neptune Club one night. He saw my set and booked me on the spot.
TEMPLE: Does Reynaud own La Mediterranee?

PETE: I don't know whether he owns it or not but he's certainly the boss. Look, why are you interested in this place?

TEMPLE: I'll tell you why. I'm investigating the Dreisler murder. During the course of my investigations, I visited a place called Salex Island.

PETE: Salex Island? Where the devil's that?

TEMPLE: It's near Henley. Anyway, to cut a long story short there's an empty bungalow on the island and I found this card in the drawing room.

TEMPLE takes the card from his pocket and hands it to PETE.

A pause.

PETE: (*Surprised*) Good Lord! I wonder how this got there.

TEMPLE: Well, presumably the owner of the bungalow must have visited La Mediterranee at some time or other.

PETE: Yes. They used to put these cards out every night. Every table had one.

TEMPLE: Yes, that's what I thought.

PETE: This island – Salex Island …

TEMPLE: Yes?

PETE: Does it belong to the chap who owns the bungalow?

TEMPLE: Yes, but no one seems to know much about him. The bungalow's only used occasionally as a sort of meeting place.

PETE: I see.

TEMPLE: Pete, tell me about this man, Reynaud. What sort of a man is he?

PETE: He's a Frenchman. Very efficient. Bad tempered. Dapper little devil. (*Shrugs*) There's not much to tell.

177

TEMPLE: Did you see much of him?

PETE: I saw him every night when I was at the club – we used to argue like blazes.

TEMPLE: Is he well known in Paris?

PETE: I suppose so, although I wouldn't really know. He's a wealthy little basket, they tell me.

TEMPLE: All right, Pete. Thank you for the information.

PETE: Information? What information?

TEMPLE: About Reynaud – and the Mediterranee.

PETE: Oh …

TEMPLE: Good night!

PETE: No, wait a minute!

TEMPLE: Yes?

PETE: You've been asking a devil of a lot of questions. Now I'd like to ask you one for a change.

TEMPLE: Go ahead.

PETE: The last time we met you told me I was going to be murdered …

TEMPLE: Oh no! Not exactly!

PETE: Well, what did you tell me?

TEMPLE: I said I <u>thought</u> you were going to be murdered. There's a subtle difference.

PETE: Well, whether there's a subtle difference or not, tell me this. Do you still think I'm going to be murdered?

TEMPLE: That's the sixty-four-thousand-dollar question, Pete.

PETE: Sure it is. That's why I'm asking it. What's the answer?

TEMPLE: The answer?

PETE: (*Angrily*) Yes.

TEMPLE: Well, let's put it in another way …

PETE: I don't care how you put it – just give me the answer.

178

TEMPLE: (*Seriously*) The answer is this … (*He hesitates*)

PETE: (*Now almost aggressive*) Well?

TEMPLE: I wouldn't like to be in your shoes, Mr Roberts.

MUSIC.

FADE UP the sound of TEMPLE's front doorbell ringing.
The door is opened by STEVE.

STEVE: Oh, hello, Paul!

TEMPLE: Sorry, darling, I forgot my key. Is Charlie out?

STEVE: Yes, he's gone to the pictures. Where on earth have you been all day?

TEMPLE: Oh, I've been all over the place. I saw Lansdale, then I went to Stepney to see … Steve, is that someone in the drawing room?

STEVE: Yes, Rupert Dreisler's here – he wants to see you.

TEMPLE: Dreisler? How long has he been here?

STEVE: Two or three minutes, that's all.

TEMPLE: What is it he wants to see me about?

STEVE: I don't know. I haven't had time to ask him. Charlie went out and left some cakes in the oven, and I've been trying to …

TEMPLE: Yes, all right, Steve. Now listen, darling, go and change and be ready in fifteen minutes. We're going to the Neptune Club.

STEVE: Oh, Paul, not tonight! I don't feel a bit like the Neptune Club!

TEMPLE: Neither do I, but I want to see Terry Gibson. It's important. (*Softly*) Fifteen minutes.

STEVE: Yes, all right, Paul.

TEMPLE passes into the drawing room.

DREISLER: Good evening, Mr Temple. I do hope I'm not intruding.

TEMPLE: Not at all. I'm sorry to have kept you waiting. Oh, didn't my wife offer you a drink?

DREISLER: Yes, but I refused, I … (*A shade tense*) Temple, I've just heard about Peter Wallace.

TEMPLE: Oh. How did you hear about Wallace? Is it in the papers?

DREISLER: No. Inspector Vosper told me.

TEMPLE: When did you see Vosper?

DREISLER: This afternoon. Apparently, someone saw me at Henley, and the Inspector was curious.

TEMPLE: I see.

DREISLER: Temple, who murdered Wallace? Was it the same person who murdered my daughter?

TEMPLE: It rather looks like it.

DREISLER: Why was he murdered – do you know?

TEMPLE: Yes, I know but – Tell me, what were you doing down at Henley, Mr Dreisler?

DREISLER: A young composer wrote to me – he's the son of a famous actress, I won't mention names – he lives near Henley, and he asked me to go down there and listen to some of his music.

TEMPLE: I see. Is that what you told the Inspector?

DREISLER: (*Surprised by the question*) But of course! Now perhaps you wouldn't mind satisfying <u>my</u> curiosity. What were you doing at Henley?

TEMPLE: I went to look at a place called Salex Island.

DREISLER: Salex Island?

TEMPLE: Yes. Have you heard of it?

DREISLER: (*Puzzled and curious*) No. Is it actually an island?

TEMPLE: Yes. It's a plot of land with a bungalow on it. In the middle of the river.

DREISLER: But why did you want to see this place?

TEMPLE: I wanted to see it for a number of reasons.

DREISLER: I'm curious. Give me one …

TEMPLE: I think your daughter went there, on more than one occasion.

DREISLER: Mary? But why should she go to this place – to Salex Island?

TEMPLE: (*Rather vague*) I think she went to meet someone. (*Suddenly, completely changing the subject*) Mr Dreisler, I'm glad you called round, because I think perhaps you might be able to help me. I'm interested in a nightclub – a place called La Mediterranee. Have you heard of it?

DREISLER: La Mediterranee? Boulevard St Germain – Paris?

TEMPLE: Yes.

DREISLER: Yes, of course I've heard of it. I've been there several times, searching for talent.

TEMPLE: Who owns the club, do you know?

DREISLER: Yes, it's run by a man called Reynaud – André Reynaud.

TEMPLE: What's he like?

DREISLER: You mean – to look at?

TEMPLE: No, as a person.

DREISLER: I've always got on well with him, but I don't know him very well. At one time there were a lot of stories about him, but – (*He shrugs*) Well, you know how it is in that business.

TEMPLE: What kind of stories?

DREISLER: Oh, people said he was mixed up in some racket or other. I don't know what it was. But why are you interested in Reynaud?

TEMPLE: Pete Roberts worked for him.

DREISLER: Did he! I didn't know that.

TEMPLE: Well, apparently, he did. Reynaud engaged him for three weeks and Pete stayed four nights.

DREISLER: (*With a little laugh*) That doesn't surprise me.

TEMPLE: Now, if you'll excuse me, Mr Dreisler. I'm going out this evening and I've got to change.

DREISLER: Yes, of course, but – Mr Temple, you said just now that you thought that Wallace was murdered by the same person that murdered my daughter.

TEMPLE: Yes.

DREISLER: Is that – Spencer?

TEMPLE: Yes.

DREISLER: And do you think you'll ever find out who Spencer really is?

TEMPLE: If I'm lucky, Mr Dreisler. If I'm lucky.

FADE OUT.

CROSS FADE to the sound of a dance orchestra playing in the restaurant at the Neptune Club. There is background noise of a crowded restaurant. The HEAD WAITER greets TEMPLE and STEVE at the entrance to the dining room.

WAITER: Good evening, madam – sir.

STEVE: Good evening.

WAITER: Have you reserved a table?

TEMPLE: Yes, I telephoned about an hour ago. Temple.

WAITER: Oh, yes, of course, Mr Temple. This way, sir.

TEMPLE: Thank you.

FADE UP and FADE DOWN the sound of the dance orchestra.

WAITER: Here you are, sir. Allow me, madam.

STEVE: Thank you …

TEMPLE and STEVE sit at the table.

TEMPLE: Shall we be seeing Miss Gibson this evening?

WAITER:	Yes, she'll be down very shortly, sir. Shall I give her a message?
TEMPLE:	No, just say I'd like her to have a drink with us when she's free.
WAITER:	Yes, certainly, sir. I'll send your waiter along.
TEMPLE:	There's no hurry – we'll have some drinks first.
WAITER:	Very good, sir.
STEVE:	Paul, isn't that Adrian Frost?
TEMPLE:	(*Turning*) Where?
STEVE:	In the doorway.
TEMPLE:	Yes, it is!
STEVE:	He's spotted you, darling.

A pause.

FROST arrives at the table.

FROST:	Hello, Temple – I thought I recognised you.
TEMPLE:	Hello, Frost. You know my wife?
FROST:	Yes, of course. Good evening, Mrs Temple.
STEVE:	Good evening.
TEMPLE:	Are you dining here?
FROST:	Yes, I'm just waiting for someone.
TEMPLE:	Well, perhaps you'd care to have a drink with us while you're waiting?
FROST:	Thank you very much.
STEVE:	Sit over here, Mr Frost.
FROST:	Thank you.
WAITER:	What can I get you, sir?
TEMPLE:	Frost?
FROST:	May I have a sherry. A medium sherry.
TEMPLE:	Certainly. (*To STEVE*) Steve?
STEVE:	Dry Martini …
TEMPLE:	Two dry Martinis and a medium sherry.
WAITER:	Yes, sir.
FROST:	It's rather curious I should bump into you, Temple.

183

TEMPLE: Indeed?

FROST: Yes. I think you'll be rather surprised when I tell you who I'm having dinner with this evening.

TEMPLE: Really?

STEVE: Who are you having dinner with, Mr Frost?

FROST: With Peter Wallace ...

MUSIC.

END OF EPISODE SIX

EPISODE SEVEN

DINNER AT THE NEPTUNE

OPENING MUSIC.
FADE DOWN MUSIC.

FADE UP background noises and dance orchestra in the restaurant of the Neptune Club.

FROST: It's rather curious I should bump into you, Temple.

TEMPLE: Indeed?

FROST: Yes. I think you'll be rather surprised when I tell you who I'm having dinner with this evening.

TEMPLE: Really?

STEVE: Who are you having dinner with, Mr Frost?

FROST: With Peter Wallace ...

STEVE: Peter Wallace?

FROST: Yes. (*Smiling*) I thought you'd be surprised.

TEMPLE: When did you make this appointment?

FROST: About five days ago. Wallace telephoned and said he wanted to see me. I was rather off-hand, I'm afraid, because as you know I've never considered him a friend of mine. Just the reverse, in fact.

TEMPLE: Was it his suggestion that you had dinner together?

FROST: Yes, it was. He said there were several things he wanted to discuss with me, and he thought it was a good idea if we got together one evening.

STEVE: Did he give you any hint as to what he meant?

FROST: (*Hesitantly*) Not exactly, but ...

TEMPLE: Go on ...

FROST: Well, he said a rather curious thing. I asked him what it was he wanted to see me about and he said: "I want you to tell me something, Frost. I want you to tell me why your name isn't on the record."

187

STEVE:	Why your name isn't on the record?
FROST:	Yes.
STEVE:	What did you say?
FROST:	I started asking questions and he said: "I'll see you at the Neptune Club on the 16th. Be there at nine o'clock."
TEMPLE:	And you haven't heard from him since?
FROST:	No.
TEMPLE:	Have you any idea what he meant – about your name and the record?
FROST:	Not the slightest. And I'm very curious. In fact, that's the only reason why I'm here.
TEMPLE:	Well, I'm sorry, but – I'm afraid Peter Wallace isn't going to satisfy your curiosity.
FROST:	What do you mean? Why not?
TEMPLE:	He's dead.
FROST:	Dead? Wallace?
TEMPLE:	Yes.
FROST:	But I can't believe it, I … Are you sure?
STEVE:	It's true. Peter Wallace was murdered. My husband and I found the body.
FROST:	But how was he murdered? Where did you find him?
TEMPLE:	We went down to look at a place called Salex Island. It's near Henley. We found Wallace in the river. He'd been drowned.
FROST:	Drowned. But I thought you said he was murdered.
TEMPLE:	He was. Someone knocked him out, tied his hands and feet and dragged him into the water.
FROST:	(*Bewildered*) You know, I can hardly believe this. I came here expecting to meet Wallace,

	to talk to him, and now you tell me that he's dead! Do the police know about this?
TEMPLE:	Yes, of course.
FROST:	Have they any idea who did it?
TEMPLE:	They think the same as I do. They think Wallace was murdered by the same person who murdered Mary Dreisler.
FROST:	I see.
TEMPLE:	(*Suddenly*) Frost, have you ever been to Paris?
FROST:	No, curiously enough, I haven't. I've been all over the Continent, but I've never actually been to Paris.
TEMPLE:	M'm.
FROST:	Why do you ask?
TEMPLE:	I was wondering if you'd been to a nightclub in Paris called La Mediterranee.
FROST:	(*Surprised*) No, but Mary went there – she went there several times.
STEVE:	How do you know?
FROST:	(*Hesitating*) I remember she mentioned it to me on one occasion. We were talking about nightclubs, and she said it was an awfully good one.
WAITER:	Two dry Martinis, and a medium sherry.
TEMPLE:	Thank you.
WAITER:	(*To TEMPLE*) Miss Gibson presents her compliments, sir, and would like to see you if you can spare a moment.
TEMPLE:	Yes, certainly. Where is Miss Gibson?
WAITER:	She's in her office, sir, on the first floor.
TEMPLE:	Oh, thank you.
FROST:	Temple, you remember the last time we spoke – on the telephone?

189

TEMPLE: Yes.
FROST: You mentioned the brooch I gave to Mary – the diamond brooch.
TEMPLE: Yes.
FROST: You said I gave it to Mary because I was under a misapprehension about her.
TEMPLE: That's right.
FROST: What did you mean by that?
TEMPLE: You know perfectly well what I meant. The very first time we met you told me to find out why you'd given Mary the brooch.
FROST: Yes, I know, but …
TEMPLE: Well, I did find out. (*He rises from the table*) Don't look confused, Frost – when you're not. (*To STEVE*) I'm going to see Terry Gibson, Steve. I'll be back in a few minutes. I'm sure Mr Frost will entertain you.
STEVE: Yes, all right, Paul.
FROST: (*Amused*) You know, your husband is a most extraordinary person, Mrs Temple.

START FADE.

STEVE: Yes, but don't under-rate him, Mr Frost.
FROST: Under-rate him? That's the last thing I should do, I assure you.

FADE OUT.

FADE IN TERRY GIBSON talking to TEMPLE. She is obviously rather annoyed.

TERRY: … But I don't see why the Inspector should have questioned <u>me</u> about Peter Wallace. Wallace wasn't a friend of mine. I hardly knew him.
TEMPLE: You say Vosper telephoned you?

TERRY: Yes, about half an hour ago. He asked me if I knew that Wallace had been murdered. And when I said I didn't he started to ask me all sorts of questions.

TEMPLE: (*Smiling*) He is investigating the case, Miss Gibson.

TERRY: Yes, I know. But why pick on me?

TEMPLE: Wallace came here quite frequently. You told me that yourself.

TERRY: So do hundreds of other people. But they're not friends of mine. Surely, Mr Temple, you must realise when you run a place like this you see hundreds of people. You get to know them in a casual kind of way, but you don't ever really get to know them. You don't know what sort of lives they lead, what sort of people they really are.

TEMPLE: Yes, I appreciate that.

TERRY: Well, I wish to goodness you'd make the Inspector appreciate it.

TEMPLE laughs.

TERRY: Now, what can I do for you?

TEMPLE: What makes you think you can do anything for me?

TERRY: We have very good food at the Neptune, Mr Temple, and a very good dance orchestra – but that's not why you came here.

TEMPLE: No, you're quite right, it isn't. Miss Gibson, do you know a club in Paris called La Mediterranee?

TERRY: (*After a barely perceptible pause*) Yes, it's in the Boulevard St Germain.

TEMPLE: It's run by a man called André Reynaud.

TERRY: That's right.

TEMPLE: Do you know him?

TERRY: Well, there you are again. I know him, but only casually. He's been here once or twice searching for talent.

TEMPLE: And have you been to La Mediterranee?

TERRY: No … (*Changing her mind*) Yes … Yes, I beg your pardon – I have, once. A long time ago.

TEMPLE: What kind of a place is it?

TERRY: It's quite nice. Rather like this, on a small scale.

TEMPLE: They tell me that Reynaud has rather a reputation. Is that true?

TERRY: A reputation? What do you mean – with women or …?

TEMPLE: (*Vaguely*) I don't really know what I mean. It was just a remark I overheard.

TERRY: He may have a bad reputation, I don't know. He's certainly a very good businessman. Now, if you'll excuse me, Mr Temple …

TEMPLE: (*Rising*) Yes, of course.

TERRY: Oh, before you go! There's something I want to ask you …

TEMPLE: Yes?

TERRY: Pete Roberts phoned me this morning. He said he was off the bottle, and he'd like to come back here, in cabaret, I mean.

TEMPLE: Well?

TERRY: I understand you've seen quite a lot of Pete recently.

TEMPLE: I wouldn't say that. I've seen him once or twice. But go on …

TERRY: Well, the point is, if I give Pete another chance, do you think I'm taking a big risk?

TEMPLE: I wouldn't know. I'm not an authority on dipsomaniacs. You'd better ask a doctor.

TERRY: No, I don't mean because of the drink. I've just got to take a chance on that.

TEMPLE: Well – what do you mean?

TERRY: I mean – well, I've told you before, I don't want any bad publicity. I don't want anyone at the Neptune to be mixed up in anything.

TEMPLE: Mixed up in anything?

TERRY: Yes, in a murder case, for instance.

TEMPLE: What makes you think Pete might be mixed up in a murder case?

TERRY: I don't. I don't think he's mixed up in anything. But it's not what I think, it's what the police think. They've questioned Pete about the Dreisler murder; so have you, Mr Temple.

TEMPLE: We've questioned a lot of people, Miss Gibson, if it comes to that – including you. If you want to take a chance on Pete Roberts, go ahead – and reserve me a table for the first night.

START FADE.

TERRY: Well, I'll think about it. About Roberts, I mean. Not about the table.

TEMPLE: (*Laughing*) Good night.

FADE OUT.

FADE UP the dance orchestra in the restaurant. Background of noises and voices.

FADE IN the voice of ADRIAN FROST.

FROST: …Yes, I agree about St Tropez, but if you go further along the coast towards Marseilles you usually find … (*He breaks off*) Oh, here's your husband.

TEMPLE: Don't get up, Frost! (*To STEVE*) Sorry to have been so long.

STEVE: We've been talking about holidays. Mr Frost went to Portugal last year and it rained every day.

FROST: Except the day I left, of course. I was furious.

They laugh.

FROST: Well, if you'll excuse me, I'll say goodnight.

TEMPLE: Won't you stay and have dinner with us?

FROST: That's awfully kind of you, but I won't if you don't mind. I've several things I want to attend to. Good night, Mrs Temple. And don't forget what I told you about Roquebrune.

STEVE: I won't.

FROST: (*To TEMPLE*) Good night, Temple.

TEMPLE: Good night.

A pause.

TEMPLE sits down.

TEMPLE: What's that all about Roquebrune?

STEVE: Apparently, it's a place near Mentone. He adores it.

TEMPLE: What do you make of Frost?

STEVE: I don't know. He's quite amusing, but …

TEMPLE: Smooth?

STEVE: No, I wouldn't call him smooth – a little actor-ified, if there is such a word.

TEMPLE: (*Smiling*) Yes, I know what you mean.

STEVE: What did Terry Gibson want?

TEMPLE: Well, apparently, Pete Roberts wants to work for her again, and she wanted my advice.

STEVE: Why your advice? You're not an impresario.

TEMPLE: She wanted to know whether Roberts was likely to be arrested or not.

STEVE: Arrested?

TEMPLE: Yes. You see, Terry doesn't want to employ him if he's going to get any bad publicity – at least, that's what she says.

STEVE: You know, I don't believe Terry Gibson, Paul.

TEMPLE: You don't believe her?

STEVE: No, I don't. Why should she worry about publicity? Surely these places thrive on it.

TEMPLE: Yes, I'm inclined to agree.

STEVE: In which case why mention Pete Roberts to you at all?

TEMPLE: Well, she may have been quizzing me, Steve.

STEVE: You mean on Pete's behalf?

TEMPLE: Yes. I've seen him several times recently. Perhaps he's worried. Perhaps he wants to know whether I really suspect him.

STEVE: And do you?

TEMPLE: (*Laughing*) I suspect everybody, darling. I even suspect that we're not going to get any dinner this evening! Ah, here's the waiter …

FADE OUT.

FADE UP the dance orchestra in the distant background. TEMPLE and STEVE are now passing through the hall of the Neptune Club.

TEMPLE: I'll meet you near the phone-box, Steve. It's next to the door.

STEVE: Yes, all right, darling.

TEMPLE: I've got to get my hat and coat and I want to make a phone call. I'll meet you near the phone-box.

STEVE: Yes, well, I'll be about five minutes.

TEMPLE: Right.

TEMPLE leaves STEVE and crosses the hall. He bumps into a man coming out of the cloakroom.

TEMPLE: I beg your pardon …

PETE: I'm so sorry, I … (*Recognising TEMPLE*) Oh, hello, Temple!

TEMPLE: Hello, Pete! What are you doing here?

195

PETE: I've got an appointment to see Terry Gibson.

TEMPLE: Oh, yes, of course. She told me about it.

PETE: (*Surprised*) She did?

TEMPLE: Yes.

PETE: When did you see Terry?

TEMPLE: About an hour ago.

PETE: (*Hesitantly*) What did she tell you?

TEMPLE: She said you wanted to come back here – in cabaret.

PETE: Yes. Yes, that's true. I've got to do something. Things are getting desperate. The Tax people have really got their claws into me this time.

TEMPLE: Yes, you told me about it. Well, I wish you luck.

PETE: Temple, did Terry give you the impression that … (*He hesitates*)

TEMPLE: Go on …

PETE: Well, how do you think she feels about the idea – about my coming back here, I mean?

TEMPLE: She's a little apprehensive. You're a pretty heavy drinker, Pete, judging from any standards.

PETE: Yes, I know but – I'm cutting down on it.

TEMPLE: I'm glad to hear it.

PETE: It's not easy.

TEMPLE: No, I don't imagine it is.

PETE: Anyway, I gather she's not completely against the idea?

TEMPLE: Would she be seeing you if she was?

PETE: No, I suppose not, but she didn't sound too friendly on the telephone. Anyway, we'll keep our fingers crossed. Good night.

TEMPLE: Good night, Pete.

A moment.

TEMPLE enters the telephone booth; the sound of the door opening and closing is heard. He dials a number and we hear

196

it ringing out. The receiver at the other end is lifted and we hear a series of quick pips and TEMPLE inserting coins in the box.

FORBES: (*On the other end of the phone*) Hello?

TEMPLE: Sir Graham?

FORBES: Yes?

TEMPLE: This is Temple.

FORBES: Oh, hello, Temple! How are you?

TEMPLE: I'm fine, thanks. Sir Graham, I want you to do something for me.

FORBES: Yes, of course.

TEMPLE: I want you to contact Interpol and make enquiries about a man called Andre Reynaud – he runs a nightclub called La Mediterranee.

FORBES: (*Surprised*) What – in London?

TEMPLE: No, in Paris – Boulevard St Germain.

FORBES: What is it you want to know, exactly?

TEMPLE: I've a shrewd suspicion he's mixed up in the Spencer affair. Find out when he was last over here and whether he's a friend of Terry Gibson's.

FORBES: Right. Will you be in tomorrow morning?

TEMPLE: Yes.

FORBES: I'll phone you as soon as I get to the Yard.

TEMPLE: Thank you, Sir Graham. Good night.

TEMPLE replaces the receiver.

FADE OUT.

FADE UP TEMPLE joining STEVE in the hall of the Neptune Club.

TEMPLE: Are you ready, Steve?

STEVE: Yes, dear.

TEMPLE: I've just seen Pete Roberts.

STEVE: Where?

TEMPLE:	I bumped into him coming out of the cloakroom. He's got an appointment with Terry Gibson.
STEVE:	Then it looks as if she was telling the truth, Paul.

The sound of the swing doors revolving.

We hear traffic noises as TEMPLE and STEVE enter the street.

COMMISSIONAIRE:	Shall I get you a taxi, sir?
TEMPLE:	No, I think we'll walk for a little while.
COMMISSIONAIRE:	Very good, sir.
STEVE:	I hope it is a little while.
TEMPLE:	The exercise will do you good, dear.
STEVE:	What do you mean – do <u>me</u> good!
TEMPLE:	I didn't want to take the first cab that came along, Steve. We'll pick one up later.
STEVE:	Yes, all right. I don't really mind walking, anyway.
PAUL TEMPLE:	It's a lovely night.

FADE DOWN the traffic noises as TEMPLE and STEVE walk down the street.

FADE UP TEMPLE and STEVE still walking. There is a background of traffic noises. During the following dialogue, a car races nearer and nearer.

TEMPLE:	Tired?
STEVE:	No, I'm fine.
TEMPLE:	Do you want to walk all the way home?
STEVE:	(*In a phoney American accent*) You don't think I can make it, do you, partner?

TEMPLE: Well …

STEVE: You're dead tootin' right – I can't! Let's pick
             up a taxi.

TEMPLE: (*Laughing*) All right, darling.

STEVE: Come on! I think there's one on the opposite
             side of the road …

TEMPLE: (*Grabbing STEVE's arm*) Steve, look out!

STEVE: (*Alarmed*) What?

TEMPLE: That car! Look out!

*TEMPLE pushes STEVE to one side as the car races towards
them. There is a screech of brakes, then the driver accelerates
and the car races past down the road.*

TEMPLE: (*Alarmed*) Steve, are you all right? I'm sorry,
             darling, I had to push you like that because …

MAN: (*From the near background*) It's a ruddy good
             job you did, mate, or he'd have knocked her for
             six!

TEMPLE: Steve!

STEVE: (*Recovering from the shock*) It's all right, Paul,
             I'm … (*Almost a little laugh*) I was so surprised
             I didn't realise what you were doing …
             (*Suddenly*) Oh, my poor stockings!

TEMPLE: I had to push you, darling. I just couldn't help
             it.

STEVE: Yes, of course … Just look at my dress!

TEMPLE: We'll get a cab – there's one over there!
             (*Calling across the road*) Taxi!

STEVE: It's taken, darling!

*TEMPLE pushes his way through the crowd, followed by
STEVE.*

TEMPLE: Excuse me! Excuse me, please!

DREISLER: (*Calling from the background*) Mr Temple! Mr
             Temple!

STEVE: (*Surprised*) Why, it's Mr Dreisler!

TEMPLE: Where?

STEVE: Look – he's just getting out of that taxi!

TEMPLE: (*Calling to DREISLER*) Is that your cab, Dreisler?

DREISLER: (*Joining TEMPLE and STEVE*) Yes, I've been to the theatre but – what happened? Are you all right, Mrs Temple?

TEMPLE: Yes, but she's rather shaken.

DREISLER: Yes, of course, I can see that! I'm so glad I came along like that. You must let me give you a lift.

STEVE: That's very kind of you, Mr Dreisler.

DREISLER: Not at all … But tell me, please, what happened? Were you in a car or just crossing the road?

TEMPLE: We were walking across the road and a car suddenly raced round the corner and made straight for us. Fortunately, I spotted it and pushed my wife to one side.

STEVE: "Pushed" is hardly the word, darling!

DREISLER: But didn't the car stop?

TEMPLE: No.

DREISLER: You mean it was done deliberately?

TEMPLE: Quite deliberately.

DREISLER: But who would do such a thing? Did you see the driver?

TEMPLE: Yes, I saw him. But I'd never recognise him again. He wore dark glasses, and he had a scarf over most of his face.

DREISLER: But you saw the car? Did you get the number?

TEMPLE: Yes. Yes, I got it. VPE 325C.

DREISLER: But this really is quite extraordinary! I didn't think such things could happen in London!

TEMPLE: Only to us, Mr Dreisler! Only to us!
MUSIC.

FADE UP a front door bell ringing. The door is opened.
TEMPLE: (*Surprised*) Hello, Vosper!
VOSPER: Good evening. May I come in?
TEMPLE: Why yes, of course, Inspector.
TEMPLE and VOSPER pass into the drawing room.
VOSPER: How's Mrs Temple?
TEMPLE: Oh, she's all right now. She's had a hot bath and she's in bed.
VOSPER: (*Smiling*) Well, you've got more nerve than I have. I daren't push my wife around like that!
TEMPLE: I had to, Inspector, or the car would have knocked her down.
VOSPER: So I understand. It's a good job you had the presence of mind.
TEMPLE: Well, is there any news?
VOSPER: Yes, we've traced the car – in fact, we've found it.
TEMPLE: You have? That's quick work.
VOSPER: Well, it wasn't very difficult. It was abandoned shortly after your little episode. We found it in Hyde Park.
TEMPLE: Oh. Was it a stolen car?
VOSPER: Yes. The car was reported stolen at ten-fifteen.
TEMPLE: Shortly before we left the Neptune Club.
VOSPER: Yes. Obviously, whoever picked it up stooged around until you and Mrs Temple left the Club, then he followed you.
TEMPLE: I see.
VOSPER: But you haven't heard the most interesting news.
TEMPLE: No?
VOSPER: Who do you think the car belongs to?

201

TEMPLE: I don't know.

VOSPER: Mr Frost.

TEMPLE: Adrian Frost?

VOSPER: Yes.

TEMPLE: But we saw Frost last night – He was actually with us till about nine o'clock.

VOSPER: (*Puzzled*) Nine o'clock?

TEMPLE: Yes.

VOSPER: But he didn't leave the Neptune until just after ten.

TEMPLE: It was just after nine when he left us.

VOSPER: Well, he telephoned Savile Row – that's the local station – about the car just after ten-fifteen. I've spoken to the man who took the message.

TEMPLE: I see.

VOSPER: I understand you saw the driver?

TEMPLE: I saw him, but I wouldn't recognise him again. He wore dark glasses and a scarf. It was impossible to see his features.

In the background the door bell is ringing.

VOSPER: Could it have been Frost himself?

TEMPLE: I suppose it could have been.

VOSPER: But you don't think it was?

TEMPLE: No, I don't think so.

VOSPER: I understand Mr Dreisler brought you home?

TEMPLE: Yes, he was passing in a taxi and gave us a lift.

VOSPER: Was that just a coincidence?

TEMPLE: Apparently. He said he'd been to the theatre.

VOSPER: Which one – did you ask him?

TEMPLE: Yes, I did. He said the Empress.

VOSPER: What time was it when he picked you up?

TEMPLE: About eleven. The show finished at ten-forty. I've already checked that, Inspector.

VOSPER: (*Amused*) Thank you.

The door opens.

CHARLIE: Excuse me, sir.

TEMPLE: Yes, what is it, Charlie?

CHARLIE: Mr Frost would like to see you …

Before CHARLIE finishes speaking, FROST pushes his way into the room.

FROST: (*Obviously worried*) Temple, forgive me for bursting in like this but … Oh, good evening, Inspector!

VOSPER: Good evening, sir.

TEMPLE: All right, Charlie.

The door closes.

FROST: Temple, I've just heard about the car incident – about Mrs Temple – is she all right?

TEMPLE: Yes, there's nothing to worry about. Fortunately, I spotted the car and pushed her out of the way.

FROST: It was my car. I suppose you know that?

TEMPLE: Yes, the Inspector's just been telling me. I was rather surprised.

FROST: I can well believe it! So was I!

VOSPER: Who told you about the attempt to run Mr Temple down?

FROST: One of your people. I've just picked the car up and he told me all about it. I was staggered. I came round here straight away.

VOSPER: Mr Frost, would you mind giving me a few more details?

FROST: Details? About the car?

VOSPER: No, about yourself, sir. What you did this evening.

FROST: Yes, certainly. Where would you like me to begin?

VOSPER: Well, what time did you arrive at the Neptune Club?

FROST: About half past eight. I had an appointment with … (*He stops, hesitates, then suddenly:*) Look – wait a minute! You don't think it was me who tried to run Temple down? You don't think I was driving the car?

VOSPER: No, sir – there's no question of that, but I would like to know exactly what happened.

TEMPLE: You arrived at the club at half past eight …

FROST: Yes. I had an appointment with Peter Wallace.

VOSPER: But Wallace is dead!

FROST: Yes, I know. But I didn't know anything about it until Mr Temple told me.

TEMPLE: That's true, Inspector.

FROST: I stayed with Mr and Mrs Temple for about twenty minutes, and then decided to go home. (*To TEMPLE*) I suppose it was about nine o'clock when I left you?

TEMPLE: Yes, it was.

VOSPER: Go on, sir.

FROST: Well, I went out to the cloakroom and just as I was getting my hat and coat a waiter came across and said that Miss Gibson wanted to see me. I went up to see Terry. She was in her office.

VOSPER: Yes – go on.

FROST: Well, to cut a long story short, Terry said she was looking for someone to write material for a new cabaret and she wondered if I'd be interested. I wasn't particularly intrigued by the idea, it's not really my cup of tea, and besides, I'm after a film contract, but we sat and talked about it for some little time.

VOSPER: What do you mean – some little time?

FROST: Well, it was about ten to ten when I left Miss Gibson.

VOSPER: I see.

TEMPLE: Did you talk about anything else, other than the cabaret act?

FROST: Yes, she mentioned Wallace. I told her I was supposed to be dining with him and I repeated what you'd told me.

TEMPLE: What did she say?

FROST: She asked me if you'd made any comment on the murder, and I said you hadn't.

VOSPER: Go on.

FROST: Well, I said good night to Terry, picked up my hat and coat from the cloakroom and left the Club.

VOSPER: What time was that?

FROST: About five minutes to ten.

TEMPLE: You didn't see Pete Roberts, by any chance?

FROST: (*Surprised*) Pete Roberts?

TEMPLE: Yes.

FROST: No. Was he at the Neptune Club?

TEMPLE: Yes. We saw him just as we were leaving – he had an appointment with Miss Gibson.

FROST: I didn't see him.

VOSPER: Go on, Mr Frost.

FROST: Well, the rest of the story you know. When I got outside, I couldn't find my car. I looked all over for it and then went back into the Club and telephoned the police.

VOSPER: And what time was that?

FROST: (*Irritated*) You know what time it was, Inspector – you've got a record of it.

VOSPER: Yes, I know but …

FROST: It was about a quarter past ten.

VOSPER: Thank you, sir.

FROST: Look, Temple, I feel pretty bad about this …

TEMPLE: There's no reason why you should.
FROST: Yes, but I do! After all, it was my car that tried to run you down.
VOSPER: (*Dryly*) But you weren't driving it.
FROST: (*Irritated*) Is that a question, Inspector?
VOSPER: No, sir – it's a statement. You weren't driving it, so you weren't responsible.
There is a pause.
TEMPLE: Frost, would you do something for me?
FROST: Yes, certainly. By all means. What is it?
TEMPLE: (*Matter of fact*) Have lunch with me on Wednesday. I'll pick you up at one o'clock.
FROST: (*Puzzled*) Yes, all right, Temple. One o'clock …
MUSIC.

FADE MUSIC.
FADE UP TEMPLE.
TEMPLE: There's still some coffee in the pot. Like some, Steve?
STEVE: No, thanks. Do be careful, Paul – you'll spill it all over the bed.
TEMPLE: (*Laughing*) You do hate having breakfast in bed, don't you, Steve?
STEVE: Yes, I do – except when I'm on holiday.
TEMPLE: Well, consider you are on holiday today.
STEVE: If you think I'm going to stay in bed all day, just because I've got a stiff shoulder …
TEMPLE: Now look, dear, we've had a pretty hectic time during the past two or three days. You've got to take it easy.
STEVE: Yes, but I'm not going to stay in bed!
TEMPLE laughs. There is a knock on the door.
TEMPLE: Come in.
The door opens.

TEMPLE:	What is it, Charlie?
CHARLIE:	Sir Graham Forbes is here, sir.
TEMPLE:	Yes, all right, Charlie. Tell Sir Graham I'll be with him in a moment.

The door closes.

STEVE:	I'll get your dressing gown.
TEMPLE:	Stay where you are, Steve! I can get it …

FADE OUT.

FADE UP a door opening.

TEMPLE:	Good morning, Sir Graham!
FORBES:	Oh, good morning, Temple! Am I too early for you?
TEMPLE:	No. No. Forgive the dressing gown, it's my wife's idea of what the popular novelist should wear!
FORBES:	(*Laughing*) How is Steve?
TEMPLE:	Her shoulder's a little stiff. Apart from that, she's fine.
FORBES:	Well, I did what you wanted, Temple. I've been through to Paris three or four times since you phoned me.
TEMPLE:	Oh, good!
FORBES:	This man you're interested in – André Reynaud …
TEMPLE:	Yes?
FORBES:	He seems to be quite a character.
TEMPLE:	That doesn't surprise me. What did you find out?
FORBES:	Well, ostensibly he runs a nightclub in Paris called Le Mediterranee and a small restaurant in Cannes.
TEMPLE:	Ostensibly?

FORBES: Yes, the French police have had their eye on him for some little time. They think his catering activities are just a blind, a cover up.

TEMPLE: A cover up for what, Sir Graham?

FORBES: They're pretty sure he's a jewel fence, but they just can't catch him. As soon as he gets the stuff, he passes it on.

TEMPLE: Yes, that's exactly what I thought.

FORBES: You think he works for Spencer?

TEMPLE: I'm sure of it, Sir Graham. When was he over here last?

FORBES: About two months ago. He's due to make another trip.

TEMPLE: How do you know?

FORBES: Well, he comes over about every two or three months, and just before he leaves, he usually goes down to the restaurant in Cannes. Then he flies over to London from Nice.

TEMPLE: Is he in Cannes at the moment?

FORBES: I believe so. Did you mention Reynaud to Terry Gibson?

TEMPLE: Oh, yes. Terry admits she knows him. So does Pete Roberts.

FORBES: Roberts played at Le Mediterranee for a short while. In cabaret.

TEMPLE: Yes, I know.

FORBES: Was he a success?

The telephone rings.

TEMPLE: Well, he was booked for three weeks, and he stayed four nights.

FORBES: Oh!

TEMPLE: Excuse me, Sir Graham.

TEMPLE crosses and lifts the telephone receiver.

TEMPLE: Paul Temple speaking.

208

VOSPER:	(*On the other end of the phone*) This is Vosper. Is Sir Graham with you?
TEMPLE:	Yes, hold on, Inspector. It's for you, Sir Graham. It's Vosper.
FORBES:	Oh, thank you. (*He takes the receiver. On the phone*) Hello?
VOSPER:	Sir Graham?
FORBES:	Yes?
VOSPER:	Oh, good morning, sir. I've just had a call through from Paris. Reynaud left Nice this morning. His plane's due in at London Airport at eleven-forty.
FORBES:	You know what to do. Contact Ritchie.
VOSPER:	I've already done so, sir. He's on his way to the airport.
FORBES:	Right! Thank you, Vosper.

FORBES replaces the receiver.

TEMPLE:	Reynaud's left Nice?
FORBES:	Yes. He's due at eleven-forty. There'll be someone on his tail from the moment he lands.
TEMPLE:	Well, I hope he's a good man, Sir Graham. Reynaud's no fool, and my bet is he's already been tipped off that we're interested in him.
FORBES:	(*Smiling*) Don't worry. Ritchie's first-class. He could follow you all over Europe and you wouldn't be any the wiser.
TEMPLE:	Ritchie? I don't think I know him, Sir Graham.
FORBES:	He's been with us about five years now. A short chap. Indiarubber face. Looks different every time you look at him.
TEMPLE:	I can't place him.
FORBES:	Exactly! Ritchie's a handful. Completely unorthodox. But he won't let us down.

209

TEMPLE: I'd like to take a look at unorthodox Mr
            Ritchie.
FORBES: Well, why not? They've a very good lounge at
            London Airport. There's no reason why we
            shouldn't be sitting in it.
TEMPLE laughs.
FADE OUT.

*FADE UP the noise of an approaching aircraft. The sound
grows louder as the plane lands.*
*FADE DOWN the noise of the aircraft to the background,
then FADE completely.*

*FADE UP background noises of the lounge and main hall at
London Airport.*
VOICE: (*From an internal relay system*) BEA announce
            the arrival of Flight 193 from Nice. Passengers
            will proceed to the Customs through Channel 4
            …
FADE UP background noises of the lounge.
TEMPLE: Let's go into the restaurant, Sir Graham. We
            can see the passengers from the window.
FORBES: Right.
TEMPLE: Do you think you'll recognise Reynaud?
FORBES: I think so. I've seen a photograph of him.
*TEMPLE and FORBES pass through the swing doors into the
restaurant. We hear background noises of the Airport, BEA
commentators, etc.*
A pause.
TEMPLE: That's the plane …
FORBES: Yes. (*Pause*) Here they are. They're walking
            across the airfield.
Pause.
TEMPLE: Is that Reynaud – in the camel-hair coat?

210

FORBES: No, I don't think so … I'm not sure … Yes, that's him – that's Reynaud … He's a pretty slick looking customer, isn't he?

TEMPLE: Where will your man Ritchie pick him up – in the Customs Hall?

FORBES: I imagine so. (*Suddenly; amused and surprised*) No, wait a minute! There's Ritchie, down there, with the passengers …

TEMPLE: Where?

FORBES: That little chap with the green hat and the briefcase …

TEMPLE: But how did he get down there – he couldn't have been on the plane!

FORBES: (*Laughing*) I never ask questions where Ritchie's concerned.

TEMPLE: Well, he's certainly on the job. He's a curious little man, isn't he? I can see what you mean about the indiarubber face. Is he English?

FORBES: No. As a matter of fact, his name's Freeberg. He was born in Cologne but came over here about five or six years ago. He was with Interpol originally.

TEMPLE: Does he speak with an accent?

FORBES: Yes. (*Watching the passengers*) They're going into the Customs … Shall we stay here or go down to the hall?

TEMPLE: I think we'd better stay here, Sir Graham. If Reynaud spots either of us it's not going to help Ritchie.

FORBES: Yes, I agree.

WAITER: Can I get you anything, sir?

TEMPLE: Yes, we'll have some coffee.

WAITER: Thank you, sir.

FADE UP the background noises of the Airport. An aircraft is taking off.
FADE ON the noise of the aircraft.

FADE UP noises of the restaurant.

TEMPLE: Yes, we'll go down. (*Suddenly*) Wait a minute! Isn't this Ritchie?

FORBES: Why, yes! (*Anxiously*) What's he doing up here – what the devil's gone wrong?

RITCHIE arrives. A dumpy little man with a slight German accent.

RITCHIE: Good morning, Sir Graham.

FORBES: What is it, Ritchie? What's happened?

RITCHIE: Reynaud's arrived …

FORBES: (*Impatiently*) Yes, I know. We've seen him. But why aren't you …

RITCHIE: He's not leaving the Airport. He's catching the next plane back to Paris.

TEMPLE: How do you know this?

FORBES: This is Paul Temple, Ritchie …

RITCHIE: Yes, I know. What was your question, Mr Temple?

TEMPLE: I said, how do you know he's returning to Paris?

RITCHIE: Reynaud's received a telegram. It was handed to him in the Customs Hall.

FORBES: Well?

RITCHIE: I've read it, Sir Graham.

TEMPLE: What did it say?

RITCHIE: Read it for yourself, Mr Temple. (*He takes the telegram from his pocket and hands it to TEMPLE*)

TEMPLE: (*Reading*) "Return to Paris immediately. Imperative make no contacts. Spencer."

FORBES:	They obviously know we were going to tail him.
TEMPLE:	Yes. How did you get the telegram?
RITCHIE:	There was an awful crush going through the Customs. It was not difficult to help myself, Mr Temple.
FORBES:	Well, I don't see what we can do, Temple. We can't arrest Reynaud, and if we start questioning him, we're liable to …
TEMPLE:	Wait a minute, Sir Graham!
FORBES:	What is it?
RITCHIE:	What are you thinking of, Mr Temple?
TEMPLE:	I've an idea … I don't know whether it will work or not, but it's worth trying …

FADE OUT.

FADE UP background noises of the main hall and lounge at London Airport.

STEWARD:	Excuse me, sir, is your name Reynaud?
REYNAUD:	(*Hesitantly, with a slight foreign accent*) Why do you wish to know my name?
STEWARD:	There's a Monsieur André Reynaud wanted on the telephone, sir. I've been asked to make enquiries.
REYNAUD:	(*Still hesitant*) Who wants to speak to Monsieur Reynaud?
STEWARD:	I'm afraid I don't know. If you're not the gentleman in question …
REYNAUD:	(*Curtly; interrupting him*) Yes. Yes, my name is Reynaud. I'm the person you are looking for. Where is this telephone?
STEWARD:	This way, if you please.

FADE DOWN of the background noises.

FADE UP the opening of a telephone booth door. REYNAUD enters the box, closes the door, and lifts the receiver.

REYNAUD: (*On the phone*) Hello?

OPERATOR: (*On the other end of the phone*) Monsieur Reynaud?

REYNAUD: Yes …

OPERATOR: One moment, please …

Pause.

REYNAUD: Hello?

RITCHIE: (*With a note of urgency in his voice; on the other end of the line*) Hello? Is that you, Reynaud?

REYNAUD: Yes – who is that?

RITCHIE: You got the telegram?

REYNAUD: Yes – yes, I got the telegram. But who is that? Who is that speaking?

RITCHIE: Don't you recognise my voice?

REYNAUD: (*Apparently recognising the voice*) Oh, yes! Yes, of course. I'm sorry. What is it you want, Dreisler?

MUSIC.

END OF EPISODE SEVEN

EPISODE EIGHT

A PARTY OF FOUR

-

OPENING MUSIC.
FADE DOWN MUSIC.

*FADE IN the voice of RITCHIE talking to ANDRÈ
REYNAUD on the telephone in a telephone booth at London
Airport.*

REYNAUD: Hello?

RITCHIE: (*With a note of urgency in his voice; on the
             other end of the line*) Hello? Is that you,
             Reynaud?

REYNAUD: Yes – who is that?

RITCHIE: You got the telegram?

REYNAUD: Yes – yes, I got the telegram. But who is that?
             Who is that speaking?

RITCHIE: Don't you recognise my voice?

REYNAUD: (*Apparently recognising the voice*) Oh, yes!
             Yes, of course. I'm sorry. What is it you
             want, Dreisler?

RITCHIE: Ignore the telegram – it's not important.
             Continue as arranged.

REYNAUD: But if it's not important why …

RITCHIE: Listen, Reynaud – do you want me to explain
             on the telephone?

REYNAUD: No, of course not, but …

RITCHIE: Then don't be stupid. There's nothing to
             worry about – the arrangements stand.

REYNAUD: All right, Dreisler.

RITCHIE: You know what to do and where to go?

REYNAUD: (*Surprised by the question*) Yes, of course.

RITCHIE: (*Quickly*) I'll see you later.

RITCHIE replaces the receiver.
FADE OUT.

217

FADE Up background noises associated with a restaurant at London Airport.

FORBES: Here's Ritchie.

TEMPLE: What happened?

RITCHIE: It looks as if he's fallen for it – he's collecting his baggage.

FORBES: Good man!

RITCHIE: I'll see you later, Sir Graham.

TEMPLE: Don't lose him, Ritchie.

RITCHIE: (*With a laugh*) I'll try not to. I'll contact Vosper immediately there's any news.

FORBES: Right!

FADE aircraft and airport noises completely.

FADE UP TEMPLE pouring a glass of port.

STEVE: Paul, I really didn't want another glass of port!

TEMPLE: Nonsense, it'll do you good, dear. How about you, Sir Graham?

FORBES: No, really, Temple!

In the background a clock chimes the hour.

TEMPLE: Here you are, Steve.

STEVE: Thank you.

FORBES: What time is that? – Ten o'clock?

TEMPLE: Yes. It's curious we haven't heard anything about Reynaud.

FORBES: I don't like it. He's either given Ritchie the slip or else …

STEVE: Or what, Sir Graham?

FORBES: Or he's contacted Dreisler.

TEMPLE: Well, it's a chance we had to take.

STEVE: You mean Reynaud may have telephoned Dreisler and found out about the phone call?

FORBES: It's beginning to look like it. It's over ten hours since he left London Airport with Ritchie on his tail.

STEVE: You know, I don't understand this business. How can Dreisler be mixed up in it? After all, it was his daughter …

TEMPLE: (*Stopping STEVE*) Just a minute, Steve!

Voices can be heard outside the room.

CHARLIE: (*Outside*) I'll see if Mr Temple's in, sir.

VOSPER: (*Impatiently*) Of course he's in. Sir Graham's with him.

The door opens.

TEMPLE: Come in, Vosper.

STEVE: All right, Charlie.

VOSPER enters. The door closes.

FORBES: Have you heard from Ritchie?

VOSPER: Yes, I had a phone call at six o'clock, Sir Graham.

FORBES: Six o'clock? (*Annoyed*) Why on earth haven't you been in touch with us?

VOSPER: Because I've been waiting for another call, sir.

TEMPLE: What's happened, Vosper?

VOSPER: Well, apparently Reynaud went to an hotel in Bloomsbury. He stayed there until four o'clock and then a car picked him up.

TEMPLE: Who was driving the car?

VOSPER: We don't know. According to Ritchie the driver wore dark glasses and a scarf. It might have been anyone.

FORBES: Go on, Vosper.

VOSPER: Ritchie stayed on their tail as far as Chingford Green, then the car pulled into a garage for

219

	petrol. Ritchie happened to be near a phone box, and he telephoned me.
TEMPLE:	That was at six o'clock?
VOSPER:	Yes. He said it looked as if they were heading for Epping Forest, and he'd telephone later. I've been waiting for the call.
FORBES:	Did Ritchie say anything else?
VOSPER:	No, sir – but he didn't sound too happy about things.
FORBES:	What do you mean – he didn't sound too happy?
VOSPER:	It's difficult to explain, sir. I got the impression he was rather worried.
FORBES:	What do you make of it, Temple?

The telephone rings.

TEMPLE:	It sounds to me as if Ritchie suspected a trap. If he did, then obviously … (*He breaks off because of the telephone*)
VOSPER:	That's probably for me. May I take it?
TEMPLE:	Of course. Go ahead.

VOSPER lifts the receiver.

VOSPER:	(*On the phone*) Hello?
RICE:	(*On the other end*) Is that Inspector Vosper?
VOSPER:	Yes.
RICE:	This is Rice, sir.
VOSPER:	Yes, Sergeant – have you got the information?
RICE:	Yes, sir. He made two telephone calls. One at two-fifteen and the other at a quarter to four. They were both to the same number.
VOSPER:	What was the number?
RICE:	734 5011 …
VOSPER:	Thank you.

VOSPER replaces the receiver.

FORBES:	Who was that?
VOSPER:	I've been checking the telephone calls at the hotel. Reynaud made two. Both to 734 5011.
TEMPLE:	That's the Neptune Club.
VOSPER:	Yes.
FORBES:	Look, Vosper, I think under the circumstances the thing to do is to contact the Special Branch. Tell them that Ritchie ... (*He breaks off*)

The door opens.

STEVE:	Yes – what is it, Charlie?
CHARLIE:	This telegram's just arrived, Mrs Temple.
STEVE:	Thank you. (*She takes the telegram*) It's for you, Paul.
TEMPLE:	(*Taking the telegram*) Thanks. (*He rips it open*)

A pause.

FORBES:	What is it, Temple?
STEVE:	Paul, what is it?
TEMPLE:	This was handed in at Faunwood Common, just after seven o'clock. It says: "In case you are interested you'll find your friend at Bellwood Heath. Spencer."
STEVE:	Bellwood Heath? Where's Bellwood Heath?
VOSPER:	It's in Essex. Near Epping Forest.
TEMPLE:	(*Urgently*) Charlie, get the car round, straight away.
CHARLIE:	Yes, sir!

MUSIC.

FADE MUSIC.

FADE UP PC Baker in a telephone booth in a country lane. He is impatiently tapping the receiver.

OPERATOR: (*Casually*) Number please?

BAKER: Put me through to Bellwood Heath Police Station. It's urgent – hurry, please!

A slight pause.

MILLMAN: (*On the other end of the phone*) Bellwood Heath Police Station – Sergeant Millman speaking.

BAKER: Sergeant, this is Baker. I'm in a callbox on the corner of Cragwell Lane. There's been an accident ...

MILLMAN: (*Matter of fact*) Okay. Let's have it ...

BAKER: There's a car in Turner's Field. It's blazing like hell.

MILLMAN: (*Alert*) Is there anyone in it?

BAKER: Yes, there's a man in the driving seat but I can't get at the poor devil.

MILLMAN: Okay, Baker. I'll get someone down there immediately.

QUICK FADE.

FADE UP the sound of a burning car; a raging, uncontrollable fire. The sound of an approaching fire engine is heard as well as many voices. The splashing of water, fire exstinguishers, etc.

Two men are struggling to get the body out of the car.

1st FIREMAN: I can't move him, Harry! He's wedged under the wheel ...

2nd FIREMAN: Get hold of his shoulders ... That's it!

1st FIREMAN: Pull! ... No, it's no use ... Other way ...

2nd FIREMAN: (*Struggling*) He never got himself in this position ... Wait a moment. I think I've moved him ...

1st FIREMAN: That's it ...

2nd FIREMAN:	(*Angrily; calling back to his colleagues*) Keep the jet over here, or we'll never get the poor devil out!!
1st FIREMAN:	It's okay, Harry … We've got him …

FADE UP the sound of the high-pressure jet, background of voices, etc.

FADE voices and general noise to the background.

VOSPER:	They've got him out of the car now, sir.
FORBES:	Did you recognise him?
VOSPER:	Just.
TEMPLE:	Is it Ritchie?
VOSPER:	Yes, it's Ritchie all right.
FORBES:	Come on, Temple – we'd better take a look at him.

FADE OUT.

FADE UP STEVE playing the piano. It is a serious piece of music.

After a pause, the door opens.

TEMPLE:	I'm going now, Steve.

The piano stops.

STEVE:	Going where?
TEMPLE:	(*Laughing*) Out, darling!
STEVE:	But it's nearly lunchtime!
TEMPLE:	That's why I'm going, I've got a lunch appointment.
STEVE:	But you never told me!
TEMPLE:	I told you ages ago. I'm lunching with Adrian Frost.
STEVE:	Oh, yes, of course! I'd forgotten about that.
TEMPLE:	Well, I hope Mr Frost hasn't forgotten.
STEVE:	(*Seriously*) Take care, Paul.

223

TEMPLE: I'm only going out to lunch, Steve. I'll be back this afternoon.

STEVE: Yes, I know but – Paul, I'm awfully worried about this business – about the Spencer Affair.

TEMPLE: Yes, I know you are, dear. But don't worry, Steve, it'll … soon be over.

STEVE: You know who it is, don't you?

TEMPLE: Yes, I know.

STEVE: Last night, after you went out, I made a list of all the possible suspects.

TEMPLE: Whatever made you do that?

STEVE: I felt so confused, I thought it might help me to think clearer if I put things down in black and white. I put six names down on a piece of paper and then I wrote down the various …

TEMPLE: <u>Six</u> names?

STEVE: Yes.

TEMPLE: Who were they?

STEVE: Well – Rupert Dreisler – Terry Gibson – Adrian Frost – Pete Roberts – Eric Lansdale – and Clutch Brompton.

TEMPLE: I see. Well, you can forget Clutch Brompton.

STEVE: Paul, who is Spencer?

TEMPLE: I'll tell you tonight, dear.

STEVE: Is that a promise?

TEMPLE: Yes. Now listen, Steve. Don't leave the flat. It doesn't matter who telephones or what happens – don't leave it.

STEVE: All right, Paul.

TEMPLE: I'll see you, later. (*He kisses STEVE*)

The door closes. After a moment STEVE starts to play the piano again.

FADE on the piano.

224

CROSS FADE to the sound of a typewriter. It continues for a time, then there is the sound of a door buzzer. The typing stops. The door is opened.

FROST: Oh, hello, Temple! Good Lord, is it nearly one o'clock?

TEMPLE: Yes, I'm afraid it is.

FROST: Sorry if I kept you waiting. I was typing.

TEMPLE: That's all right.

They go into the drawing room.

FROST: Would you care for a glass of sherry?

TEMPLE: I don't think so, thank you. (*Pleasantly*) What are you writing? A play?

FROST: Well, I'm trying to. Of course, you write novels and things, don't you?

TEMPLE: Mostly novels.

FROST: Oh, I didn't mean …

TEMPLE: That's all right. As a writer I know how irritating it is to be interrupted, so if you don't feel like lunch …

FROST: Not at all, I'm looking forward to it. It's very nice of you to ask me.

TEMPLE: Well, I thought it would be a good opportunity for us to have a little talk.

FROST: What is it you want to talk about?

TEMPLE: Well, for one thing, I thought you might be interested to hear about Reynaud.

FROST: Reynaud?

TEMPLE: Yes, André Reynaud. He runs a nightclub in Paris.

FROST: Oh, yes. Yes, I remember. You spoke to me about Reynaud once before.

TEMPLE: That's right. Well, he arrived in London yesterday. A man called Ritchie – a Scotland Yard official – was told to follow him.

225

	Unfortunately, Ritchie made a mistake. He was murdered.
FROST:	What?
TEMPLE:	Last night.
FROST:	Murdered by Reynaud?
TEMPLE:	Reynaud and a gentleman called Spencer.
FROST:	What happened exactly?
TEMPLE:	They knocked him out, put him in a car and set fire to it.
FROST:	Does this man Reynaud work for Spencer?
TEMPLE:	Yes.
FROST:	I see.
TEMPLE:	Frost, I hope you won't think me presumptuous, but … (*He hesitates*)
FROST:	Yes?
TEMPLE:	I'd like to give you a piece of advice.
FROST:	I'm not good at taking advice. Even from friends.
TEMPLE:	There's a first time for everything.
FROST:	(*A shade angry*) Look, Temple, what is it you want? Why did you really come here today?
TEMPLE:	You want to know?
FROST:	Of course I want to know.
TEMPLE:	(*Pleasantly*) Right, I'll tell you. But first of all, tell me something.
FROST:	(*Still irritated*) Well?
TEMPLE:	Why are you going to America?
FROST:	(*Apparently surprised by the question*) Going to America?
TEMPLE:	Yes.
FROST:	Whatever gave you the idea that …
TEMPLE:	(*Interrupting FROST*) You've made a reservation on the "Queen Elizabeth", haven't you?

FROST:	(*A moment*) My agents got me a Hollywood contract; I shall be there until November. I – I didn't want to say anything about it because I haven't got my visa yet.
TEMPLE:	I see.
FROST:	(*A note of sarcasm*) You appear to be very well informed, Mr Temple.
TEMPLE:	I wouldn't dream of giving you advice if I weren't well informed, Mr Frost.

MUSIC.
FADE MUSIC.

A door opens.

CHARLIE:	Have you finished with the coffee, Mrs Temple?
STEVE:	Yes, thank you, Charlie. You can take the tray.
TEMPLE:	And I think we shall want some logs before the evening's out.
CHARLEY:	Okey-dokey, I'll see to it.
STEVE:	When you've got the logs, you can go out, Charlie, if you like. Go to the pictures.
CHARLIE:	Oh, thank you, Mrs Temple.

The front door bell rings in the background.

TEMPLE:	See who that is …
CHARLIE:	Yes, sir.

CHARLIE goes out.

STEVE:	Are you expecting anyone?
TEMPLE:	Sir Graham said he might drop in …
STEVE:	Well, I hope it isn't Sir Graham, or the Inspector!
TEMPLE:	Why?
STEVE:	Because I want to talk to you, Paul. Remember what you promised. You said … (*She breaks off*) Yes, Charlie?

CHARLIE: There's a Mr Dreisler – he says he'd like to see Mr Temple if it's convenient. I said I wasn't sure if you were in or not, sir.

TEMPLE: Yes, all right, Charlie. Ask him in.

CHARLIE goes out again.

STEVE: What on earth does Dreisler want?

TEMPLE: I'll lay six to four he wants to talk to me about Pete Roberts.

STEVE: What makes you think that?

TEMPLE: Oh, I don't know. It's just a feeling I've got. A sort of intuition.

STEVE: That's my department!

CHARLIE returns with RUPERT DREISLER.

CHARLIE: Mr Dreisler, sir.

CHARLIE goes out. The door closes.

TEMPLE: Good evening. It's nice of you to call.

DREISLER: (*Obviously a little nervous*) No, no, I must apologise for intruding. I should have telephoned you, but … Oh, good evening, Mrs Temple, we meet again.

STEVE: Yes. Good evening, Mr Dreisler.

TEMPLE: May I offer you a drink?

DREISLER: No – no, that's very kind of you, but if you don't mind … (*He hesitates, almost lost for words*)

TEMPLE: Well, what can I do for you?

DREISLER: I've decided to go away – to leave England for a little while. I thought under the circumstances, I had better tell you this.

TEMPLE: But only the other day you told me you had no intention of leaving.

DREISLER: Yes, I know, but – it's no use my staying here. I get depressed and I'm neglecting my business. Also, I hope you'll forgive me for

228

saying this, but – I don't think either you or Scotland Yard are making much headway. I don't think you'll ever discover who murdered my daughter.

TEMPLE: It's a difficult case, Mr Dreisler.

DREISLER: Yes, of course – of course. I'm sure it is. Please don't think I'm criticising – that's the last thing I should wish to do.

STEVE: When are you going away?

DREISLER: In two days' time. I'm sailing to New York on the "Queen Elizabeth".

TEMPLE: Alone?

DREISLER: (*Surprised by the question*) No – I'm taking Pete Roberts with me.

TEMPLE: Pete Roberts?

DREISLER: Yes. An American friend of mine is producing a new musical and his leading man has been taken ill. I've persuaded Roberts to give an audition.

TEMPLE: Do you think Pete is good enough for Broadway?

DREISLER: Yes, I do. I think he could be a big star, if only he would keep off the drink.

TEMPLE: Well, I think you may be lucky. I've a shrewd suspicion he'll keep off the drink all right.

DREISLER: (*Surprised*) Well, I hope you are right! I sincerely hope so! But what makes you so optimistic?

TEMPLE: The way he shaves.

DREISLER: (*Puzzled*) The way he – shaves?

TEMPLE: Yes.

DREISLER: Forgive me, I don't understand. Do you understand what your husband means, Mrs Temple?

STEVE: No, I'm afraid I don't.

DREISLER: Is it a joke, perhaps?

TEMPLE: (*Laughing; dismissing the matter*) Yes, it's just a little joke, Mr Dreisler. Well, thank you for calling. I hope you'll have a pleasant trip to the States.

DREISLER: Thank you. If you want to get in touch with me. I shall be at the Waldorf Astoria. You might tell Scotland Yard that.

TEMPLE: I will, indeed.

DREISLER: Goodbye, Mrs Temple.

STEVE: Goodbye, Mr Dreisler.

TEMPLE: I'll see you out.

TEMPLE and DREISLER go into the hall.

The telephone rings. STEVE lifts the receiver.

STEVE: (*On the phone*) Hello?

VOSPER: (*On the other end of the line*) Mrs Temple?

STEVE: Yes.

VOSPER: (*Brightly; obviously pleased with himself*) This is Inspector Vosper, Mrs Temple. Could I speak to your husband?

STEVE: Yes, just a moment, Inspector.

TEMPLE returns.

TEMPLE: Is that for me?

STEVE: It's Vosper. He sounds very pleased with himself.

TEMPLE: (*Taking the phone*) Hello, Vosper?

VOSPER: Temple?

TEMPLE: Yes.

VOSPER: I've got some news for you. We've picked up Reynaud.

TEMPLE: Oh, good. What happened?

VOSPER:	The Harwich people picked him up this morning; he was trying to get through to Amsterdam.
TEMPLE:	Has he talked?
VOSPER:	Not yet. But we're not worried.
TEMPLE:	I've got some news for you too, Inspector. Rupert Dreisler is leaving for America. He sails on the "Queen Elizabeth".
VOSPER:	Yes, I know. (*Pleased with himself*) Suite 23, A deck.
TEMPLE:	Oh? And Pete Roberts?
VOSPER:	Cabin 27.
TEMPLE:	And Adrian Frost – did you know about Adrian Frost?
VOSPER:	Yes, indeed. Cabin 19, B deck.
TEMPLE:	Quite a party, Inspector.
VOSPER:	As you say – quite a party. Well, I'll keep in touch.
TEMPLE:	Thank you, Vosper.
VOSPER:	(*A deliberate afterthought*) Oh, by the way …
TEMPLE:	Yes, Inspector?
VOSPER:	Miss Gibson's in Suite 38, in case you're interested.
TEMPLE:	(*Amused*) I'm interested. Good night, Inspector!
VOSPER:	(*Chuckling to himself*) Good night.
MUSIC.	

FADE MUSIC.

FADE UP background noises associated with Southampton Docks.

CROSS FADE to noises on board a liner.

A swing door opens and closes. We are in the cocktail bar on the "Queen Elizabeth". The bar is comparatively empty.

DREISLER:	Good evening, Louis.
LOUIS:	Good evening, Mr Dreisler.
PETE:	Good evening.
DREISLER:	Are we going to have a smooth crossing?
LOUIS:	Well, I hope so, sir. What can I get you gentlemen?
PETE:	A whisky and soda.
LOUIS:	Thank you, sir.
PETE:	What time do we sail?
LOUIS:	Oh, we should be away by eleven tomorrow morning.
PETE:	Do most passengers come on board the night before?
LOUIS:	Most of the first-class passengers, sir. (*As TERRY arrives*) Good evening, madam!
TERRY:	Good evening.
LOUIS:	What can I get you?
TERRY:	Nothing, thank you.
PETE:	Hello, Terry!
TERRY:	(*Tensely*) I want to talk to you – both of you. Come over to the table near the window.

FADE DOWN the background noises and conversation.

FADE UP TERRY, DREISLER and PETE at a quiet table near the window.

DREISLER:	(*Amused*) What's the matter, Terry? You look as if you've seen a ghost.
TERRY:	I have.
PETE:	What do you mean?
TERRY:	Temple's on board.
PETE:	Temple?
DREISLER:	That's nonsense!
TERRY:	It isn't nonsense, I've seen him.

DREISLER:	But why should Temple be on board – he's not going to America?
TERRY:	How do you know he's not going to America?
PETE:	Where did you see him – on deck?

ADRIAN FROST arrives at the table unnoticed and interrupts them.

FROST:	Good evening, may I join you?
DREISLER:	Frost! What are you doing on board?
FROST:	I came to see you, Dreisler. And Mr Roberts. And, of course, my old friend, Terry Gibson.
TERRY:	Look, what is this? What are you doing here?
FROST:	Well, since I'm on the "Queen Elizabeth" and we're still in Southampton Dock, the natural assumption is that I'm going to America.
DREISLER:	Look, Frost, I don't know what this is all about …
PETE:	Here's Temple!
TEMPLE:	Don't you know what it's all about, Mr Dreisler? … No, don't get up, Miss Gibson, please! … (*With authority*) Sit down, Roberts. (*A moment*) May I introduce Sir Graham Forbes?
TERRY:	Sir Graham Forbes!
TEMPLE:	Pull up a chair, Sir Graham. Dreisler, several days ago you sent for me and asked me to find out who murdered your daughter.
DREISLER:	Yes.
TEMPLE:	Why did you do that?
PETE:	What do you mean – why did he do it? He's the girl's father … Isn't it natural that he should want to know …
TEMPLE:	Dreisler already knew the answer to the question, Mr Roberts – he knew the name of

233

the murderer. He knew why his daughter was murdered.

DREISLER: That's not true!

TEMPLE: I think it is true, Dreisler.

TERRY: Mr Temple, don't you think you'd better begin at the beginning and tell us what you know about this affair?

PETE: He doesn't know anything – he's bluffing!

DREISLER: Be quiet, Pete! You say I know the name of the murderer?

TEMPLE: Yes.

DREISLER: Then why did I send for you? Why didn't I just go to the police?

FORBES: Because you thought that by sending for Temple you were covering up. You wanted to give the impression of a …

FROST: (*With sarcasm*) A distraught father, clutching at every straw, determined on revenge …

DREISLER: Look, Frost, what the hell are you doing here? How do you fit into all this?

FROST: Shall I tell him, Temple?

A slight pause.

TEMPLE: Yes. Go on, Frost – tell him.

FROST: Many months ago, I fell in love with your daughter. I was under the impression that her sole ambition was to become an actress. But I soon discovered that this wasn't so. I found out that she was a member of a group who smuggled stolen property from the Continent. I begged Mary to give it up and she promised me she would. In October she went to Paris to tell her father – or so I thought – that she intended to break away from him. When she returned, she told me that she had done this,

234

and I was so delighted that I gave her a diamond brooch. But, as Mr Temple has since pointed out, I was under a misapprehension. Mary hadn't the slightest intention of breaking away from the organisation. On the contrary, she had another, and far more lucrative proposition in mind.

DREISLER: What the devil are you talking about?

TEMPLE: Mary Dreisler knew the identity of every member of the group. Encouraged by a certain Peter Wallace, who was a professional blackmailer, she made a gramophone record. The record was indeed just that …

TERRY: What do you mean?

FORBES: The record was a record of the actual activities of the organisation. Names, identities, secret routes from the continent, foreign representatives …

DREISER: I don't believe a word of this.

TEMPLE: You know it's true, Dreisler. (*A moment*) The head of the outfit was a fence, who called himself Spencer. He heard about the record and thought that Mary Dreisler was completely responsible for it. He went to her flat, murdered her, and took what he believed to be the incriminating record. But Wallace was a jump ahead. He'd already spread the rumour that the vital record was called "My Heart and Harry" and he'd planted a record with that label on it in Mary Dreisler's flat.

TERRY: And are you trying to tell us that Peter Wallace had the real record – the one that Mary Dreisler made?

FORBES: Of course he had! He persuaded her to make the record in the first place. You don't think that once he'd made it, he was going to let it slip through his fingers?

TEMPLE: When Spencer discovered that he'd got the wrong record he realised that not only was he up against one of his own outfit, but he was also up against an outsider – a professional blackmailer.

PETE: And the record? Does it still exist?

TEMPLE: I doubt it, since Peter Wallace was murdered. But an excellent copy of it exists, Mr Roberts.

PETE: What do you mean – a copy?

TEMPLE: Records can be copied, you know. Indeed, a few days ago I broke into Wallace's flat, and, with the aid of an excellent tape recorder, I made …

PETE: (*Speaking without thinking*) You're bluffing! I know you're bluffing because it was me who broke into …

TEMPLE: It was you who what, Mr Roberts – or should I say, Spencer?

PETE suddenly rises and turns the table completely over.

FORBES: Temple, look out!

There is an immediate buzz of astonishment from the other occupants of the cocktail bar.

FROST: He's making for the door!

FORBES: It's all right, he won't get far, Vosper's outside!

From outside the cocktail bar there is the sound of angry voices; a struggle; then a revolver shot. For a brief moment there is silence and then a babble of voices can be heard, both in the bar and in the corridor outside.

SERGEANT:	(*Shouting from the background*) The Inspector's been hit, sir!
FORBES:	Come on, Temple!

FADE DOWN the noises of the cocktail bar.

The swing door is pushed open.

FORBES:	What happened?
SERGEANT:	He pulled a gun on us, sir, just as he came through the door!
TEMPLE:	Vosper – are you all right?
VOSPER:	(*In pain but not seriously hurt*) Yes, it's only my arm, but unfortunately …
FORBES:	Get a doctor straight away, Sergeant!
TEMPLE:	Which way did he go?
SERGEANT:	He went through the door on the right, sir – he's making for the deck!
TEMPLE:	Come on, Sir Graham!

FADE COMPLETELY.

FADE UP the sound of a lift drawing to a standstill. The lift doors open. PETE rushes into the lift.

ATTENDANT:	Which deck would you like to … (*Words freeze on his lips as he sees the gun*)
PETE:	(*Desperately*) Close the door! Close it!

The lift door closes.

PETE:	This revolver isn't a toy – and this isn't a gag!
ATTENDANT:	(*Terrified*) N-o, sir …
PETE:	Take me to the top deck – quickly!
ATTENDANT:	Yes – yes, sir!

The lift starts to ascend.
FADE the noise of the lift completely.

FADE IN open air noises; background of Southampton Docks.

FORBES: Well, Sergeant?

SERGEANT: (*Breathlessly*) We've been all over, sir. There's no sign of him.

FORBES: Look, Sergeant, he's on this boat somewhere. (*A second police official arrives*) ... Any news, Harris?

HARRIS: No, I'm sorry, sir – there's only the swimming pool and the gymnasium left.

FORBES: Well, get someone down there immediately before ...

HARRIS: There's Morgan, sir – he's just come out of the gym! (*Shouting down to MORGAN*) Any luck?

MORGAN: (*Shouting from the background*) No, the place is deserted – he's not down there!

HARRIS: What about the pool?

MORGAN: No, we've been to the pool!

SERGEANT: There he is, sir!

FORBES: Where?

SERGEANT: On the top deck – Mr Temple's after him!

FORBES: (*Shouting across the deck*) Get up there, Smith, straight away!

SERGEANT: Temple's caught him, sir! He's got him!

Quick CROSS FADE to TEMPLE struggling with PETE on the top deck.

TEMPLE: ... Drop the gun, Pete! ...

PETE: Temple, I warn you, if you don't leave go ...

TEMPLE: (*Struggling*) Drop – it!

The gun drops but the struggle continues.

PETE: … (*Grimly; determined to escape*) You're not
                 going to stop me, Temple … If it's the last
                 thing I do …

The struggle continues.

*CROSS FADE to FORBES, HARRIS and the SERGEANT on
the deck below.*

HARRIS: (*Watching*) Temple's got him! I think
                 Temple's got the upper hand, sir.

FORBES: I'm not so sure …

HARRIS: You're right. He's breaking away …

FORBES: He's going for the side – he's going to jump
                 for it!!!

HARRIS: (*Tensely*) No, it's all right, Temple's got him.

FORBES: (*Alarmed*) What's he trying to do?

HARRIS: They'll both go over the side if they're not
                 careful!

FORBES: (*Alarmed; calling*) Temple, look out!
                 Temple, for Heaven's sake watch yourself!

HARRIS: They're both falling!

FORBES: (*Shouting*) Temple!

*There is a wild scream from a woman onlooker as PETE and
TEMPLE fall from the top deck.*

FADE UP the sound of TEMPLE and PETE hitting the water.

FADE UP a tugboat hooter giving warning blasts.
FADE OUT.

*FADE UP the sound of a high-powered launch racing
towards TEMPLE in the water. The motor launch slows
down.*

RADLEY: There he is! … Okay, Fred!

FRED: (*Shouting to TEMPLE*) We'll soon 'ave you
                  out, don't worry, sir!

The motor launch stops.

RADLEY: Get hold of his hand, Mr Temple!

The sound of TEMPLE in the water; he is a shade breathless.

FRED: (*Holding TEMPLE's arm*) Okay, that's it!
                  Give us a pull, Radley.

TEMPLE is slowly pulled out of the water onto the launch.

RADLEY: Steady now … That's it!

TEMPLE: (*Taking a deep breath*) Phew! By Timothy!

RADLEY: Are you all right, sir?

TEMPLE: Yes … (*Taking a deep breath*) That's better.

RADLEY: We've picked up the other man, sir.

TEMPLE: You have? Where is he?

RADLEY: He's down below. It's all right, Mr Temple –
                  the police have got him.

TEMPLE: Oh … Well, do you think I could get out of
                  these clothes?

RADLEY: (*Laughing*) Yes. Come along, sir. Come down
                  below!

FADE UP background of noises.
FADE OUT.

*FADE UP TEMPLE, STEVE and SIR GRAHAM FORBES
sitting in front of the fire in TEMPLE's flat.*

STEVE: Do let me make some sandwiches.

TEMPLE: Yes, and have another drink, Sir Graham.

In the background the clock chimes.

FORBES: No, thank you both very much. I must be
                  making a move. I promised to drop in on
                  Vosper.

STEVE: How is the Inspector?

FORBES: Oh, he's going along nicely, thank you, Steve.
                  It's nothing serious.

STEVE:	You know, the thing I don't understand …
TEMPLE:	Here we go, Sir Graham!
FORBES:	Here we go, Temple!

They all laugh.

STEVE:	No, but seriously, Paul …
TEMPLE:	(*Quite seriously*) Yes, Steve?
STEVE:	I don't understand why Peter Wallace threw suspicion onto Adrian Frost. Frost wasn't a member of the organisation. Wouldn't it have been much better from Wallace's point of view if he'd picked on someone in the group – say Dreisler or Terry Gibson?
TEMPLE:	No. Although he wasn't a member, he didn't want us to suspect the group.
FORBES:	You see, Wallace had the record and was proposing to blackmail them. It was virtually to his advantage that we shouldn't solve the murder.
STEVE:	Yes, I see. But surely Frost was implicated. After all, he went to the Bronze Heart one night.
TEMPLE:	He went to the Bronze Heart because he was curious about Pete Roberts. He suspected that Pete was the leader of the group and decided to investigate. I became worried about this because I knew what would happen if he became too deeply involved. That's why I saw Frost and had a serious talk with him. I persuaded him to tell me everything he knew. Also, I warned him about Wallace. Wallace knew so much about Frost, I felt sure that he had access to his diary.
STEVE:	But what about the record? Pete Roberts deliberately drew your attention to it. He

	actually mentioned the song and told you he'd made a recording of it.
TEMPLE:	Yes. And he did that for a particular reason. He knew we'd heard about the record, and he was determined that we should think it was simply a song. The last thing he wanted was us to suspect that the record contained vital information about the group.
FORBES:	In short, a deliberate mystery was created about "My Heart and Harry" in order to stop us from realising what was actually on the record.
STEVE:	But what happened to the record, Sir Graham? Was that the genuine record that Vosper saw? The one that disappeared from Mary Dreisler's flat?
TEMPLE:	No. Wallace had the original record, but he'd planted a dummy in the flat …
FORBES:	… A recording of "Oklahoma" bearing the label "My Heart and Harry" …
TEMPLE:	When Pete realised it wasn't the genuine record, he sent it back with the note, "Adored every minute of it. Love. Spencer."
STEVE:	But why should he do that?
FORBES:	What was your impression when you heard about the note, Steve?
STEVE:	I didn't think it was important. It just sounded as though someone called Spencer had borrowed a record and was returning it.
FORBES:	Exactly. And that was our impression. In fact, we shouldn't have given it another thought if it hadn't been for your husband and Clutch Brompton.

STEVE:	But it was after that that the record disappeared.
TEMPLE:	Yes. And that's how Judy Milton comes into the story. Judy was a friend of Mary Dreisler's and she knew about the record. In fact, she came to the conclusion that Mary had been murdered because of it. One day, she went to the flat, secured the record – the Oklahoma one – and took it away with her.
FORBES:	She decided to take it to Terry Gibson because she thought Terry was a good friend of Mary's and would advise her what to do with it. When she arrived at the Club, she overheard a conversation between Terry and Pete Roberts, became suspicious, and left the record in the Ladies' Cloakroom. Then she got in touch with your husband.
STEVE:	But how do you know this, Sir Graham?
TEMPLE:	She told Adrian Frost. Frost was worried about Judy and made her write me a letter. He was frightened that something might happen to her before we had a chance to talk – which indeed it did.
STEVE:	And was it Pete Roberts who murdered Judy?
TEMPLE:	Yes.
STEVE:	But the night we came back from the Neptune Club they smashed our radiogram.
TEMPLE:	Of course they did! Roberts thought Judy had got hold of the real record and obviously he didn't want us to play it.
STEVE:	But, Paul, you told Pete Roberts that _he_ was likely to be murdered – why did you do that?
TEMPLE:	I overheard part of a telephone conversation between Terry Gibson and Pete Roberts.

They were talking about Wallace, but I wanted to cover up that I knew, so I deliberately told Roberts about the conversation. I gave him the impression that I thought he was the person that was likely to be murdered. I then asked Vosper to check the phone calls at the Neptune Club.

FORBES: And this confirmed your suspicions it was Pete Roberts that Terry Gibson had been talking to.

STEVE: I see. You know, Roberts must have been an extraordinary man.

FORBES: He was, he was indeed. But there was just that kink, I suppose. He was certainly a good singer, and a pretty good actor too, if it comes to that.

TEMPLE: A good impersonator, yes – but not a good actor, Sir Graham. He never really convinced me that he was a dipsomaniac.

FORBES: (*Amused*) That's because you saw him shaving.

STEVE: What do you mean, Sir Graham?

TEMPLE: His hand was as steady as a rock.

A pause.

FORBES: (*Rising from his chair*) Well, that's the end of the Spencer Affair …

TEMPLE: Yes, Sir Graham.

A tiny pause.

FORBES: And now I really must go.

TEMPLE: I'll get your coat.

FORBES: Good night, Steve.

STEVE: Good night, Sir Graham.

FORBES: Take care of yourselves!

STEVE: We'll try!

STEVE moves across to the piano; she plays a few bars – or hums to herself.

TEMPLE returns.

TEMPLE: Well, darling? Are you ready for bed?

STEVE: Yes. (*A yawn*) What are you doing tomorrow, Paul?

TEMPLE: I don't know. I've just been thinking. I'm rather at a loose end. I've finished the new novel, the Spencer Affair's over, and … (*Suddenly*) I say, Steve! Why don't we go to America?

STEVE: America?

TEMPLE: Yes – there's nothing like a trip to the States to pop you up.

STEVE: We'd never get a berth, not at a moment's notice!

TEMPLE: That's what you think!

STEVE: What do you mean?

TEMPLE: There's four empty berths on the Lizzie!

STEVE: (*Laughing*) By Timothy, Paul – you really are the limit!

TEMPLE: (*Gay; laughing*) F.B.I. – here we come

STEVE laughs, then stops dead.

STEVE: What do you mean – F.B.I.?

TEMPLE laughs at STEVE.

MUSIC.

THE END

Press Pack
press cuttings about *Paul Temple and the Spencer Affair* ...

Wednesday will be a day of dual importance for author Francis Durbridge. For while viewers are watching his seventh tv serial, *A Time of Day*, Light Programme listeners will be hearing his latest Paul Temple series.

It was Paul Temple who established Durbridge as the most successful thriller writer of the day.

The voice of Temple in the new series will belong to 44-year-old Peter Coke, who has played this role over the past two years.

Temple's wife, Steve, will again be played by Marjorie Westbury, who has been automatically associated with the part since she first took it in 1945.

Paul Temple made his initial radio appearance in 1938. The last series was heard in April 1956.

Michael Ray

Paul Temple Back in New B.B.C. Serial
Paul Temple, a radio character who has become a household name, returns to the Light Programme for eight weeks in a new series which begins at eight o'clock tomorrow night.

As in the past few years, he will be portrayed by Peter Coke, who besides appearing in many West End plays has also written and had published several dramatic pieces. Born at Southsea, he was educated at Kenton college, Kenya, and Stowe School.

Coke studied at R.A.D.A. and his first stage appearance was at the Grand Casino, Mentone, France, in 1934.

Playing the part of Steve, Paul Temple's wife, is Marjorie Westbury, who made her first appearance in this role in September, 1945. She was born in Birmingham and when only 20 won a scholarship to the Royal College of Music, specialising in lieder and Mozart.

It was Martyn C. Webster, the producer of the Paul Temple series, who gave Marjorie her first break in a burlesque called *The Fifth Form at St Pontefracts*. Since then she has taken part in numerous plays in the Home Service and Light Programme.

Paul Temple was first heard on the air in 1938 after Martyn C. Webster and writer Francis Durbridge had a meeting in Birmingham. The last series was heard in April, 1956.

Others taking part include Isabel Dean as Terry Gibson, Thomas Heathcote (Pete Roberts), Simon Lack (Adrian Frost), Lester Mudditt (Sir Graham Forbes), Hugh Manning (Det. Inspector Vosper) and Brewster Mason (Rupert Dreisler).

Sunderland Echo

New Durbridge Serials

Today will be notable in the annals of that prolific writer of thrillers, Francis Durbridge, for he has a new serial starting on B.B.C. Television, and a new Paul Temple series starting in the Light Programme. *A Time of Day* is Durbridge's seventh B.B.C. television serial, and the fourth to be produced by Alan Bromly who has been responsible for *Portrait of Alison, My Friend Charles* and *The Other Man*. It will be in six weekly episodes. In a rather different vein from its predecessors, its central characters are a husband and wife who are on the verge of separating after a certain amount of emotional conflict. Clive Freeman is a research scientist who has been working for the Government in a secret but poorly-paid job. At the opening of *A Time of Day* Clive and Lucy become involved with other mysterious matters which take their minds off their personal relationship. Stephen Murray plays Clive Freeman and Dorothy Alison his wife Lucy.

Paul Temple, a radio character who has become a household name, returns to the Light Programme for eight weeks in a new series. As in the past two years, he will be portrayed by Peter Coke, and playing the part of Steve, Paul Temple's wife, is Marjorie Westbury, the Birmingham radio actress who made her first appearance in the role in September 1945.

Paul Temple was first heard on the air in 1938 from Birmingham in a play produced by Martyn C. Webster.

Birmingham Post

Durbridge Doubled by Jean Blair

A combination of the old and new mediums and some slick dial changing last night brought us the first instalment of two new Francis Durbridge serials.

At 8 o'clock on the air there was *Paul Temple and the Spencer Affair*, then a quick move over to TV at 8.30 for *A Time of Day*.

It is, of course, too early to pass any real judgement on these as thrillers, but there is no doubt that the old master's hand still has its cunning.

In both, Durbridge got things moving quickly, and he contrived neat climaxes to bring us back next week.

And I don't think it should be difficult to keep the two quite separate in our minds, for Durbridge has been wise enough not to put Paul Temple on the screen.

We all have our own mental picture of that cool young man (though he can't be so young now), and no actor could ever bring him to life without annoying a great many of his fans.

The Bulletin and Scots Pictorial

The Man Who Makes Crime Pay

Between eight and nine o'clock on Wednesday evening, the work of one author will attract a radio and television audience of at least 11,000,000 people. Impossible? Think again! The author is master of mystery, Francis Durbridge.

Every Wednesday for the past four weeks over 4,500,000 listeners have been tuning in to the Light at 8 p.m. to hear *Paul Temple and the Spencer Affair*, the fifteenth serialised Temple adventure to be broadcast since Durbridge began writing them in 1938.

Half an hour later, at least 7,000,000 BBC viewers will have settled down in front of their sets to lap up 30 more minutes of Durbridge mystery, namely *A Time of Day* which also began four weeks ago.

They say crime doesn't pay. Done the Durbridge way it does.

He looks like any fairly successful businessman you'd encounter on a late morning train to Town. Medium height, 45, well-built, with thin dark hair, his only concession to flamboyance is a pink shirt under his expensively cut blue-grey suit.

A graduate of Birmingham University, he began writing seriously for radio in the early thirties when *Promotion*, a play he wrote about life in a department store, was received with acclaim.

"The man who encouraged me most in those days was Martyn C. Webster, who still produces the Paul Temple series," he said.

Since those days he has written millions of words about the adventures of Temple which have appeared in books, strip cartoons and films as well as on radio.

Since 1952 Durbridge has written seven serials for BBC television. Remember The *Teckman Biography, Portrait of Alison, The Other Man*?

"When a writer creates someone like Paul Temple," says Durbridge, "it sometimes happens that the character ruins the life of the author. I decided that wouldn't happen to me. That's why I accepted when the BBC commissioned me to write television serials for them. It meant new characters, a new medium."